A THEORY OF GREAT MEN

A THEORY OF GREAT MEN

DANIEL GREENSTONE

ACADEMY CHICAGO PUBLISHERS

Published in 2011 by
Academy Chicago Publishers
363 West Erie Street
Chicago, Illinois 60654

© 2011 by Daniel Greenstone

First edition.

Printed and bound in the U.S.A.

Library of Congress Cataloging-in-Publication Data

Greenstone, Daniel.
A theory of great men / by Daniel Greenstone.
p. cm.
ISBN 978-0-89733-613-0 (pbk. : alk. paper)
1. High school teachers—Fiction. 2. Self-realization—Fiction.
3. Chicago (Ill.)—Fiction. I. Title.
PS3607.R4664T47 2011
813'.6—dc22
2010053280

CHAPTER 1

You know all those movies and books where some saintly teacher goes into a desolate classroom and saves a bunch of tough but deserving kids. Well, this is not one of those stories. I've been teaching history at Edgemont High School, in the suburbs of Chicago, for fifteen years, and it's a job not a calling. Not for me, anyway. Sure, there are some holier-than-thou types who come in all afire, trying to change the world, but they usually don't last long. Most of the time they wind up frustrated and bitter. Then they quit, blaming the system. Eric Goldstein, my student-teacher, was just like that when he showed up on an October morning, during my preparation period.

I was on my way to the bathroom, when I saw him walking down the hallway, gazing up at the room numbers stenciled onto the panes of glass above the doorways, as he lugged a backpack and a pair of Starbucks coffee cups. Even though I wasn't expecting him for another twenty minutes, I could tell it was him. It had to be, the way he moved cautiously through the hall, wearing a pressed shirt and new tie, stopping to peer at the trophy cases and bulletin boards. Still, I didn't say anything when he made a wrong turn toward the gym, past the wall-sized mirror that runs down the PE corridor. I've had student-teachers before, and I've learned that they have to figure things out for themselves.

When he finally found the teacher's lounge, he knocked on the door, even though it was propped open. "I'm looking for George Cavaliere," he said.

"Yeah, that's me. Come in."

Eric Goldstein was tall, with olive skin and haphazard tufts of dark brown hair. With his slender build and uneven wisps of facial hair, he was an unimposing figure.

"Oh, too bad," I said, when he introduced himself. "I was hoping you'd be a girl." This was partly a joke. I'd known he was going to be a male, since the college had sent over his name earlier in the week, but I had in fact requested a girl. The first thing you have to do to help a student-teacher is break them down, and it's easier with the females. They start out humbler.

"Sorry to disappoint you," Goldstein said, chuckling uncomfortably.

"Where's the funeral?" I said.

Goldstein looked down at his suit. It was a nice one, too nice for school. The standard issue all-purpose suit—weddings, funerals and job interviews—that a college kid gets from his folks before his senior year.

"Sorry. I guess I'm overdressed," he said. "The woman who coordinates the student teaching program at Xavier, Ms. Barton—she said we should wear our best outfit on the first day."

"I don't know what planet that Barton is on," I said. "She's been out to this school a hundred times, and she knows goddamn well nobody dresses up anymore."

I was wearing battered trousers and a faded golf shirt. Inelegant though my ensemble may have seemed, it was a better fit for the surroundings than Goldstein's suit. The teacher's lounge was a dank little office, with an opaque window that looked across a service shaft onto the other side of the building. There was a black and white television, a few rickety chairs and a couple of dusty books—a history of rocketry, an introductory guide to accounting—on an old card table.

"Do you drink coffee?" Goldstein said, offering me one of the Starbucks cups. "I bought an extra, just in case."

"No thanks," I said, pointing at the table. "I've got some already."

"That's one cool coffee mug," Goldstein said. "Do you mind if I take a look?"

"Help yourself," I said. Actually it was more of a tankard than a mug. The base was ceramic, with a pewter lid and maroon bands. On one side was a hand-painted illustration of Andrew Jackson shooting Charles Dickinson in a duel. On the other side, a quotation of Jackson's was embossed in gold.

"That's awesome!" Goldstein said. "Is it original?"

"Yeah, 1839," I said. "It was a gift. From the principal, actually."

"The principal?"

"Elaine Jorgenson. She used to teach history." I had been her student-teacher, and she gave it to me when I got my job here.

"That's the famous duel, right, where Jackson fooled Dickinson with the size of his coat?"

"Yeah," I said. "That's right. Did you take Lister's class on antebellum America?"

"No. Actually this if my first year at Xavier," he said, looking at the floor.

"Oh yeah? What, did you transfer?"

"Yeah, actually, I did."

"From where?"

"Harvard, actually." He mumbled the word Harvard, like he was proud as heck he'd gone there, but he thought it better to couch the information in some half-assed admission, so as not to intimidate me. I took another long look at him before saying anything. There was nothing particularly remarkable about him. Just a scrawny, eager kid, who happened to have a good resume.

"Harvard, huh. Why would you come back here then?"

"Oh, I just wanted to be closer to my family," he said.

"You must have done pretty well on the SAT," I said.

"Huh?" he said, blinking twice. "Yeah. I guess so."

"What did you get?"

"Excuse me?" he tilted his head to the side.

"What was your score? 1400? You can tell me. I won't feel threatened. I did pretty well, too. Not that I went to a fancy college. Couldn't afford it. I went to ISU. I was working my way through school."

"1600," he said. "Yeah, I got a perfect score."

He was lying. I could tell the way he spit it out like that, just like my delta students do when they're pissed off. "You know all that Harvard stuff won't help you much here," I said.

"What are you talking about?"

"This ain't the Ivy League. All those hours in the library aren't gonna make it any easier for you to connect with these kids. Look around you," I said, pointing at the busted radiator and leaking faucet. "You're not in the ivory tower here. Believe it or not, I worked with a teacher from Harvard before. He didn't make it."

"You don't know a thing about me," Goldstein said, his fists clenching. "Not one."

"Good for you," I said. "You just passed your first test. You didn't back down; that's a good sign."

Goldstein forced a grin at this.

"Don't get a big head about it. I do know something about you. Two things. Harvard and you're wearing a suit. And I wouldn't put either of those in the plus column. But time for chitchat is about over. I've got a class coming in."

"What class is this?" he asked, as we walked from the teachers' lounge to my classroom.

"It's my AP class," I said. "AP means Advanced Placement. They take a test at the end of the year for college credit."

"I know. I took AP when I was in high school," Goldstein said.

"Right, Harvard," I said. "Of course you did."

"Is this a good group of kids?" Goldstein said.

"They're like any group. Some are nice. Some are pricks."

"No, I guess I mean what makes them AP kids?"

"Obviously they're the best students at Edgemont, though they're not necessarily the smartest."

"What's the difference?"

"There are plenty of kids in the regular track who are smart enough, but not motivated. A lot of bright African American kids don't want to be one of just two or three black kids in their class. The black kids who are in AP tend to be more like the white kids than like most other black kids."

"More like them how?" he said, raising an eyebrow.

"You know, they're like you. They're a well-heeled group—the parents are college educated. The kids drive better cars than I do. The boys are all either on the soccer or the lacrosse teams; the girls run cross-country and play field hockey. They're pretty and thin, and some of them are anorexic because they see their fathers too little. During the week, these guys go to practice or music lessons, and do their homework while barraging each other with dozens of inane texts. On weekends, the popular ones have a party at the house of whoever's parents are out of town, where they make out and drink too much. They're good students, but mostly conformist and dull."

Goldstein pursed his lips, as though he was about to contest what I'd said, but he decided against it. The bell rang then anyway, and the students rushed in from the hallway, still chattering as they took their seats.

"Take out your notebooks, ladies and gentleman," I said, "and let's begin our press conference. President Jackson is ready to entertain your questions now." The students were quiet and ready with pen and paper within thirty seconds. AP kids may be dull and conformist, but they rarely pose discipline problems. I donned my fake beard and top hat, hit play on the CD player and, to the bouncing chords of "Hail to the Chief," strode over to the podium. This is one of my favorite activities, where I play the part of a president, and the students play reporters, asking questions about specific policies or actions.

The first question got us off to an excellent start. "Mr. Jackson, I understand your wife Rachel is the daughter of a prostitute," Peter Boyle said. "And, furthermore, that she is married to another man. Would you care to comment?" Pete's a nerdy kid, who seems to always be wearing a *Lord of the Rings* T-shirt and the same pair of tired jeans. He's one of my favorite students.

"You, sir," I said, scowling my fiercest scowl, "what's your name?"

"Peter Boyle, Mr. President."

"How dare you impugn the good name of my wife, Mr. Boyle," I said, with a wink. "If you be not a poltroon nor a coward, you will give me an opportunity to meet on the field of honor, so that I may exact satisfaction."

"Indeed, sir, let's have our seconds arrange it," Peter said.

I waited for another question, but Peter and I had lost the class. No hands went up until Anne Burch said, "Wait, Mr. Cavaliere, is Peter making that stuff up?"

"No. Not really," I said. "The origins of Jackson's wife are disputed. She was from New Orleans, and some of his enemies claimed her mother had been a prostitute, though we'll probably never know the truth of it. And as far as the bigamy, in a sense it's true. Before she met Andrew, Rachel had been married to a playboy, who abandoned her. Apparently she never bothered to get a legal divorce before she married Jackson."

"How does he know all that?" Shelley Krawcyk said, meaning Peter, not me. "None of it's in the book." Shelley is my least favorite type of student, hardworking but expedient. Having no real interest in history, she did exactly what I asked of her and not a whit more. Worse, she was a dogged grade grubber. Twice a week, she tried to get me to tell her what percentage she was earning.

In the last fifteen years, teachers have started using a spreadsheet program to register their grades. It's cool in some ways; you don't have to break out your calculator at the end of each term and do all that tedious arithmetic. But the downside is the students have gotten completely spoiled. Some teachers, especially in math, give out their grades once a week. I saw Shelley standing in front of the foreign language office once, waiting for her grade with the grim tenacity of a slot jockey hoping for a payout. But I refuse to be badgered into weekly updates. That's the whole point of the nine-week report card. Besides, giving students too much information only empowers them. Unfortunately, Shelley got an A during the first quarter. I tried to tweak her average by giving her a D for class participation, but it wasn't enough. Her tests are always A's.

"How *do* you know all that stuff, Peter?" Anne said. She was nerdy, too, but she had a pretty face and if she'd worn spaghetti straps and tight pants, like some of the other girls, instead of baggy overalls and a college sweatshirt, she would have had more boys after her than she could count. But she seemed way more interested in politics. Anne was an old school lefty. Her backpack was filled with dog-eared copies of *The Nation,* and she said things you don't hear sane people say anymore, like the Rosenbergs were innocent. Or that communism might actually work if only we gave it a real chance.

"I dunno, I guess I learned it in middle school," Peter said, looking down at his desk.

This was a lie. Peter went to the same middle school as the rest of the students. The truth is he was a genuine buff. But Peter was so lacking in confidence, that even in an AP class, he feared he'd be mocked if the other kids found out.

"I will not entertain any more questions of a personal nature," I said. "Let's stick to policy. Yes, ma'am," I pointed to Anne.

"Mr. President, how do you defend the Indian Removal Act of 1830, when it means displacement for thousands of Native Americans? Plus it's based on massive treaty violations."

"Which treaty has been violated?" I said.

"You know," Anne said, flustered, "that treaty with the Cherokee—"

"Which treaty with the Cherokee? There are several."

"I don't remember the name, but you know which one I'm talking about—"

"Yes, I do," I said, breaking character, "but your job is to know this stuff, including the details. That was your homework. So, go on, look it up."

While Anne leafed through her textbook, Maurice Lowes asked, "What about the Trail of Tears? U.S. soldiers rounded up old Cherokee women and children and drove them from their homes at gunpoint and forced them to move hundreds of miles to a new and strange—"

"The Treaty of New Echota—" Anne chimed in.

"Yes," I said, ignoring Anne. "The fate of the savage peoples of this continent is indeed sad. And it was with regret that I chose the path of removal for my red children. But the time for nostalgia for their primitive way of life is long past. In fact, my removal policy is the last best hope for these unfortunate children of the forest."

"The last best hope!" Anne was apoplectic now. "The last best hope for them is to steal their land, send them on a cross country journey, hundreds of miles away, and a quarter of them will die on the trip?"

"Yes," I said, calmly. "That's correct. Look at the tribes that once populated this continent. What has become of the Choctaw, the Creeks, the Narragansett, even the once proud Iroquois? Extinction. All of them are gone, or nearly so. Is it not clear, after two hundred years of experience, that there is no hope for the savage when he encounters a civilized society? Is it not clear we do the savage a great disservice by strangling him to death slowly? Shall we not learn from our history and see that if the children of the forest are to survive at all, they must remove to the far side of the Mississippi. There, given time and patient, Christian instruction, they may practice at the arts of civilization and, God willing, one day take their rightful place at the table of mankind, alongside the other civilized members of the family of nations."

"But you can't call the Cherokee savages," Anne said. "I mean, in the article you gave us, they said Sequoyah invented a Cherokee alphabet, and they even had a daily newspaper they published. And some of them owned plantations and farmed, and lived in big mansions, and even had African American slaves."

This was a good answer. Jackson's critics like to point out the hypocrisy behind the Cherokee removal since, in the 18th century, the Cherokee, having witnessed the destruction of their neighbors, buried the hatchet and took the advice of U.S. government officials, assimilating more than any other tribe.

"Sure," I said, "there are a few half-breeds who ape the ways of the white men, but most of the full-blooded ones live in a liquor-induced stupor, savage as ever."

Some of the kids shook their heads, and one girl, Colleen West, gave a little gasp at the phrase half-breed. I looked over at Goldstein to see his reaction, but he was staring at his shoes.

"You know, Mr. Cavaliere," Colleen West said, "I'm part Cherokee, and I don't think those are very nice things to say."

Colleen was one of the biggest whiners in the class. She was a marginal AP student, but unlike most of the kids at the bottom tier of the class, who were pretty quiet, she complained incessantly about the amount of reading I assigned and about how hard the tests were.

"You gotta remember," I said, "I'm playing a role, and these are the actual things President Jackson said. I can show you the speech he made." I gestured to my bookcase. "There were some Whigs who criticized him on exactly the grounds Anne raised, and Jackson made just the sort of defense I gave. You have to be able to distinguish between the message and the messenger. You may not like the phrasing Jackson used, but it's a critical point."

I paced in front of the class, for effect, before continuing. "Jackson's point, and my point, is that all of these events were beyond Jackson's control, beyond anyone's control. People want there to be heroes and villains in history. They don't like what happened to the Cherokee, so they want to blame someone, and Jackson is a handy villain. These folks subscribe to what's called the 'Great Man' school of history. That's the theory that our leaders change the world. But I'm afraid that's a naïve view of the way the world works. It really just amounts to hero worship."

The class was silent for a minute, but finally Jimmy Civiatelli spoke. "But what about Jefferson?" he said. "I mean, without him there would have been no Declaration of Independence and maybe no revolution." Jimmy rarely did his reading, and he really wasn't all that bright, but neither of those facts was enough to keep him quiet.

"Does anybody disagree with that?" I asked. It should have been obvious from my question that I did, but I prefer to have the students challenge each other whenever possible.

No hands went up. "What do you think of Jimmy's point, Louis?" I said. Louis Sterling, the lone black boy in the class, was one of my top three students, right up there with Anne and Peter.

"I don't know," he said, looking away from Jimmy as he spoke. "I mean, after all, Jefferson was only one of five men appointed by the Continental Congress to work on the committee to draft the Declaration. And if he hadn't been there, Adams would have written it. Anyway, by the time they appointed him, the Congress had pretty well made up their minds to declare for independence."

"Good answer, Louis," I said, smiling. "People who don't understand history like to think of great heroes and great villains marching across the stage, as if they were characters in a soap opera. It's a romantic idea, childish really. But the more history you know, the more you'll come to understand that individuals are basically powerless to shape their own lives, let alone the fate of their country. We're all pushed along by circumstance. Part of growing up, part of becoming a wiser person, is recognizing that."

"But what about Lincoln?" Peter said. "Wouldn't you say that he saved the Union?"

"You've got a better case with Lincoln than with Jefferson," I conceded, "but even so, it's easy to get carried away with the importance of any one man. Near the end of the war Lincoln himself once said—well, wait, let me get the quotation exactly." I pulled one of my Lincoln biographies from the shelf. "He said, 'I claim not to have controlled events but confess plainly that events have controlled me.' It was really the Union armies that saved the country. This was the point Jackson understood, the point I'm trying to make. Jackson couldn't have saved the Cherokee. Nobody could have. And unfortunately they're still in sorry shape today."

"But Mr. Cavaliere," Anne said, "isn't it true that the Native Americans are doing well now because of casinos?"

"Yes and no," I said. "There are a few casinos that make big bucks. The Pequot in Connecticut have the biggest casino in America. There are only about a thousand of them, so they're really rich, but they don't share it with other tribes. And most tribes don't live in populated areas, so they can't build huge casinos.

A lot of younger people from the western tribes are moving to big cities, but they tend to be really poor. Lots of them are alcoholics. I don't know what it's going to take to get them into the middle class. I guess they need to come up with their own version of the burrito or the egg roll."

A couple of kids laughed at that. But Colleen West didn't think it was so funny. She grabbed her books and stormed out of the room, fumbling with her backpack. "I'm going to see my guidance counselor," she spat as she left.

Normally, I wouldn't allow a kid to walk out on me like that. But in this case, I thought it was best to let her go. "Why don't we switch to another topic," I said. "We've just got time to discuss the national bank."

"Mr. Jackson," Louis said, "everybody knows you vetoed the national bank, which set off a financial crisis. So lots of people say it's your fault that the Panic of 1837 occurred. What do you say to that?"

"Nonsense. The Panic of 1837 was the result of international trade problems with China and England, not because I put a stop to the bank, that scourge of the common man."

"But you didn't even do it legally," Anne said. "The Senate asked you for documents about the veto, and you wouldn't even turn them over. That's why they voted to censure you. You're the only president in history to be censured by the Senate. How do you defend yourself?"

"The United States Senate," I thundered, "is a rogues' gallery that has placed itself in the service of that infamous brigand, Henry Clay. My lone regret is that I did not shoot Clay when I had the chance. As far as the censure, I will not legitimize it with a reply." I grabbed my Old Hickory tankard from my desk and read the quotation from Jackson aloud. "Suffice it to say that I have lived in vain if it be necessary to enter into a formal vindication of my character."

After class as we walked through the hallway, Goldstein said, "Jackson's a hero of yours, huh?"

"I don't like the word hero," I said. "But, yeah, Jackson's my guy."

"What is it you like about him?" Goldstein said, "I mean he was a slaveholder, dueler, Indian fighter . . . ."

"True," I said, "but for me it's more about style. He was, I don't know, I guess the word for it is theatrical. I like drama. And playing him certainly provides it."

"It's a great idea for a lesson," Goldstein said. "Do you mind if I borrow that and do a news conference for another president later on in the year?"

"Be my guest," I said. "No one owns any of these ideas. You should borrow liberally. It's all been done before by somebody else, anyway. Hey," I looked at him, "you don't think the kids got too bent out of shape by my little speech, do you?"

By now we had reached the faculty mailroom, and I reached my hand into my box. There was just one folded-over sheet of paper in my cubbyhole. "*Call me,*" was all it said. But I recognized Dara's handwriting. I crumpled it up and shoved it down deep into the recycling bin.

"What?" Goldstein said. "You mean the bit about the burrito?"

"Yeah."

"No. I'm sure they're fine," he said. But he mumbled it unconvincingly, looking straight ahead.

"Come on," I said. "Don't bullshit me."

"I don't know. You were so convincing in the role, it almost seemed like you kind of relished saying *savage* and *half-breed.*" He looked nervously over at me, "Like maybe you blurred the distinction a little yourself."

"What distinction?"

"Between message and messenger."

I thought about that for a second before answering. Maybe Goldstein had bigger stones than I'd given him credit for. "I don't deny that I enjoy being at the center of attention." We'd reached an intersection of hallways, and I said, "The cafeteria is that way, but if you don't mind, we'll take a quick detour on the way to lunch."

"Sure," Goldstein said.

"I want to pop into the guidance counselor's office real quick," I said. "There's someone I've got to talk to." Someone was Dara Jurevicius, the secretary for the guidance office, and I was planning to tell her to knock it off with all her notes. But when we reached the office, I pushed the door open and took only a half step in before retreating. Dara was talking to Colleen West, of all people. Colleen was standing to the side of Dara's desk, gesticulating animatedly as she spoke. Dara patted her on the shoulder and nodded sympathetically at whatever she was saying. As the guidance secretary, Dara was the gatekeeper for Josh Wentworth, the school's guidance counselor. She had as much contact with the kids as Wentworth did, and was actually pretty popular with them. I wondered if Colleen was complaining about me. If so, then she had something in common with Dara. "You know what," I said to Goldstein, "this can wait. Let's go get lunch."

There was still a line when we got to teachers' cafeteria, and I pointed to the daily menu, written in curlicue marker on a whiteboard behind the serving line, while we waited. "Don't get your hopes up," I said. "The food is pretty average." Actually, I was being kind because Betty, the server, was waiting to take my order. "Grilled chicken and jalapeno poppers, Betty," I said.

Betty dropped a charred breast into a bun and used her tongs to pick out three small jalapenos from her tray.

"Can I get one that's a little less burned, Betty? And maybe some bigger poppers. Those are kind of puny."

"We can't take special requests," Betty said, handing me the plate. "Everybody would want them." It wasn't like Betty to be difficult, and I was going to say something, but she moved away from me and was already asking Goldstein what he wanted. I watched with envy as she served Goldstein four fat poppers.

When we had both got our food, I surveyed the tables to find the best place to sit. Since this was the first day of the second academic quarter, a lot of teachers had new schedules, and the usual lunch groups had been scrambled. Unfortunately, few options were attractive. A table of secretaries was out of the question. The other large table, full of teachers, was not much better. The men sitting there were driver's-ed instructors, members of the Christian Coalition, or both. The best option was a smaller table with a mix of teachers from different departments. Though, judging from the conversation wafting across the room, it was by no means ideal. They seemed to be talking about the redesigned quarters and dollars the Treasury Department has been issuing.

"I just got the one with Georgia on it," said Josh Wentworth. "It's got a peach on the back."

"Does anyone have the one from Illinois yet?" asked Cynthia, a new French teacher. I'd had lunch with her last quarter, and she seemed unable to avoid the mindless banter that takes place on small-town AM radio. Lots of amiable talk about collectibles, real-estate prices and school assemblies. On the plus side, she was nice to look at. And from the way she dressed—tiny black skirts that accented her bulbous ass—you could tell she knew it.

"No," said Wentworth authoritatively. "You wouldn't. It won't be available for another six months."

"Anyway," I said to Goldstein, loudly, as we sat down, "The only one who seemed bent out of shape was Colleen." I prefer to be in the middle of a discussion when I arrive at a lunch table, because it gives me a chance to redirect the conversation.

"Which one is she?" Goldstein asked, his gaze darting around the table at the other teachers.

"The one who claimed she's part Indian."

"Why do you say claimed?" Goldstein asked.

"Because she's lying?"

"Lying?" Goldstein furrowed his brow.

"That's right."

"Do you know her family?"

"No."

"Then how can you say—"

"They're all lying," I said, taking a bite of my sandwich. Though I'd slathered it in barbecue sauce, the meat was still tough and bitter.

"Who is *they*?"

"Everybody who says that."

"Everybody who says what?" Wentworth said. The conversation about currency had fizzled, and he looked annoyed. Wentworth was extra short, maybe five-feet-two in dress shoes, and he had a major-league Napoleon complex.

"That they're Indian," I said.

"What do you mean?" Wentworth said, taking over the argument from Goldstein.

"I mean they're lying or at the very least mistaken. People think there's something cool about it. You know, back in the 60's, Bob Dylan told anybody who would listen that he was part Sioux. That's how he laid Joan Baez." I shook my head in envy at the prospect of doing just that. "But now it's not so much cool as it is romantic. At least to the middle class white population around here, who'd like to claim some connection to the glorious lost cause of a non-materialistic, environmentally sensitive lifestyle that seems so much more virtuous than our own mass-consumption, spiritually impoverished lives. I suppose it's tempting to identify with Indians, when the view from the bay window in your subdivision isn't marred by empty bottles of Colt 45, rusting automobiles and seedy bingo parlors."

"But there *are* kids who are part Native American," Cynthia said. "I did a survey of the kids at the beginning of the school year, and several said they were."

"How many said that?" I asked, softening my tone.

"I don't know, seven or eight."

"Ha! Seven or eight in a class of twenty-five," I said. "There you go."

"What do you mean?" Cynthia said, frowning.

"Do you know the actual percentage of the U.S. population that's Indian? Like one percent, only. And this kid Colleen, she said it was her grandmother who was Indian. Ask your kids, Cynthia, and you'll see the relative is always a female—it has to be because the last names are never Indian. And the grandmother being part Indian is distant enough that no one could ever contradict them."

"Well, maybe—" Wentworth started to say, but I overrode him.

"And notice that this kid said she was Cherokee."

"So what?"

"It's a total giveaway," I said. "Everybody, absolutely everybody claims they're Cherokee or Sioux. They're the only tribes anybody has ever heard of. At least Dylan was from Minnesota; I mean, it was somewhat plausible. And they always claim some improbable ratio of Indian blood, too, like they say they're one fifth Indian."

Nobody spoke for a moment, and I guess it was sort of an awkward silence. Then Cynthia said, "Aren't you going to introduce us to your friend?"

"Yeah, sorry," I said. "This is my student-teacher, Eric Goldstein. He's from Xavier College."

"I can't believe they still let you have student-teachers, Cavaliere, after what happened the last time," Wentworth said. "And to think, you'd take one that's not female. Well, I guess you're never too old to be surprised. What convinced you? The extra free periods?"

The bit about the girl was such a cheap shot. As Wentworth knew full well, that case was more than four years old, and I had been exonerated. Why else would the college have agreed to set me up with another student-teacher? And to be honest—sure, the extra free periods I would get when Goldstein took over my classes were a big incentive. That's the main reason anybody has a student-teacher, and anyone who tells you different is full of shit. But lunch was ending and there wasn't time to say all this before the bell rang, so I called Wentworth an asshole, bused my tray and went back to class.

The next class was delta level World History.

"Delta?" Goldstein asked, as we hustled through the hall.

"Yeah, we have tracking—you know, ability grouping. It goes from alpha, which is AP, down to delta."

"Alpha to delta," he said, "you mean like in *Brave New World?*"

"You got it," I said. "Horrible, isn't it? I think the administration is too stupid to get the reference. They've never heard of Aldous Huxley."

"Don't the parents complain?" Goldstein said.

"The only ones who would know what the terms mean are the parents of the top kids, and it's not really their problem. The parents of the deltas—well, I guess they've got other things to worry about."

I was just starting my lesson on the pyramids of Egypt, when a kid I didn't know came in the room. "I'm Billy Jackson," he announced, interrupting me.

"Yeah," I said. "What can I do for you?"

"I'm new," he said, as though I might be expecting him. "History, right?"

"Yeah, this is World History," I said. "Let me see that." I pointed to the schedule he was clutching in his left hand. A glance told me he was in the right place. His counselor had given him a full plate of remedial classes.

"So they put all the rough Negroes up in this room," Billy said, surveying the class.

"Who you calling rough?" Sean Robbins said, sitting up straight in his desk-chair for the first time all period. I was a little surprised to hear Sean take exception to Billy's characterization. After all, Sean spent a good deal of effort cultivating his tough guy image. He wouldn't be caught dead with a backpack. Every day he came to class with a pen wedged behind his ear and a few random sheets of paper jammed in his back pocket. And he talked loudly about how his brother was a gang member in the drug-infested neighborhood in Chicago that borders Edgemont. All this made him an odd fit at Edgemont, which is one of those rare places where blacks and whites send their kids to the same school. While there are some poor kids, mostly black, the majority of our students are headed to college at some level. The few street-hardened kids we have, like Sean, are almost always in delta. Since Goldstein was only going to be working with AP and delta, he was going to get a really skewed view of the school. The very top and the very bottom.

Billy was black, so I guess he felt entitled to observe the demographic facts of the class. And as he'd said, this was a tough looking group.

"Why don't you sit over there, Billy," I said, pointing to an open desk between Goldstein and Anisha Carter.

"How come he gets to sit there?" Sean asked.

Sean was not angling to sit next to Goldstein. Like nearly every other male in the room, Sean had begged me to let him sit next to Anisha, who is gorgeous.

"Mind your business," I said to Sean. To spare the poor girl the attentions of her fawning classmates, I hadn't, up to that point, let anyone sit next to Anisha. But I put Billy next to her because I had a hunch he was not going to get along with the other boys—usually if kids leave one school to go to another at mid-year, there's a reason. And the space next to Anisha was the only spot left in the room where he wouldn't have to sit next to another boy. But, as I explained to Sean, none of this was his concern.

Billy seemed to notice Goldstein before he did Anisha. He plopped his books on the desk, and looked Eric up and down. "You musta pissed off the principal to get put up in here."

I could see why Billy was confused. Though his dress clothes set him apart from the RocaWear jerseys and gaudy "gold" chains of the kids, Eric definitely looked young enough to be a student.

"No, Billy," I said. "Mr. Goldstein is my student-teacher. He's observing the class today is all. He'll be teaching next week."

"You mean you gonna be my teacher," Billy said, his face lighting up in a jack-o-lantern smile. "My bad." Billy extended his hand by way of apology.

Goldstein looked at me, to see if he should shake it. I shrugged and Eric reached for Billy's hand. The two of them performed a seamless sliding shake that ended in a snap. I'd seen kids do this plenty of times, but never a teacher.

Billy evidently hadn't seen a teacher do it either. He was so pleased he blurted out, "You're pretty down for a teacher, Joe." The class laughed at Billy for calling Goldstein, 'Joe.'

"You're pretty OC for your first day, Joe," Sean said to Billy, using the slang term for out of control.

Anyway, Luther Watkins gave a great belly laugh in response to Sean's dig. It was quite a noise; Luther's balloonish frame jiggled over the top of my chair as he guffawed. He had to sit there because he couldn't fit in the desk-chairs, which are old and narrow, with peeling yellow paint. Relics of a slimmer age.

"All right, Luther and Sean, settle down." I understood that Sean felt the need to challenge Billy, since he was the new kid. Still, I questioned his judgment. Billy's jack-o-lantern smile had curdled into a snarl, and his biceps bulged impressively through his thin, white tank top. A wife-beater, the alpha kids call it. And he had a bull neck, crooked yellow teeth and angry mounds of acne that had already scarred his face for life. He was a nineteenth-century, pre-cosmetic kind of homely. Only poor kids look like that.

"*Everybody* settle down," I said. "Let's get back to the Egyptians." The collective posture of the class slumped as I handed out a worksheet on the construction of the pyramids. But after a little muttering, they all got to work.

After class ended, Goldstein made his way over to the chalkboard.

"What do you think?" I said. "Most people can tell whether teaching suits them after just a few hours in a classroom. What about you? Do you have a gut feeling about it?"

"Yeah," Goldstein said, "I suppose I do. I really think this is for me. The place just seems so alive with opportunities."

"Opportunities?" I said, squinting skeptically at him.

"Yeah," Goldstein said, "you know, opportunities to really make a connection with these kids."

"That's why you want to teach, isn't it?" I said. "To make a difference."

"Sure," he said, frowning, "isn't that why you do it?"

"No," I said, "it's not. If you think you're gonna come in and change the world, you've got a hard road ahead of you."

Goldstein was fresh from all those horrible education courses, so I wasn't surprised at his attitude. It's a great irony that education programs are the worst taught and least practical classes available at most colleges. They tend to be run by people with a Ph.D. in education, but no classroom experience, or by former teachers who hated teaching so much they did whatever they could to get out. They preach a messianic brand of education, so far removed from reality that loads of new teachers burn themselves out in frustration when their efforts to transform the lives of America's youth are blithely ignored by their students.

"But if you don't think you do any good, why do you teach?" Goldstein said, rubbing his scalp. "If you can't help people to change their lives, what's the point of this job? How is it any better than investment banking or working in a law firm?"

I thought about why I like teaching before I answered. "There are a lot of reasons this is a good job. First of all, you have to enjoy it. I love history and this job allows me to continue learning more of it every year. And you have to enjoy hanging out with teenagers. I have a lot fun goofing around with them, dressing up like a president, joking around. Not many people get paid to do that. And don't underestimate the vacations. You know the old saying about teaching: the three best things about this job are June, July and August."

"But all of those reasons are about you," Goldstein said. He looked genuinely troubled. "What about helping the students?"

CHAPTER 2

LATER THAT NIGHT, I was stripped down to my boxers, clicking through cable TV and drinking a glass of whiskey, when the first visitor ever to my apartment rang the bell in the lobby of my walk-up. I'd never heard the bell before, and the sound made me jump, so that the ice cubes rattled against the skin of the glass. Actually, the sound was more of a buzzer than a bell, like the hum of an old light bulb with faulty wiring. I got up off the futon and walked toward the door, tossing the ice and a puddle of watery whiskey into the sink on my way to the intercom.

"Who is it?" I said, as I held down the talk button.

"It's me, George," a voice crackled back.

"What do you want, Dara?"

"Just let me come in for a minute and have a cup of coffee. I'm too tipsy to drive right now. And it's raining."

I looked out the window. She was right; though I hadn't noticed it; fat drops of rain were lashing the windows. I buzzed her in. While she walked up the stairs, I raced to my bedroom and grabbed a pair of sweatpants, pulling them over my boxers. By the time I got back to the hallway, she was knocking on the front door.

"Easy there," I called, fumbling with the locks. "I'm coming." My apartment was in a seedy area, and in addition to the lock on the doorknob, the landlord had installed a turnkey, a deadbolt and a chain. The locks, though, seemed mostly for show, because the door was so hollow and cheap, it felt like one good kick would splinter it.

"This is a nice place," Dara said, meeting my gaze with a goofy smile, as I finally opened the door.

"No, it's not," I said. "It's a dump, and I wouldn't be here if it wasn't for you."

I'd already taken my contacts out for the night, and I squinted at her as she stood in the doorway, water dripping from her bottle-blond hair onto the floor. She smelled like a saloon, smoky and stale. The water began to pool around her shoes. Thin black straps and stiletto heels, terrible shoes for a rainstorm.

"What are you doing here?" I said.

"They all bought Gwen and me drinks at McGuire's," she said, her voice twittering like she'd just been elected homecoming queen.

"Who did?"

"There was a convention of top salesmen from all over Illinois. They're meeting at Roosevelt Plaza." She pronounced Roosevelt so that the first syllable sounded the same as the last in kangaroo. Just from that one word, you could tell she was from Beverly, the same working class neighborhood, on the southwest side, that I'm from. Unlike Dara, I'd worked hard to scrub the Beverly off of me.

"Shut up about the salesmen," I said. "What are you doing *here?*"

"I told you," she said, "I can't drive after all that Midori. Anyway, I wanted to see you," she pursed her lips. "You know we'll have a good time."

Dara was, in fact, a lot of fun. Actually, she was the most social person I'd ever met. She'd been at the school less than two years, and already she'd managed to make friends with just about everybody. I first met her when she came by my room one day to collect for the school nurse's retirement gift. Normally I don't pony up for those kinds of things, but Dara was smart about it. Instead of coming right out to ask me for the money, she started off by saying, "George Cavaliere, right? I'm Dara Jurevicius."

"Yeah," I said, "good to meet you."

"Same here," she said. "I hear so many things about you in the guidance office. It's nice to finally meet you."

"You're new," I said. "It doesn't seem fair that you got stuck collecting money."

"I volunteered," she said. "I love getting out of my office and meeting people. Think about it," she said, smiling, "if I just sat at my desk all day, I wouldn't have gotten to meet you."

"Well, I'm glad you did volunteer," I said. Before I knew it, I was ten bucks poorer, and I'd agreed to meet her and the other secretaries out for drinks after work on Friday. That night, as was her habit, Dara had too much to drink, and I gave her a ride home. Suffice it to say we had a lot of fun in the car, after I pulled up to the curb in front of her house. And we'd had been having good times for almost a year.

Yeah, Dara was fun all right. But, unfortunately, as I'd learned six weeks ago, she was also demanding, vengeful and reckless. That was when, after I refused to move in with her, she called Amy, my wife, and told her about our affair. Yeah, I'm married. Technically, anyway.

"Admit it, George," Dara said, "we've always had fun."

"Yeah, sure, a great time," I said. "But explain something to me. If you were having such a great time, why you didn't think telling my wife was gonna ruin it?"

"We've had fun," she said, "but it's time for something more."

"Well it's not gonna happen," I said. "I'll call you a cab and get you some coffee." She gave me a pouty look, and I turned to go get the phone before she could say anything else.

After I got off of the phone, I went to the tiny kitchen area to make a pot of coffee. I had only two burners on my electric stove, and the rings were rusted red. The stove did work, though, and soon I had a pot of water going. But it wasn't until the water reached a boil that I realized I didn't have anything to grind the coffee beans with, so I made her a mug of tea instead.

When I came back, Dara was talking into her cell phone, and smoking a cigarette. "All right, sweetie," she said. "Call me first thing in the morning and tell me what happens." She looked up at me, "Sorry, that was Gwen. She's having trouble with her husband again. He just will not—"

"Here," I said, cutting her off and handing her the cup. The trials of Gwen, the mail lady, and her insensitive husband piqued my interest less than Dara imagined. "I'm out of coffee. All I've got is tea."

"Sit down, George," Dara said, her voice slipping from a gossipy pitch into a husky drawl. Caressing the futon with one hand, she dunked the cigarette into the steaming mug of Earl Grey with the other. Then she uncrossed her legs.

I looked back and forth, first at her then at the empty seat on the futon. The fabric of her blouse was damp, and I could see the outline of her breasts, round and firm.

I'd moved out of my house in a hurry. Actually, it's probably more accurate to say Amy kicked me out, since my clothes were packed when I came home from school. After a couple of nights at a motel, I signed a lease for the crappy little studio where Dara found me. Anyway, the long and the short of it is I'd moved in a rush, and though I suppose half of the furniture in our old house was mine, it didn't seem like a good idea to press Amy on it. And what with school and all, I hadn't had time to furnish my apartment properly. Anyway, it seemed silly to buy a ton of furniture until it was pretty certain things weren't going to work out between me and Amy. In fact, the futon was literally my only piece of furniture. I'd picked it up at Ikea, and I'd been using it as sort of a one-piece dining room set, couch and bed. I'd been meaning to get a real bed, a table and some dining room chairs. I'd actually been to a couple of garage sales to look, but I hadn't found anything decent. So, what I'm trying to say is, despite my oft-repeated vow to have nothing further to do with Dara—a vow to which I had thus far been one-hundred percent faithful—there was nowhere else to sit.

The second ever visitor to my new apartment ruined my orgasm. Well, maybe visitor isn't the right word, since the cab-driver had no intention of staying. He'd honked several times, just after I entered Dara, and for a moment I thought about getting up and telling him to go away, but the prospect of putting all my clothes on and running out in the rain was too daunting. And besides, I thought (irrationally in retrospect) if I hurried, Dara might still have time to catch the cab. Anyway, the driver quit honking after a minute, and I figured he must have left. But then the doorbell began buzzing incessantly. I managed to cum before I got up to answer the door, but just. Not satisfying.

"How did you get my new address, anyway?" I asked Dara, after I had slipped the cabbie a twenty. It was with Dara in mind that I had requested an unlisted phone number.

"Susie, in payroll," she said, looking up at me from the couch.

"Sure, your little cabal," I said.

"My *cable*?" she said, squinting back at me.

The secretaries and the lunchroom and support staff at school were like their own little sorority, with Dara as pledge-master. In fact, based on the number of evil looks I'd received in the weeks since we'd broken up, Dara seemed to have taken nearly every member of the support staff into her confidence. I don't know how she managed it, but she seemed to have convinced her friends *I* was the one at fault, which is insane, since we're both married and she's the one who ratted to *my* wife and wrecked *my* marriage.

The good news is the secretaries and teachers don't mix much, and as far as I could tell, none of my colleagues knew about our fling. To this point, I'd managed to avoid telling anyone at school that I'd even moved out.

"Come on back and lie down, George," Dara said, rolling onto her side so there was room for both of us on the futon.

"You should be getting home," I said, still standing. "Tim will be wondering about you."

"Fuck Tim." She yawned as she said her husband's name. "You know I'd rather be with you." She reached her arm out over the edge of the futon and caressed the back of my calf. "You should feel lucky, you know."

"How's that?"

"You're not the only man at work interested in me."

"Oh yeah?"

"Josh Wentworth has been flirting with me," she said, as she tickled my leg.

"That doesn't bother you?" I said. "What with him being your boss."

"Bother me," she laughed. "Josh is harmless. It just means I can get him to do what I want." Her fingertips pressing against the hairs on my shin felt scratchy and dry, like an old wool blanket. The lights in the room were off, but there was a street lamp, just outside the window, that sprayed enough yellow light into the room so that I could make out the expression on her face. Her brow was crinkled and her lips were drawn in a smug smile. Dara was up for anything, she was a fine friend to Gwen and her whole crowd, and she was damn good looking, but the more I got to know about her the less attractive I found her. Wentworth was a jackass, but even so, the callous, calculating way she talked about him bothered me.

"Listen," I said, breaking her hold with a shake of my leg. "This is it, the last time. We can't do this anymore."

"What do you mean?" she said, her eyes widening.

"I mean that's the last time. I can't see you again. Go home and see your husband before you don't have one anymore."

"Are you threatening me?" she said, sitting upright as her eyes flashed. "Is that what this is about. Revenge? 'Cause if you want me to apologize for calling Amy, I'm not going to. If she couldn't keep her man happy—"

"You're so goddamn obnoxious," I said, cutting her off. "None of this has ever been about Amy. You know what, fuck you!" I grabbed her cell phone. "I'll call him right now."

I expected Dara to protest, but instead she did the strangest thing. She lay back on the futon as though I was about to lay her again.

Tim picked up the phone on the first ring. "Dara?" he said, his voice scratchy and low. There was a short, shitty silence, and he said "Dara?" again.

I turned off the phone.

"What are you doing," Dara said, sitting up again. "You're not afraid to talk to him, are you?"

"Get out," I said.

"What?" Her voice dropped a register.

"I should never have let you in," I said, scooping her clothes off the floor and chucking them at her.

"What! You're throwing me out!" She was standing up now. "You just *came* inside of me, and now you're throwing me out?"

"Don't even start with that bullshit," I said.

"What bullshit?"

"The 'you used me like a piece of meat' bullshit. You knew the fucking deal when this whole thing started. You're the one who fucked everything up by telling Amy. You know what, I was gonna tell Tim. I really fucking was gonna. Except it's so obvious from your annoying little smirk that that's exactly what you want me to do. You're the only one who would be happy if I did. Then maybe

33

you could get Tim to finally fucking leave you, and you could make me feel guilty enough to let you come live with me. Besides, calling Tim would make us even. Well, I don't want to be even with you. Look at me. Just fucking looking at me. I'm living by myself in this shit hole. Amy's got a goddamn lawyer, and she won't return my phone calls, and it's all your fucking fault."

I was wasting my breath with that speech. When Dara makes up her mind about something, she stops listening. More to the point, after slipping into her heels, wrapping her skirt around her waist and putting her top on backward, Dara left. I chased her down the staircase, to the first floor landing, still shouting, until I heard the front door slam behind her.

I was standing there in my boxers, no shirt on, when the door to one of the apartments on the first floor creaked. I jumped back. But before the door opened, the chain caught on its slide. Two blue eyes peeked around the edge of the frame. I met their gaze, and the door closed as suddenly as it had opened.

CHAPTER 3

I DRINK FOUR OR FIVE TUMBLERS of whiskey every night, though I rarely get tanked, and I firmly believe grading papers is the main cause of my drinking habit. It's hard to explain to a non-teacher exactly what is so soul-crushing about grading. After all, I'm a compulsive reader, especially history. But there's something about student writing that makes you want to shave your teeth. Maybe it's the poor grammar (the phrase "they should of" is a particular pet peeve of mine), or maybe it's just that I resent working diligently at home on some piece of crap assignment a kid dashed off, while shoving a hot dog down his throat during lunch. In any case, I find it almost impossible to grade for longer than thirty minutes without a little lubrication. So the absolute best thing about having Goldstein as my student-teacher was I would have fewer papers to grade.

Still, the prospect of more free time was a mixed blessing. I've been known to get into trouble unless I keep myself busy. With that in mind I took a job coaching eighth grade basketball at William Lloyd Garrison Junior High, one of the feeder schools for Edgemont. I love basketball; I've played all my life, so it seemed a good fit. And with a pending divorce, I needed the extra cash. There was just one potential problem. I'm not too fond of young kids. Even ninth graders rub me wrong. That might sound like an odd thing for a teacher to say, but I'd rather work a furnace, like my old man did, than teach primary school. My wife Amy teaches third grade. We met in grad school, about four years ago, when we were both getting our master's in education, which is the easiest way to move up the pay scale. Anyway, whenever I've asked Amy how she can stand working with such dependent children, she'll smile and say she loves kids. I've never understood that answer. Sure, I can see why she likes the sweet ones, the nice ones, the shy ones. But it completely escapes me how she has the patience to deal with the needy pests, who need help wiping their noses.

I took some solace from the fact that Garrison school mostly serves the wealthiest part of Edgemont. I figured there wouldn't be much social work, and I could just concentrate on basketball. When I showed up at the school for tryouts on Friday afternoon, the kids were crammed into a little hallway outside the gym, moving around like cars jockeying for a parking space at the mall. We had to wait in the hall until the girls finished practicing. Some of the boys were so excited they were actually hopping, holding one foot in the air, showing off the gleaming white leather of their new shoes. Others were bouncing balls against the cinderblock walls. It made an awful racket.

"Hey," I said, when a stray one rolled toward me, "knock that off."

I snaked my way to the end of the hallway, where a couple of guys were hanging out by the gym door, peering in at the girls as they huddled around their coach. "Gentlemen," I said, "back away from the door."

Most of them cooperated, but one kid still stood there. He was tall enough to look into the gym without standing on his toes. As I walked over to him, he rapped on the pane of glass at the top of the door. His knocking caught the attention of a couple of the girls, and when they looked back at him, he smooched the window, leaving a perfectly formed mist imprint of his lips.

"Are you deaf?" I said, poking him in the shoulder. "Get away from there until the girls are done."

"Sorry, sir." He did a double take when he saw me, as though shocked at the sight of an adult. Then he hung his head. But he did it too quick, in almost a practiced way, as though he was used to getting in trouble. He was tall, about five-feet-nine with greasy brown hair, a pocked complexion and a few mousy whiskers above his lip.

"Are you trying out for the team?" I asked.

"Yes, sir."

"Well you're not off to such a good start." He looked totally crestfallen, and there was an awkward moment where I didn't know what to say, so, finally, to break the silence, I asked him his name.

"Morris Spicer Jr., sir." He said it in such an eager tone of voice I half expected him to salute me.

"All right, Morris. You don't have to call me 'sir.' Coach is fine."

He nodded nervously, like he was afraid he'd offended me again.

"How come no shorts, Morris?" I asked, pointing at his pants. It came out harsher than I meant it, and he studied the floor without answering. I felt a little bad I had embarrassed him, but, I mean, he was wearing blue jeans and a belt. What he was think- ing coming to tryouts like that?

Since I didn't know their names, I had them fill out player profile sheets while they stretched. Morris was the last one to finish, and I put his profile at the top of the stack. I blew my whistle and got them started in a drill. While they shot jump shots, I read over the sheets. Morris's handwriting was sloppy and boyish, and his spelling was horrible. He claimed "rebonden and deefens" as his strengths, but conceded his "driblling" needed work.

He was right about the dribbling. I watched him during the drills. He used his palms instead of his fingertips, and he looked down at the floor while he bounced the ball. Still, he was tall, and he wasn't the worst player out there, not even close. Little Adam Garcia looked more like a ventriloquist's dummy than a basketball player. According to his profile sheet, he was 4-feet-9-inches and 75 pounds.

When they were loose and had burned off some nervous energy, I began the introductions. "Good afternoon, men. I'm the new eighth grade coach. My name is George Cavaliere. My friends call me George. You can call me Mr. Cavaliere."

They sat there in stony silence.

"That was a joke," I said. "Just call me coach." My old YMCA coach started practice with that line every year. I thought it was pretty funny, but I guess he must have delivered it better than I did.

"Now," I said, "I want to say a few words about the tryout process. We can't carry thirty guys on this team. We're going to have to limit the squad to twelve. That's just how it's done."

One of the boys, a kid with a shock of blond hair and a T-shirt from Michael Jordan's basketball camp, nodded his head in agreement. He was a little guy, not as small as Adam Garcia, but definitely pre-pubescent.

"Because I don't work at this school," I said, "I can guarantee you I'm coming to this without any prejudices or biases. I think that's a big advantage. I'm going to be completely objective in deciding who makes the team. Everybody gets an equal shot."

While I ran them through some more drills, I tried to match each kid with his profile sheet. The blond boy was named Dan Wexler; the other kids called him Wex. He was a decent little guard—a good handle, nice shot, but on the small side. He looked like he was really having fun out there, though. He smiled during the drills and shrugged his shoulders bashfully when he made a mistake.

After a while, I blew the whistle and started them scrimmaging. When I turned around, Coach Gresecki was waiting to talk to me. He was huge, with the cartoonish muscles of a guy who spends half his life in the weight room.

"Coach Cavaliere, is it?"

"Yeah, nice to meet you," I said, returning his handshake. His grip felt like a nutcracker crushing a lobster claw, and he held onto to my hand for too long. When he finally released it, I looked down to see if the marrow was oozing from my fingers.

"Hey, welcome aboard." He spoke in a loud, coach's voice, even though we were standing so close I could smell the musk scent of his deodorant. "How'd you end up coaching here?"

"I work over at the high school, and I saw a posting—said they needed a coach."

"Terrific. Well I'll let you get back to your tryouts. Just one thing. Some of your men interrupted my practice today, knocking on the door and pointing at my girls. I'd appreciate it if you'd talk to them, explain that our practices are closed."

"Were they? Hey, I guess I didn't see it," I said. Dislike for Gresecki surged through me. I never react well to being told what to do. Especially by some middle school muscle-head. "I'll talk to the guys about it."

I let the guys scrimmage for about an hour, taking notes on their strengths and weaknesses. Two or three of the stronger players, including Colin, a point guard, and Mitch, a lanky forward, were clearly going to be the core of the team. And there were about fifteen kids who looked like they'd never picked up a basketball before. You had to wonder why they even bothered to try out. But there was a group of eight or ten, including Dan Wexler and Morris Spicer that were pretty evenly matched. I put them all in at the same time.

The play was ragged, lots of turnovers and missed shots. Of course, you'd expect that. None of them were used to playing under pressure. Since I was busy taking notes, I wasn't able to officiate, and I told the guys to call their own fouls. It worked all right at first, but as time ran short, some of them started to get testy. A boy named Quentin went up for a lay-up, and Morris Spicer tried to block his shot. He got a piece of the ball, but not without knocking the kid to the floor. Quentin landed heavily on his rear, and Morris picked up the ball and started dribbling up-court, like there was no foul.

"Hey, Spicer," Quentin screamed, "that's a *foul*! You nearly took my head off!"

"Spicer is such a psycho," someone else said.

I looked up to see who'd spoken. It was Wexler. From the way the other guys were nodding on the sideline, you could tell Spicer was not a popular kid. By now, he had stopped dribbling and was looking at me, pleadingly.

I blew my whistle. "All right, all right," I said to Quentin, "take the ball out of bounds." It was a hard foul, but not intentional, by no means a dirty play. I considered saying something in Spicer's defense, but I didn't see what I had to gain by taking sides.

I'd slowly been making choices, and finally it came down to Morris Spicer and Dan Wexler for the last spot. Their basketball skills were pretty evenly matched. But with his height, Spicer had a small edge. I was set to pick him, but then I thought about how he'd rapped on the door, ogling the girls, and how the other kids disliked him. I crossed his name out and circled Wexler's.

"All right, boys," I said, whistling the scrimmage to an end, "have a seat on the floor." They formed a semi-circle around me.

"Believe me," I said, "this is not something I've been look-ing forward to. It's the worst part of coaching. But it's time to make cuts."

I didn't want to shy away from the tough part of my job, so I tried to make eye contact with the kids while I read the list. But every time I looked at one of them, he averted his eyes.

After I finished reading the list, I didn't have anything more to say, and I waited for the kids to leave. But they must have expected me to keep talking, because nobody moved. Finally, one of the kids I'd cut got up to go. When I didn't tell him to stop, the others began to leave. A few of them hung their heads or pursed their lips, as if they might cry. But most of them were fine. I was glad it was over.

Well, almost over. Little Adam Garcia came by to ask me why he didn't make the team. I didn't know what to tell him. It didn't seem particularly helpful to point out that his lack of height was nearly matched by his lack of skill.

"Yeah," I said, "you could work on your defense."

He nodded earnestly, as though I'd given him an especially sage piece of advice.

I had to wait around until they changed, so I could close up the locker room. The kids streamed out in twos and threes. Those who made the cut talked to each other in excited tones. Those who didn't left quickly and quietly. Morris Spicer came out alone. I felt a little bit bad for him. He had played hard.

"Sorry it didn't work out," I said. But Morris just steamed by, lower lip jutted, spitting quiet curses at me as he marched away. I was glad I'd cut him.

Dan Wexler was the last one to leave the locker room. He was beaming. "Congratulations, Wex," I said, walking out to the parking lot with him.

"Thanks, coach. What do you think I should work on at home?"

"Let's see. Do you have a basement big enough to do some dribbling?"

"Yeah, I can fold up the Ping-Pong table."

"Good. Do some dribble figure 8's and maybe work on your crossover."

"Okay. Hey, there's my mom."

She was driving an enormous, imported SUV. The power window whined down, and she leaned over into the passenger seat, her eyes wide with expectation. She was athletic and pretty, and had the same blond hair as her son. For some reason I found it disconcerting that she looked about my age, though I shouldn't have been surprised, since I'm 38, which is definitely old enough to have a child in eighth grade.

"I made it!" Wex shouted, his little boy's voice cracking in excitement.

She unbuckled her seat belt and got out of the car, beaming. She looked as though she was about to hug him, but she thought the better of it and shook my hand instead.

"It's wonderful to meet you, coach. This is a *big* day at our house." She looked down at Dan, "We'll order from Plazzio's tonight to celebrate."

"This is going to be such a fun season," she said, as they climbed up into the SUV.

The next day was Saturday, and I had scheduled practice for the morning. Since there was only one other car in the parking lot at Garrison, I was surprised to find a man already in the equipment closet, when I went to get the rack of basketballs and some orange cones.

The sound of the door opening must have startled him, too. "Oh," he said jumping a little. "You must be the new basketball coach." He was heavy-set, with gray hair and a gentle voice.

"Yeah, George Cavaliere," I said, offering my hand.

"Dick Fitzgerald." His grip was soft and lifeless, like an empty glove. "I teach special-education. I didn't realize you were having practice now. I suppose you'll be using the gym."

"Yeah, I'm pretty sure I signed it out," I said.

"Oh, of course, I should have checked. That's my mistake," he said. "Say, do you mind if I borrow one ball?"

I looked at the ball-rack. There were twenty-four leather balls, way more than I needed. "Help yourself," I said.

"So I understand Morris Spicer didn't make the team," Fitzgerald said, as he grabbed a ball.

I hesitated for a second before answering, wondering where he was going with that. "No, he didn't." I spoke slowly while considering the best way to phrase it. "He's not, uh...Well, I guess you could say he's got poor fundamentals."

Fitzgerald nodded warmly at me. It was easy to see why he taught special-ed. I couldn't muster much annoyance with him, even though he was obviously meddling.

"We were hoping he would," Fitzgerald stopped and shook his head. "I'm sorry, I know it must be hard to make cuts. It's just, it would have been really important to him, and, well...Morris has had some problems at home. You know, no father around."

I smiled sympathetically. Too sympathetically, Fitzgerald kept going.

"His mother's got this boyfriend..." He shook his head.

"Yeah, divorce is tough," I said, gathering the cones in my arms.

"Yes, it is," Fitzgerald agreed. "But this fellow, this boyfriend, he's nasty. *Really* nasty. Last year, Morris's gym teacher spotted some bruises on his legs. He's no kind of father figure. I guess that's why we were hoping he'd make the team."

Father figure? I gave him a generic, non-committal nod, as though he was some nut in a bus station giving me the real story behind the Kennedy assassination. I backed out of the closet, propping the door with one hand and pulling the ball rack with the other.

"Watch where you're going," an angry voice called from behind me.

I started to apologize, but as I looked up I did a double take.

It was Morris Spicer. He was standing in the doorway, and I'd almost hit him with the rack. I wondered what he was doing there, and he looked just as surprised to see me as I was to see him.

"Hi, Morris," I managed to say.

He didn't answer. Instead he stared through me with glassy blue eyes. For a second I thought he might cry. But he didn't, and finally he moved out of the way. I shrugged my shoulders and was about to move on, when Fitzgerald stepped out of the closet and into the gym.

"Hey, Morris," Fitzgerald said. "I think the adaptive gym is empty. We'll just push some cafeteria tables out of the way. We can go work on some things in there." Fitzgerald bounced his ball. He started his dribble up at his chest, way too high, using his forearm but not his wrists. Terrible form. The ball landed on his toe and scooted away.

It's not too late, I thought. I could carry an extra kid on the squad. But how would I justify it? How would I explain why I've changed my mind? I could just tell the other guys I'd made a mistake when I read off the list. No, it wasn't too late.

Wait, Morris, I made a mistake. The words rose in my throat, but I swallowed them. This kid was such a project. I thought about my problems with Amy and Dara. I couldn't do it. Maybe when I was younger, but not now. No, I just didn't have it in me.

"Thanks again, coach," Dick Fitzgerald said. "Thanks for the ball."

He put his hand on Morris's shoulder, and they walked off together. I blew my whistle and started practice.

CHAPTER 4

"WHAT'S THE LESSON FOR TODAY?" Goldstein asked me, when he came back on Monday morning to see the AP class again.

"Slavery," I said.

"Wow. You guys are really moving along."

"Yeah, no choice," I said, peeking up at the door as I spoke. "I could talk happily about Jackson for another week, but with the AP test hanging over our heads, there's really no time to linger."

The AP, or Advanced Placement U.S. History test, is given to students nationwide every May. It's a hard test, but if the kids do well they earn college credit. My students, the good ones, anyway, fear it, which gives me a great motivational tool. The downside, though, is there isn't any time to dwell on a topic, no matter how interesting. So I was done with Jackson and on to slavery.

"How do you approach slavery?" Goldstein asked.

"Slavery is tough," I said. "It's such a depressing subject." I glanced up at the door again as I spoke, checking for the kid who works for the audio-video department. "Slavery is a hard thing to get kids excited about. The key is to hook them into it at the beginning. I play them a record of some old spirituals, and that gets us talking about slave culture and stuff. The record player should be here any second."

"How could you possibly have a recording of slave spirituals?" Goldstein asked. "There weren't any record players back then."

"Obviously," I said, "I don't. Have you ever heard of Alan Lomax?"

"No."

"He was an ethnomusicologist, who toured the South during the Great Depression. His mission was to record all kinds of folk music before radio and industrialization completely homogenized the culture. The recordings he made are fantastic. Unbelievable, really. And maybe the best thing Lomax found was a series of spirituals from the South Carolina Sea Islands. Do you know anything about them?"

"Not much," Goldstein said.

"They're a chain of islands that were settled by Englishmen, who made their fortune growing sugar in Barbados. In the 1600's, some of the English moved from Barbados to South Carolina, bringing whole plantations of slaves with them. And these Sea Islands were cut off from the mainland, so they really didn't change all that much after emancipation. In fact there are still a few Sea Islanders who speak this dialect called Gullah. It's like an African-English pidgin language. Anyway, when Lomax went there in the 30's, there were still people singing these old slave songs. One in particular, called Buzzard Lope, is incredible. It talks about how the slaves didn't have time to bury their dead properly, and had to leave the corpses exposed to the buzzards."

"That sounds awesome," Goldstein said, nodding his head. "You really have some cool ideas. All my teacher in high school did was lecture and go over the readings he'd assigned."

Ever since I'd met Goldstein, I'd felt this distinct vibe of disapproval coming from him, so I gave him a hard stare to see if there was any hint of sarcasm in what he'd said. When I realized there wasn't, I looked away.

"Yeah," I said. "Well the record won't do me much good without the record player." Just one minute until class started and still no sign of AV. When the bell rang, the kids filed into their desks and stared up at me expectantly.

"Good morning," I said. "We'll get started in just a second. I'm waiting on a record player. I'll tell you what, while I call about it, we'll have Mr. Goldstein here introduce himself. He's going to be student-teaching later this year."

The kids began murmuring as Goldstein stepped up to the front of the room. They had seen him last week and must have been wondering who he was. I picked up the phone and dialed AV, while Goldstein talked to the class.

"Good morning, AV. Grace speaking."

"Grace, this is George Cavaliere. Where's my record player?"

"What record player?" she said, her voice losing all of its pleasantness.

"I left a note in your box. I need one this period."

"I didn't *get* any note," she said. "I don't know what you're talking about."

Her tone gave it away. The way she stressed the word *get*, with that snotty edge to her voice, I knew she was messing with me. Dara must have told her about our fight.

"Look," I said, "I don't have time to argue with you about the note. Just bring me a record player."

"I'll see what I can do," she said.

Grace was a pain in my ass, but if this was Dara's idea of revenge, it was a pretty thin broth. While I was talking to Grace, I'd tuned out what Goldstein was saying to the class. But the way the kids were smiling and laughing, it must have been funny.

"We should get started," I said, interrupting Goldstein. "The record player is on its way. While we're waiting, why don't we brainstorm about slavery. See what you know already." The kids raised their hands and I wrote down their comments on the chalkboard. They shouted out Harriet Tubman and the Underground Railroad, Frederick Douglass and the abolitionists, the horrible suffering, etc.

"Yeah, that's all true," I said, stepping away from the chalk-board, "but it's pretty basic stuff. Does anybody know anything other than the blatantly obvious?"

"Yeah, go ahead, Anne," I said. Anne Burch was looking extra attractive. It must have been picture day for some club or team she was on, because she was uncharacteristically done up, with makeup and a black dress. Anne was my most enthusiastic student, and I kind of suspected she had a crush on me.

"Well, slavery broke down the black family," she said. "That's why there are so many single parents in the black community."

"No, that's not right," I said, shaking my head. "That's a myth. Yes, the black family was broken apart during slavery. And, yes, the black family is a shambles today. But slavery is *not* the reason why there are so many illegitimate children in the black commu-nity. In fact, after emancipation black families married in roughly the same numbers as white families. Not until relatively recently, after World War II, did the black family fall apart."

"Oh," Anne said. "Well then why *are* there so many... so many," she paused, weighing her words, "so many African American children born out of wedlock?"

"That's a disputed question," I said. "Some say it's because of the decline of manufacturing jobs in the inner-city, but if you ask me, it's a lot simpler than that. I think when you break it down, too many black men are lazy and selfish. They just don't support their families. I mean, you can call it racism or poverty, whatever, but facts are facts, two thirds of black men abandon their families."

The room had gone silent. There weren't any of the usual hushed whispers, no rustling of paper. Nearly everyone was look-ing down at their desks. Everyone except two students. One was Louis Sterling, the only black boy in the class. Louis was normally a shy kid. But now he bit his lip and looked right at me, and then softly, but loud enough for me to hear, he said, "Fuck you."

Shit, I thought, I shouldn't have said that. I remembered now I'd got a memo at the beginning of the year from Wentworth, saying Louis' father had just left his family.

The only other kid to meet my gaze was Colleen, the one I'd offended with my comments about the Cherokee. I looked at her, expecting to see daggers flying from her eyes. But she did the strangest thing. She smirked and rocked her head, as if stifling a laugh. Then she started writing furiously in her notebook.

At that moment a kid came into the room, pushing a wheeled cart. On the top shelf of the cart was a dust-covered, metal machine that looked like it was designed to withstand a minor atomic attack. The kid looked up at me and said, "Where do you want this 8-track?"

* * *

Anisha Carter, one of the two girls in my World History class, was staggering: shiny ebony complexion and high cheekbones, a dancer's body and braided hair. Since good looks and academic achievement both tend to be reflections of wealth, people who look like this in a delta class, are, to say the least, rare. So to have someone like Anisha in there was pretty bizarre. Not that she was in the wrong class academically. According to her IEP, she read at a fifth grade level.

The sixteen boys in the class didn't know what to do with Anisha. Since they'd spent their whole high school careers in the delta track, they were accustomed to seeing the same few females in all of their classes. And most of those girls looked more like Jackie, the only other girl in this class, who was perhaps 100 pounds overweight, with bad skin and thick glasses. With Anisha in their midst, the boys were like a pack of hungry dogs that mysteriously woke up one morning in a bakery. They were totally psyched, knowing the ultimate prize was in reach, but they had no idea how to get up to the counter, where all the eclairs are.

All year they'd tried to talk to Anisha, or rather Sean, the leader of this particular pack, talked to her. But Sean was so completely out of his league—a fact at least as obvious to him as it was to Anisha—that instead of talking to her directly, he would stand near her and brag loudly about all his "bitches." I can't say if Sean truly had as many bitches as he claimed, but I would bet you dollars to donuts, none of them looked as good as Anisha. Sean was actually not a bad looking guy—some of the girls call him "pretty eyes"—but Anisha was clearly underwhelmed with Sean's boasting. Occasionally she would roll her eyes when he said something stupid about pimping, but mostly she just ignored him.

As ham-fisted as Sean's courtship of Anisha had been, since he was the top dog, nobody else could even step up to the plate. Nobody until Billy Jackson arrived. He had come so late on his first day that he didn't have time to talk to her. But on his second day he chatted her up every chance he got, before the bell rang, while I returned homework and when I passed out new worksheets on Ancient Greece. Billy's chatter didn't bother me, though, because he showed respect for the class. He only talked when we were between activities, and never over me. I tried to catch what he was saying, as I moved about the room, but he spoke in such a rumble it was hard to make out his words.

I was so used to seeing Anisha's complete disdain for the boys who drooled after her that I had a hard time believing she could have any interest in Billy, especially considering his acne problem and jack-o-lantern grin. But to my surprise, she laughed fetchingly at whatever it was he was saying. I wasn't the only one intrigued. There were a few seconds left at the end of class, before the bell rang, and I had collected all of the worksheets already. Nobody except for Billy was talking. But only Anisha was watching him. Everyone else, including Goldstein and I, were watching Anisha watch Billy. Something he whispered to her made her laugh uncontrollably, and as she leaned forward, she touched him on the elbow. Just then the bell rang, and as Billy rose, he said, "How 'bout I holler at you tonight, Anisha?"

"I'm in the book," Anisha said, smiling as she left.

Luther Watkins nudged Sean's elbow with one of his doughy mitts. "Hey, Joe, you hear that? Anisha just told Billy he could holler at her."

Sean had most certainly heard it. He gripped the top of his desk, seething. I could tell from his knitted brow that he was trying to think of something to say to Anisha. But verbal agility was not his strength. Instead he sidled up behind Billy, who was whistling to himself as he picked up his books, and shoved him so that Billy tripped and sent a desk clattering to the floor.

But, in a surprising bout of coordination, Billy caught his balance, and he spun around to face Sean. Before Sean could muster any real defense, Billy dragged him to the floor and applied a chokehold to Sean's neck. I raced over to break up the fight, but they were penned into a tight space, between the toppled desk and the wall, and it was hard to get between them.

"Stop, Billy! Stop!" I yelled over and over, as I tried to pry his fingers from Sean's neck. "Stop!"

Billy couldn't hear me. His forehead was furrowed into tight folds, and his expression resembled his jack-o-lantern grin in the way his features remained rigid, but the usual glint of humor was replaced by grim concentration. And his eyes were vacant and remote. I pried at his fingers, but he was phenomenally strong. Finally, I managed to loosen one hand, using two of mine. But he kept on choking Sean with the other. By now, Goldstein was there with me. At last we got Billy off of Sean, who was beginning to turn purple, and held him against the wall. Goldstein wrapped Billy up from behind in a bear hug. Gradually, Billy's eyes seemed to return from wherever he had been.

Sean was recovering, too. You could see the finger marks on his throat, and he rubbed his neck, eyeing Billy.

"Go, Sean," I said. "Just get the hell out of here. I'll deal with you later."

Sean did go. But not before he spat, with great precision, straight into Billy's eyes.

Billy started to flail again, and I yelled "Hold him!" to Goldstein, while I hustled Sean out of the room and slammed the door behind him. When I turned around I was pleasantly surprised to see that Goldstein still had Billy in a bear hug, though Billy's torso was shuddering and shaking.

"Okay," I said to Goldstein, "you can let him go. Just come over here and stand by the door with me."

Goldstein released Billy and joined me at the door.

Free now, Billy raged across the room in wide circles, bulling his way through the rows of desks, turning some over onto the floor and kicking others. "I didn't fucking do nothing to him! I didn't fucking do nothing to him!" he shouted. He repeated the same phrase, over and over. But gradually his voice lost some of its intensity, and after a while his words took on an almost pleading tone. Once, he made his way toward the door, but seeing Goldstein and me physically blocking the way, he didn't come closer than a few feet. "It's over, Billy," I said to him. "Sean is long gone now."

Billy didn't answer, but as the fury drained out of him, he marched around the room in smaller circles, and now, instead of knocking over desks, he began picking them up. Finally, when the desks were all straightened, he stopped moving altogether and raised his arms in the air, as though he was being arrested.

"You okay now?" I said.

"Yeah," Billy said. "I'm sorry about your room, Mr. Cavaliere. Sometimes I just lose my temper."

"Here," Goldstein said, handing Billy a wad of Kleenex.

Billy wiped the spit from his face.

"You too," Goldstein said, handing me some tissue.

"He didn't spit on me," I said.

"You've got blood on your cheek," he said. "A bad scratch."

"Blood?" I wiped my face and looked at the Kleenex. He was right. I looked down at Billy's hand. He had long fingernails. Disgustingly long. He must have scratched me while I was prying him off of Sean.

"Oh, damn. My bad, Mr. Cavaliere," Billy said. "I'm sorry." He shook his head. "I messed up. I made you bleed. And you're a good teacher, too."

When we had both cleaned up, I said, "We've got to go down to the discipline office now. You know I've got to write you up."

"I know. They're gonna give me ten days, ain't they?"

"Yeah," I said. "You've been in trouble before, haven't you?"

"That's how come they sent me here," Billy said. "I ain't bad. Really, Mr. Cavaliere. I just got a temper."

Billy's self-assessment felt about right to me. He wasn't a totally bad guy. It was really kind of endearing, the way he'd cleaned up the desks and apologized for scratching me. He was genuinely sorry. But he did have an awful temper.

"Hey," I said to Goldstein, as I opened the door. "Good job. You've got a cool head. You might just work out."

We stepped out into the hall, where a tiny freshman was waiting, holding a note in shaking hands. Her face was pale, and she looked away from the bloody tissue I was still clutching.

"It's all right," I said, throwing the tissue in the trash. "Everything is under control."

I unfolded the note. "*George,*" it read, "*See me immediately after school. Elaine.*"

Elaine Jorgenson is the principal of Edgemont. But principal or not, immediately after school was out of the question. Covering your ass in school is about half of the job these days. So getting a kid punished takes a ton of paperwork. By the time I finished writing Sean and Billy up and got down to the administrative wing, it was 3:30.

The principal's office is the best kept area of the school. There's a huge oak desk, that supposedly has been passed down from principal to principal since the school was founded in the 1870's, and several high-backed leather chairs that ring a mahogany conference table. As I walked in, afternoon sun lit up a wall of windows that looked out on the playing fields. The football team was practicing, and you could hear a few low burps from a tuba, as the band tuned up.

"Jesus, George, where'd you get that?" Elaine said, pointing to the scratch on my forehead.

"It's been a long day."

"I'm afraid it may get longer," Elaine said. "Have a seat." She pointed to the chair on the other side of her desk. Elaine had been my mentor teacher when I student taught and for my first few years at Edgemont, before she became an administrator, she'd been in the classroom next door to mine. There are two things you should know about her. First she's one of those earth-mother type freaks. When she taught, she used to wear hippie skirts, beaded necklaces and Mayan jewelry. Even weirder, she buried the placenta of her daughter in her backyard, under a ginkgo tree. No kidding—she showed me a picture of it. Red and veiny and dripping with mucous, it was absolutely foul.

The second thing you ought to know about Elaine is that I've seen her naked. She got divorced eight years ago, when she found out that her husband—he worked in business, or something boring like that—was having an affair. And one night, soon after, a bunch of us teachers went out for beers. Elaine and I were the last two there. One thing led to another, and, to make a long story short, we wound up mashing on the couch at my apartment—this was before Amy. And pretty soon, we were naked. But before I could do anything, she looked at me and said, "We can't do this, George."

So we put our clothes on and she went home. And neither of us has ever mentioned that night again. Not once. You might expect having something like that between us would be really awkward, but it totally isn't. If anything, it's been kind of like sharing a private joke. But I have to say not following through is one of my big regrets. Even with the age difference between us—she's eight years older than me—and the braids, which I was no fan of, Elaine was one of the best looking women I'd ever fooled around with—tight body, the cutest little mouth and a deep, sexy laugh.

Anyway, when her husband left her, Elaine went into administration. I'm not a 100 percent sure that's the reason she quit the classroom, but the timing was suspicious. First she became head of the history department, and my boss. Then she was assistant principal, and now principal. Since we've never had anything but stiffs in our administration, I was hoping Elaine would liven things up. Unfortunately the opposite occurred. Being in charge dulled her. First, she changed her appearance. When she was department chair, she got rid of her funky skirts, then when she was promoted to assistant principal she straightened her hair, and when she got the principal's job, she lost the beads. Now she acts so phony, it makes me nuts to watch her. Every morning she stations herself at the front door, gushing "Good Morning! Good Morning!" like a Wal-Mart greeter.

"George, I've known you for more than fifteen years," she said, as I sat down. "And I know you're a great teacher." She pulled her own chair around from behind her desk and wheeled it next to mine. That right there was the reason Elaine could be an administrator and I never could stand it. It was such a bullshit gambit, trying to make me feel comfortable by coming down from her perch behind her desk and descending to the level of us ordinary teachers. "So, George," she went on, "when something like this comes to my attention, I find it really—"

"Jesus, Elaine," I said. "Do you hear yourself?"

She blinked twice. "Do I hear what, George?"

"I mean, listen to yourself," I said. "It's obvious that you're pissed at me, so save all this bullshit about fifteen years and how I'm such a great teacher and all. What are you pissed about? Get to it, so I can get out of here and you can get back to planning the pep rally or whatever it is you do."

"All right, George," she said, as her smile soured into a bitchy frown. "I've received a complaint that you made a racist remark in your class."

She seemed to be expecting me to make some sort of reply to this, but I figured it wouldn't do me any good to look defensive, so I just sat there waiting for her to finish.

"Several racist remarks, actually," she said.

"Who told you that?"

"It's not important who, George."

I knew who it was, just the same. I thought back to Colleen's smug little smile as she wrote in her notebook.

"According to the report I have here from the child's guidance counselor, you said something insulting about Native Americans, Mexicans, Chinese and last, but certainly not least, African Americans."

"Let me see the report," I said.

It was written on one of those old carbon style forms—four layers of paper, each a different color. I read it aloud. "According to the student, Mr. Cavaliere made offensive remarks on two occasions in the last week. First the student alleges that he called Native Americans drunken savages. Additionally he used the term half-breed to describe mixed-race individuals. Even worse, Mr. Cavaliere then went on to denigrate Chinese and Mexican immigrants. But since this appeared to be a one time offense, I encouraged the student to write down any subsequent remarks Mr. Cavaliere made, before taking action. Then, just today, the student came back to me alleging Mr. Cavaliere insulted African Americans by disparaging the African American family." I looked down at the bottom of the page. It was signed in a bouncy cursive by Josh Wentworth.

"Wentworth is such an ass," I said. "That's a bullshit way to handle a problem."

"Is it true?" Elaine said.

"I mean, if the girl was upset, then he should have come and talked to me about it. Don't you think? But instead he set a trap for me and used this kid to do his dirty work."

"So it *is* true." Elaine's eyes turned icy.

"No," I said. "Not really. The first part is total bullshit." Elaine flinched at the word bullshit. Here was another thing I didn't like about her. She used to curse like a sailor. But since she went into administration, she'd lost her edge. "Like it says in the report, it was a *role play*. I was Andrew Jackson. Everything I said to them was just a repetition of what Jackson said himself."

"You really used the term half-breed?" she said, stroking her forehead.

"That's a term Jackson used."

Elaine exhaled deeply, like a smoker trying to blow a ring.

"He did," I said. "I can show you the quotation."

"What did you say about the Chinese and Mexicans?"

"Nothing. That's a crock."

"You said nothing about them," she said. "Absolutely nothing?"

"Well, not nothing. All I said was that if Native Americans want to succeed in modern life, they should find something comparable to the egg roll or the burrito. What's wrong with that? Small business is part of the—"

"Stop!" Elaine barked. "Save the speech. What did you say about African American families?"

I got up out of my chair and looked out of the window at the marching band before answering. A couple of kids in wheelchairs were laughing about something. The band director was a great guy. He'd gotten several handicapped kids to participate in the program. They played simple stuff like cymbals, but it was a nice thing. I turned to Elaine. "First, I'm not saying it was my best moment. But you need to know the context."

"What did you say, George?"

"First, the context," I said. "We were doing a brainstorm on slavery, and one of the kids—not me, but one of the kids—said slavery was responsible for the breakdown of the black family, even today. So I corrected her. I pointed out that while the black family had suffered during slavery, that it had recovered after emancipation and had only really broken down after World War II."

"That's all you said?" The crinkles in her brow melted.

"Well, no. So the kid asks me why there are so many out of wedlock children born in the black community, if not because of slavery. And I said you could come up with whatever kind of excuses you want, but that what it comes down to is too many black men are selfish and lazy and won't support their families."

Elaine slumped in her chair.

I felt a little bad. This was going to be her headache, just as much as mine. "I'm not saying I phrased it well. But what exactly is wrong with that idea? I mean, we're always telling our students they need to take individual responsibility and that they shouldn't blame others for their problems. And here the fact is two-thirds of the black men in America don't—"

"You're not getting it, George," Elaine said. "You rarely *do* get it. This is not about whether or not you know your history, or whether your facts are well supported."

"What are you talking about?" I said. "I teach history. You used to, too. How can you say the truth isn't important?"

"You do teach history, George. But you are not a professor at some university. Do you remember when I was department chair, and I used to tell you that you should go on to get a Ph.D. and try to teach at the college level?"

"Yeah."

"Well you always thought it was a compliment, and in a way it was—you have the best academic mind of anybody at Edgemont. But it was also meant as a criticism, though I guess it was too subtle."

"How is that supposed to be a criticism?" I said.

"This job is more than just arguing about history. If that was all it was, you'd be the best teacher on staff. Yes, you do teach history. But you teach it to young people. To children. And with children, you have to adjust your approach to their developmental level. Sometimes people are not mature enough or simply not able to hear what you think is the truth. And if they aren't, you can really alienate them when you hit them broadside with your unvarnished ideas."

I nodded in approval. I like speeches, and it was good to see that the cheerleader in Elaine hadn't totally buried her real personality.

"Here's how I'm going to handle this," Elaine said. "I'll call the parents of this kid and invite them in, and we can try to smooth this over, here in my office. I've dealt with enough angry parents to know that the best thing to do is to pounce on this before bad feelings have a chance to ferment. So get out of here and I will call them right now. I want them to hear from me before they hear from their daughter."

"Thanks," I said.

She looked at me hard, to see if I was being sarcastic, which I'm kind of known for. "Really," I said. "Thanks for sticking up for me."

"You're welcome," she said. "But I can't do this on my own. You're gonna have to eat some crow here, George. I hope you realize that."

"Yeah, sure, if I have to."

"Goddamn it, yes you have to. I don't need to remind you that you are already on probation."

"No," I said. "I am aware of that."

CHAPTER 5

AFTER MY MEETING with Elaine, I raced over to Garrison school for a special, second chance tryout with Morris Spicer Jr. I'd called him on Sunday morning to arrange it. The phone rang half a dozen times, and I was just about to hang up, when the receiver at the other end clicked.

"Hello," an adolescent voice said.

"Hi, Morris?" I said.

"Ye-ah," he said, drawing out the end of the word into a second syllable.

"This is Coach Cavaliere."

"Oh."

"Listen, Morris," I said. "I made a mistake. I've been thinking about it, and as hard as you played in the tryouts, we really could use your energy and height on the team. So what I'd like to do is to have you come before practice and work out with me, one on one. I'd like to give you another chance."

"Oh." You could tell Morris wasn't much of a talker on the phone. "Okay."

He sounded so unenthusiastic I half suspected he wouldn't show up for the tryout. But when I had finished changing and emerged from the coach's locker room, he was waiting for me on the court. This time, thank goodness, he was wearing shorts. I chucked him a ball and told him to take some shots. As he moved around the three point-arc, hoisting the ball, it was even clearer now that he'd never been coached at all. There was no rhyme or reason to the way he warmed up. His first few shots came from way past the three-point line. None of them was close.

"It's not good to begin with three-pointers," I said. "Try starting closer to the hoop and move across the court in a semi-circle as you shoot. Then each time you reach the baseline, you can extend the arc a couple of feet."

Morris stopped dribbling and stared blankly at me. "Do what?"

"Here. Watch me. You always want to start in close to the hoop, because your body needs to loosen up and find its form before you're ready to take longer shots."

When I finished, Morris did the drill, while I rebounded for him. "Okay," I said, when he finally got the hang of where to go and when to shoot. "Let's work on your form. You're bringing your left hand way across to the far side of the ball; that's why your shots come off with that crazy spin."

"What should I do with my hand?" he said.

"Here," I said, "give me the ball. Okay, now move the left hand further away and let the right hand do all the pushing. The left hand just guides the ball."

"Oh, yeah," Morris said. "Yeah, I got it."

He did have it. But he had barely been able to follow a simple instruction. I remembered his poor spelling from his profile sheet and what his teacher, Mr. Fitzgerald, had said about how he struggled in school. He obviously had a severe of learning disability.

We worked on shooting for a little while longer, and Morris made surprising progress. The rotation on his ball improved almost immediately, and the curve on his shot straightened out quite a bit. Then I had him guard me on defense for a few plays. He was solid. Quick feet and good instincts.

"All right," I said. "It's almost five o'clock, and the other guys will be here soon. So why don't you take a break and get some water, so you'll be fresh for practice."

"Does this mean I made the team?" Morris said, his voice quivering.

"Yeah," I said, chuckling, "you made it."

"All right!" he shouted, pumping his fist in the air.

At no point, I realized, until just then, had I told him he definitely made the team. But I had assumed he understood that was the whole point of this second tryout. Instead he really thought it was possible I had invited him back in order to humiliate him and cut him a second time.

My suspicions that Morris was unpopular were confirmed when Mitch and Dan Wexler came into the gym. When Mitch saw Morris, he said, "Jesus, Spicer. Get a freaking life. You got cut, or are you too stupid to remember?"

"Yeah, Wexler said, snickering. "Why don't you go to the playground and stalk some sixth grade girls?"

"Okay, *stop* right there," I said, bending down into Mitch's face, so that he backed up as I talked. "Morris is here because I asked him to come. He is now a member of this team. If *you* want to stay on the team, then start treating him like a teammate."

That shut them up pretty quick, but I don't think it made Morris feel a whole lot better. As the team gathered together, he stood a few feet behind the rest of the huddle.

I didn't have a strong sense of how many kids had been coached before, so I asked who had played on the seventh grade team.

"Everybody but Morris," Colin said. He was short and built like a bulldog, but he was also the best ball-handler on the team. A good candidate for point guard. "I was the captain," he added, in a matter of fact way, so it came across as not being boastful.

"What kind of stuff did you guys run last year on defense?" I asked.

"A 2-3 zone," Colin said.

"What else?" I said.

"That's all," Colin said.

"That's it? You never ran any man-to-man or presses?"

"Just zone."

"That is such garbage," I said, moving closer to the huddle. "No offense to your seventh grade coach, but it's a terrible idea."

"It worked pretty well," Colin said. "Most teams didn't score a lot on us."

"Sure it worked well," I said. "Seventh graders can't shoot a lick, neither can eighth graders for that matter. The problem isn't that zones don't work, it's that they don't teach you anything. For the rest of your life, when you play ball, you're going to need to know how to play man-to-man. Every pick-up game on every playground is man-to-man, and high school coaches will expect you to know it, too. You'll see. Who's our first game of the season?"

"Altgeld," several of the kids said simultaneously.

"We play them next Friday," Colin said.

"All right," I said, "then Altgeld may have a little surprise coming, when we match up in man-to-man."

"That's not going to work against Altgeld," Mitch said, shaking his head emphatically.

"Oh yeah," I said, raising an eyebrow. "Why not?"

"We can't play those guys man-to-man?"

I already disliked Mitch. "And why not?"

"Have you seen those guys," he said. "They'll kill us. They can jump like crazy, and basketball is their whole lives. That's all they care about."

Altgeld is also a feeder school to Edgemont. And it's predominantly black, whereas Garrison is nearly all white. In fact, we had only one black kid on our team, a boy named Chris, who was one of our worst players.

"Are you afraid to play them just because they're black?" I said. "That's the worst possible attitude. In fact, let me promise you now, I will *not* put players on the floor, if they're afraid to play."

"I'm not afraid," Mitch said, "I'm just telling you they're gonna kill us."

Several of the other kids nodded their heads in agreement at this. I looked at Colin to see what his reaction was. "I go to camp with those guys in the summer," he said. "They're really good, but if we played well, we could give them a game."

"Whatever," Mitch said.

"If I'd known this was going to be such a whining bunch of little brats," I said, "I might not have taken the job. But the good news for you guys is I've got plenty of time before the first game to make sure you believe in yourselves. Tell you what; let's start by running those negative attitudes out of your system. Let's go, suicide sprints."

"How many?" Colin said.

"We'll see," I said. I blew the whistle and they were off and running. Normally, I would expect two or three as a max, but I made them keep going.

"When can we stop?" Mitch gasped as he ran by me in the middle of his fourth.

"When *I* get tired," I said, yawning as I leaned back against the bleachers.

Finally after five suicides, I blew the whistle. By this point the players were stretched out across the floor. Colin was the first one in, Morris was second and Mitch brought up the rear.

After some water, I gathered them around for a shooting lesson. Eighth grade is the pivotal time for most young ballplayers because, before then, most kids can't shoot with proper form. They don't have the strength to reach the hoop, so they hitch at their waist, which gives them the distance but messes up their rotation. And if you don't break that habit by the time you reach high school, you're really going to have problems. The team watched me as I went to the foul line and demonstrated proper technique. "The best way," I said, shooting as I talked, "no, the only way to really improve is through repetition." I sank another free throw. "Constant repetition."

I made another and said, "If you want to get better, come to practice early and shoot a hundred free throws, exactly the same way. Develop a routine before each shot. It doesn't matter what the routine is, but you have to do it exactly the same each time. For me, it's three dribbles, spin the laces of the ball, so it lines up even with my body, take a deep breath and release on the exhalation." I made my fifth straight.

"How long did it take before you could shoot like that, coach?" Colin said.

"I practiced for an hour a day, every day from eighth grade through senior year. That's an hour just on shooting. But you have to be a perfectionist. Like right now, I'm not happy with that last shot," I said.

"But it went in," Morris said. "If I hit six in a row, I'd be psyched."

"Yeah, but it hit the rim. I'm always working for the perfect shot." I waited for somebody to ask what the perfect shot looked like, but nobody did. "The perfect shot is when the ball hits the net, exactly dead center, and then the net jumps over to one side of the rim. You guys have seen it before on TV. When it happens, the ref stops the game, and the ball boy gets a chair to stand on, so he can untangle the net." I picked up the ball. "Now you guys go work on your free throws, and take your time and build good habits."

They fanned out to all six hoops in the gym and shot for twenty minutes. I went around and watched them. It was good; they were taking my advice seriously, shooting with real concentration. When they were done, I blew the whistle and we worked on help-side positioning, an integral part of man-to-man defense that none of them, not even Colin, seemed familiar with. One pleasant surprise was that Morris was a born defender. He blocked several shots, including one of Mitch's.

After more water, I drew up our first play on the chalkboard. It was a pretty simple pick and roll set, but I noticed Morris fidgeting as he stared up at me with his blue eyes. When his squad tried to run the play, it became clear why he was so nervous. He drifted around the court in all the wrong places, almost at random. At first, it wasn't that big of a deal; Colin was the only one who knew where to go on the first try, and most of the other guys needed a couple of chances. But after five or six run-throughs, everybody but Morris knew what to do.

And then when I put defenders on the guys, so they could run it under game conditions, Morris was a disaster. He tried his best, but he was always in the wrong place, mucking up the routes of the other players. As the point guard on Morris' team, Colin ran the show, calling the play and making the initial pass. Three times in a row, Morris got in his way, and though Colin did his best to keep his temper, on the fourth mistake, he slammed the ball off the court. Knowing he was at fault was too much for Morris. Now he just sat in the far corner on the baseline, letting the play unfold without him. While he didn't actively mess anything up that way, he was still a handicap to his team. It was like playing four on five.

Since we had thirteen players on the squad, and they couldn't all be on the court at once, Mitch and Dan were watching from the baseline. From behind me, I heard one of them say, "What a dumb ass."

We finished practice with a few more sprints, and as the players were heading to the showers, I pulled Mitch and Dan aside. "I'm giving you one last warning," I said. "If I have to make this speech to you again, you're off of the team. Never, ever make fun of a teammate in his presence. A teammate is a brother, and Morris is your teammate. You don't have to like him, but you will work with him. And if you feel you can't, then you should walk out of here and not come back." They nodded their heads sullenly, and turned to go to the locker room. "Not so fast," I said. "You guys owe me five extra suicides." I blew the whistle.

They looked at me in disbelief. "Five more?" Mitch said.

"If you don't want to run them," I said, "then don't bother coming back."

They ran them.

After I closed up the locker room, I found Morris waiting to see me. "Coach, I quit," he said.

"What do you mean?"

"I'm not gonna be able to learn the plays. I can't do stuff like that."

"Stuff like what?"

"Like school. You can ask anybody," he said, his voice trailing lower as he spoke. "I'm kind of dumb."

"You can do this, Morris," I said. "It takes a while to get the hang of these plays. This is only your first practice. We've got lots of time left before the first game."

"I don't think so, coach," he said. But he didn't leave.

"What are you doing after dinner tonight?"

"I dunno," Morris said, cocking an eyebrow.

"Make you a deal," I said. "Let's see if you can learn this one play tonight. If you can't, then you can quit. But if you do learn it, then that means you can learn the rest of the plays, too. Right?" He'd stopped listening. I made a mental note that with Morris the shorter the speech the better. "Look at me," I said.

"Ye-ah?"

"Do you know where 1224 Sangamon Avenue is?"

"Uh, yeah."

"Can you get there on your own tonight at 8:00?"

Morris did a double take, and finally said, "Ye-ah."

"Okay, I'm in apartment three. Meet me there at 8:00. I'll teach you the play."

At precisely 8:00, there was a loud rap on the door to my apartment. "How did you get in the building, Morris?" I said, as I opened the door.

"A key," he said, peering at me through skeptical eyes.

"You have a key?"

"Ye-ah."

"How did you get a key?" I was starting to think he was messing with my head, and he must have come in while one of my neighbors went out. But the idea of him toying with me seemed so incongruous with the rest of his character. I could think of a lot of adjectives to describe Morris Spicer Jr., but sly wasn't one of them.

"From my mom."

"How did your mom get one?"

"Coach," he said, as though I were very stupid, "I live downstairs."

Downstairs. I looked at his eyes. Bright blue. Shit, I thought. That was him in the doorway, behind the chain, after my fight with Dara. He'd seen the whole thing: doors slamming, me in my underwear, the screaming and cussing. I don't get embarrassed often, but right then I could feel my face burning red.

When I had mustered enough composure to be sure my voice was normal, I said, "How do you learn things most easily at school?"

"I don't learn things easily," he said.

"Okay," I said, "but what about Mr. Fitzgerald. Isn't that the name of one of your teachers?"

"Yeah."

"Okay, well what do you do with him when you're trying to learn something new?"

"We usually draw it first. I see stuff better than I hear it."

"Great," I said, "that's what we'll do."

We spent the next hour and a half going over that one play. I made Morris diagram it on a notepad, over and over. It took him ten tries to get it right, and then I made him do it ten more after that, just to be sure.

"Now go get your Nerf hoop from your bedroom and bring it up," I said.

"How did you know I have a Nerf hoop?" Morris said, smiling.

"Come on. A boy your age, who loves basketball—of course you do. Go on and get it and we'll run through the play up here."

He was gone for several minutes, and I started to think he wasn't coming back. But then, finally, there was a soft knock on the door, which was weird because I'd left it propped open.

"Yeah, come in, Morris," I said.

A brown head peeked around the door. But it wasn't Morris. Instead there was a tall woman with an unfortunate collection of buck teeth.

"Hi, I'm Morris' mother," she said.

"Oh, yeah," I got up off of the futon. "Nice to meet you Mrs. Spicer. I'm George Cavaliere, Morris' basketball coach."

"Yeah, he told me," she said. "It's awful nice of you to help him out and all, but I just want to be sure he's not a bother to you."

"He's not a bother. I invited him."

"See, Ma," Morris said. "I told you."

"Are you sure, Mr. Cavaliere?" she said. "Because I know how my Morris can be. Believe me, I know."

"It's fine," I said. "Really."

She pulled a receipt from her pocket book and scribbled something on it. "Listen, I'm going off to work now, but if he gives you a hard time, you call me. This is my work phone. Just have the manager page me."

To make her feel better, I took the number. When she was gone, we shoved the futon against the window and ran through the play in my living room, with him, me and three pillows for our starting five. And when we were finished with that, I challenged Morris to a game of HORSE. He thumped me. Nerf balls are hard to shoot if you're not used to it.

"Thanks, coach," Morris said, when we were through.

"Any time," I said. "It was fun, actually."

He turned to leave, but then stopped with the door half-open. "Hey, coach, can I ask you something?"

"Shoot."

"How come you're so different now from how you are other times?"

"Different how?"

"Like, you know, so much nicer."

I thought about that for a while before answering. I mean, really thought about it. "I don't know, Morris," I said, finally. "I really don't."

CHAPTER 6

THE MEETING WITH COLLEEN and her parents didn't go well. For one thing, that asshole Wentworth was there. Colleen's parents sat to her left, at the big conference table in Elaine's office, and Wentworth was on her right. Colleen didn't look at me as I came in the room, and neither did Wentworth. He was so little he had to stretch up to the table, just to jot notes onto a yellow pad. I was dying to peek underneath, to see if his feet hit the ground.

"What's he doing here?" I murmured to Elaine.

"Who, Josh? Oh, Mr. and Mrs. West thought Colleen would feel more comfortable if her counselor were here to support her. He's only going to observe." Elaine looked over at the Wests. "Well, I'm glad we could all be here today. I want to thank you, Mr. and Mrs. West, for taking time off of work to meet with us. And Mr. Cavaliere, you should know the Wests have heard Colleen's account of what happened last week, and they have also read Mr. Wentworth's report, so to start with, I wonder if you have anything you'd like to say?"

She said that last bit in her most condescending voice, like she was talking to a four-year-old who had just tripped his little sister. I had to wrestle with my temper before responding. Colleen's parents looked expectantly at me. The father was tall and thin, with a hawk nose, a huge Adam's apple and bags under his eyes. He was wearing a silk tie and a French-blue shirt, but no jacket. If he wasn't in marketing he should have been. The mother was short, with a long face and sharp features. She shared her daughter's slight build, but not her poor posture, and it seemed obvious from the way the father took his cues from her—tilting his head in her direction every time she squawked—that she called the shots in this family.

"Yeah," I said. "Let me just say I regret using the language I used in referring to Native Americans. I realize it was not appropriate for the developmental level of the students."

They kept staring at me, I guess wanting more. "And as far as the comment about the African American family, I'm sorry if anyone took offense at what I said, or maybe how I said it. Though I stand by the accuracy of what I said, which is that the breakdown of the African American family is not the result of slavery."

There was a long silence and then Mrs. West turned toward Elaine. "That better not be his idea of an apology. He hasn't even addressed the horrible things he said about Mexicans and Chinese. And let me assure you I didn't cancel a meeting with the other partners so he could express regret that my daughter *misunderstood* him."

"George," Elaine said, her eyes flashing, "perhaps you could be a little clearer."

I stroked my chin for a moment, while I thought about what to say. The Wests seemed to have come expecting me to kiss their ring in return for their dispensation. From her mention of the "other partners," I gathered Mrs. West was some kind of big shot lawyer, and you could just tell from the way she directed her remarks to Elaine, not to me, that she considered teachers beneath her. This is a common problem in Edgemont, at least with the AP class. The parents generally make a lot of money and are usually convinced they're smarter than I am, and it can difficult to disabuse them of that notion.

"I'll try to explain this again," I said, in my most didactic tone. "The objection Colleen had was to a comment I made during a role play. The comment was a quotation from President Jackson. Is Jackson's phrasing offensive to modern sensibilities? I suppose it is. And, as I said, I regret now that I did not at the time sufficiently appreciate the impact those words might have on some adolescents. Yet those ideas are a perfectly legitimate area of historical inquiry. And let me remind you, the AP course is a college level course, for which, if she performs well enough on the AP test, Colleen will receive college credit. So it would be unrealistic for me to shy away from controversial areas of study.

"In regard to the remarks about Mexicans and Chinese, all I said is it would be a good thing for Native Americans to have some small businesses, like the Chinese and the Mexicans have developed, as a launching pad into the middle class.

"Finally, as for the comment about the black family, again, in retrospect, my phrasing was unfortunate. I should not have used such frank language when talking to teenagers, and I'm sorry if Colleen or any of the other kids took offense at what I said. But let me ask you, Colleen, were you *personally* offended by what I said about the black family?"

Colleen jutted her lip and looked at her father.

"You don't need to answer that, Colleen," the mother said. "This is not about you. It's about him. Ms. Jorgenson, I've heard plenty. I want Colleen out of that class. Today. Who else teaches AP US History?"

Elaine scrunched her nose as she answered. "I'm afraid we only have the one section of AP U.S. History. Mr. Cavaliere is the only teacher who teaches it. If you insist on switching Colleen, we could place her in a regular class, beta level—"

"No, she's not going to that dumping ground." She shuddered as she pictured the inferior breed of kid in the beta level. "And I fail to see why my daughter is the one being punished for

Mr. Cavaliere's offenses. Why not remove him from this AP class as a punishment?"

"I'm afraid that's not a realistic option," Elaine said. "It would be unfair to the kids in the AP class, most of whom work well with Mr. Cavaliere, and it would be unfair to the other class we switched him to, because they would lose their teacher. In any case, Mr. Cavaliere is easily the most qualified teacher we have for the AP course."

"Well, I was warned you might stick up for Mr. Cavaliere," Mrs. West said. She pulled a bound pamphlet from her briefcase, and tapped the table with it. "So I've done my homework. I have your faculty handbook here, and it says a teacher can be dismissed for creating a hostile learning environment, either through sexual harassment or through racial discrimination."

I wondered where she had got her hands on our faculty handbook. Not that it was a top-secret document, but it seemed like odd reading material for a parent.

"I am not sticking up for Mr. Cavaliere," Elaine said, measuring her words as she spoke, "and I assure you I will deal with Mr. Cavaliere later, but that is not the issue at this particular meeting."

"I think it is *exactly* the issue. I would like to know how you intend to punish him?"

"A teacher's personnel records are confidential," Elaine said. "I can't discuss any action I might take."

"Maybe so," Mrs. West said. "But my understanding is Mr. Cavaliere is already on probation."

Elaine and I looked at each other uneasily. Where the hell had she heard that? I stared at Wentworth.

He looked away, the bastard.

"I don't know what your source is," Elaine said, "but I'm not at liberty to discuss an employee's personnel records."

"You're not going to be able to hide behind that for long," Mrs. West said. "As I see it, this is a civil rights case. You are forcing my daughter to endure a hostile learning environment. I can subpoena Mr. Cavaliere's employment file, secondary to a lawsuit. And if I find out you are not following your own discipline code, that's an actionable cause. So I would think very carefully before allowing this man to return to the classroom—"

"*I* think," Elaine said, in her most commanding voice, "that all this talk of lawsuits is not helpful. Even if Mr. Cavaliere were to be dismissed, which I think is exceedingly unlikely, he is entitled to due process, as I'm sure you know. And so, for the time being, I have no intention of switching him out of the AP class and disrupting the schedules of two entire classes."

"Then how are you going to make me whole?" Mrs. West said.

"Colleen," the husband said, nudging her with his elbow.

"What?" she barked.

"How is she going to make *Colleen* whole, not us."

"Right," Mrs. West conceded, though she didn't look happy about being corrected. "How are you going to make our daughter whole?"

"I'm afraid she has only two choices," Elaine said. "One is to remain in Mr. Cavaliere's class. And let me assure you he will speak more carefully from here forward, or she can move to a regular class."

"What do you want, Colleen?" Mr. West said.

Colleen squeezed one eye shut and looked at her father with the other. "I want to switch classes," she said.

Elaine rose from her chair and pointed the Wests toward the door. "I'm afraid I have another meeting now," she said. "But thank you for coming in, and if I can be of help in the future, please let me know."

"Oh, you will be hearing from us again," Mrs. West said.

After AP History that morning, I hit the lights the moment the bell rang. I can't stand wading through the sea of students that clogs the halls during passing periods, so on most days I hang out in my classroom for a couple of minutes after the second bell rings, before I head for lunch. But today I turned to Goldstein and said, "Come on. We've got to get to the caf early today."

"Okay," he said, grabbing his book bag. "Any special reason?"

"Got a little score to settle," I said. "I need to stake my claim at the lunch table."

He looked puzzled, but he didn't press it. Fortunately the cafeteria was still empty when we got there. And Josh Wentworth was the next to arrive, which was ideal, because there was no reason for everyone else to see me bitch him out. Wentworth slid into a chair without a word or a glance in my direction. "You can't possibly be thinking about sitting at my table," I said. "Not after that bitch-ass performance."

"Who says this is your table?"

"Aren't you embarrassed?" I said. "I mean what kind of a back-stabbing wimp are you? If you've got a problem with me, be a man and settle it face to face. But you can't do that, can you? You're such a wuss that you sent that kid in there to spy on me and report back to the principal."

"This isn't about you and me," Wentworth said, dumping his fork onto his tray. "It's not about me at all. This is about you and your student. You're the one who did wrong here." He grabbed his tray and stood up. "But for the sake of peace, I'll sit somewhere else. And you know what, it'll be a pleasure. It might come as a surprise to you, since you're obviously lacking self-awareness, but you're not exactly my idea of good company."

"Not your idea of good company?" I said. "You mean I'm not prone to flaccid conversation about tag sales and gardening?"

"No," Wentworth said, his cheeks turning red. "I mean you talk too much. You never listen to what anybody else has to say. Never. And if you don't like the topic, you bully people out of talking about it until you get your way."

"You're a short, dull man," I said.

"I'm not the only one who thinks so," Wentworth insisted. "Everybody at this table talks about you behind your back. On the days when you don't come to lunch, we're all ecstatic."

"You're full of shit," I said.

"Wait and see," Wentworth said. "Just wait and see who sits with you today. And if this poor kid here," he pointed at Goldstein, "if he didn't have to kiss your ass, I bet he'd leave, too."

After Wentworth left, it was quiet for a minute. I tried to eat, but my potatoes were so soggy I wondered if they'd been soaked in water, and the first bite of my chicken Vesuvio tasted cold and fibrous, but juicy. I spat it out, gagging. The inside was pink and bloody, barely cooked at all. I was all set to get up and return it to Betty, when it occurred to me that all of my meals in the cafeteria had been terrible lately. Sometimes Betty gave me runt portions, sometimes burnt food, and now uncooked chicken. Then it hit me, Betty was Dara's friend. She was giving me the dregs from the kitchen, the bitch.

I had nothing to eat, and I didn't feel like getting back in line to argue with Betty, so I just sat there fuming. But Goldstein hadn't said anything since Wentworth left, and he looked pretty darn uncomfortable, so finally I started telling him about my team I was coaching. I tried not to watch the rest of the lunch crew file in while I talked, even though I wanted badly to see who the other regulars would choose. Not that I wanted their company, or cared whether they liked me—they were mostly dullards. But I didn't want Wentworth to think he had gotten the best of me. So I have to admit, it kind of bummed me out when, one by one, they filed right past my table and sat with Wentworth, on the far side of the room. All of them except Cynthia. She came out of the lunch line, clutching her tray as she peered back and forth between Goldstein and me, on one side, and Wentworth and his crew of losers on the other. She headed straight for us, and stopped in front of the table, standing.

"How's it going?" I said.

"Oh, fine, I suppose," she said. Her breasts stretched her black blouse so that the outline of her nipples peeked out over her plate of salad. "Why is everybody sitting over there?"

"Long story," I said. "Philosophical differences, you could call it. But it's probably for the best. You know, addition by subtraction."

"Oh, I don't quite know what you mean," she said, but she pulled a chair out and sat down.

"Not much of a story, really," I said. "Wentworth wanted a change of pace, I guess. I was just telling Goldstein here about this eighth grade basketball team I'm coaching."

"Oh, that sounds like lots of fun," Cynthia said.

"Yeah, I'm getting a real kick out of it," I said. "You should come by and check out a game sometime. The kids are really cute."

"That would be fun," Cynthia said. "What do you say, Eric? Do you want to go sometime?"

"Sure," Goldstein said. "Definitely."

"We play this Friday, right over at Altgeld School," I said. "They're our big rival. It should be fun." I was pretty pleased with myself there. By inviting Cynthia to the game, I'd managed to show her I was a decent guy, who spent his free time coaching kids. Plus, all in the same stroke, I'd slipped a social invitation past the goalie. If she came to the game, it wouldn't be hard to get her to go out for a drink afterwards.

But I didn't have long to savor my triumph. Doug Feeney, a football coach and math teacher, in that order, bounded up to our table. "You guys look a little shorthanded today," he said. "Think I'll join you."

"Help yourself," I said, without enthusiasm. Feeney's big gut and chapped bald head made him look a bit like one of those dodge balls little kids play with. He usually sat with the driver's ed and PE teachers, which was fine by me, since he was conversational death. For some reason, though, he thought I was his buddy. Maybe it was because two years ago I'd dragged Amy over to his place for this really depressing Super Bowl party. He lived in a dank garden apartment, with dirty dishes stacked on the counters and used Q-tips spilling out of the wastebasket. Aside from Amy, there wasn't a single other female at the party, unless you counted the swimsuit models plastered on all of the walls. And Doug's friends were all borderline misogynists. Not one of them even said hello to Amy. Which was probably for the best, since the conversation alternated between profanity-laced criticisms of the play calling and profanity-laced ogling of the girls in the beer commercials. We left at halftime, and I hadn't hung out with Feeney since then. But he was always threatening to meet me out for a beer.

"It's nice to meet you," Cynthia said, smiling at Doug. "What do you teach?"

"Idiots," he said.

Cynthia and Eric both stared at him, waiting for a punch line, but Doug tore into a chicken leg without further explanation. I peered jealously over at his food. His chicken was nicely browned and the potatoes looked crisp.

"Doug teaches all delta level," I said. "Essentials of math. It's starting to wear him down. Wherever you wind up, make sure you teach at least one honors level class. Otherwise you could end up like this guy."

"Did you see the game last night?" Doug said to me, as I played with my fork.

"Which game?"

"Bulls-Celtics."

"No."

"How about you, buddy?" he said, turning to Goldstein.

"No, I don't have cable," Goldstein said. "I'm just a student. I don't think you can even get it in the dorm."

Cynthia chuckled and said, "I have cable but I never watch it during the school year. Maybe it's because I'm a new teacher, but I don't seem to have the time to watch much. I've always got so much grading."

"I grade with the TV on," I said.

"Really?" Cynthia said. "Doesn't that slow you down?"

"Oh, definitely," I said, "but if I didn't I probably would have gone nuts by now."

"I know what you mean," Cynthia said. "I'm finding the grading really overwhelming. What about you, Doug?"

"I'd rather have cable than heat," Feeney said, spearing a potato with his fork.

"Yes, but how do you handle the grading?"

"I don't take work home," Feeney said.

Cynthia searched Feeney's face for a hint of levity, but his lips stayed frozen in a stolid smirk. "What? Really?" she said.

"Never," Feeney said. "It's my rule."

"Well how late do you stay at work?" Goldstein asked.

"Union hours, except during football season."

Cynthia and Goldstein both gave me blank looks.

"Union hours are 7:30 to 3:30," I said. "You have to be on the premises for at least that long."

"You must be really efficient," Goldstein said.

"There's one good thing about deltas," Doug said, as he choked down a hunk of chicken skin. "Only one. They don't turn in their homework, so I don't have to grade it."

Mercifully, the bell rang then, and we all began gathering our trash. Doug crumpled his greasy napkin and tossed it onto his tray. "I'll call you, Cavaliere," he said, as he pushed back from the table. "I'm going to Hi-Tops to watch the game on Sunday."

"Take it easy," I said.

He grinned as he stood up. "Always do."

We were all ready to go, but the tables in the cafeteria are so tightly packed that only one person can get through at a time.

Doug was closest to the exit, but he said, "Hey now, ladies first." And he backed away from our table, against the wall, to let Cynthia go. But the space was small, and with Feeney's gut in the way, it was a tight squeeze for her. She peered up at him uncertainly and pursed her lips, as if she was going to say something. But she thought the better of it and slipped past him silently.

As she walked ahead of him, Doug's eyes went wide and a sly smile spilled across his lips. For a second I thought he might actually cop a feel, right there in the cafeteria. He didn't, but as she moved through the room, weaving in and out of the tables, he elbowed me in the ribs and pointed at her ass. "See that," he mouthed, "hard as a rock." I shook my head at his comment, but I have to confess, before I turned my head away, I snuck a quick look. It was a hell of a view.

* * *

Snow started coming down in fat flakes right after lunch. So I called over to Garrison, and they said they'd already canceled practice. I needed to grab some things from my old house, so I scraped my car off and headed over there. It was only five o'clock when I arrived, but already the sun had set. Usually it's the darkness more than the cold that bums me out about winter. Today, though, the night sky was speckled with white, and the snow glistened in the moonlight and the glow of street lamps. There were already five or six inches of powder on the ground. Half of the block seemed to be out and about, shoveling and scraping their windshields, dusting their walks with rock salt, and pushing their cars out of snowdrifts. But the blanket of snow muffled the sounds of scraping shovels and sputtering tires, giving the evening a dreamlike quality.

Our house was dark, which didn't surprise me because Amy had a longer commute than I did. And with the storm, the traffic must have been brutal. I grabbed a shovel out of the garage and started clearing the sidewalk in front of our house. The snow was deep, but airy and easy to push. As I worked the flakes swirled around my head, melting on my face and mixing with beads of sweat. Every minute or two I glanced down the street for a sign of Amy's car, but she seemed in no hurry to get home. She was really dedicated to teaching, a quality that was obvious when I first got to know her in grad school.

We'd met during the worst class in our master's of education program. It was summer school, a condensed schedule, so the class was held for three and a half hours on Tuesday and Thursday mornings. Professor Germiny was the most brutal lecturer in the whole education school, so there wasn't much else to do but check out the women in the class. The ratio in our program was about three to one, so getting a date figured to be a breeze. And this was a nice crop, but right away I set my sights on Amy. Even from all the way across the room, her eyes were striking—huge green pools, swimming with flecks of silver. I couldn't figure out a way to talk to her the first day, but for the second class, I got there early and staked out the chair next to hers. We made small talk for a few minutes, while Germiny got himself organized, and over the next couple of weeks we got to know each other a bit. Amy was friendly but not flirtatious, which made her a bit hard to read, but did nothing to discourage me.

By the third week, it was early July, and a heat wave had descended over the Midwest. The kind of moist heat that clogs salt shakers and keeps your toothbrush damp overnight. When I got to class, a blue-coated maintenance guy was out in the hall, holding a pair of needle nose pliers and fiddling with the thermostat. The air conditioning had blown a circuit. I poked my head in the lecture hall. It was a modern design, with rings of built-in desks funneling down a circular terrace to the floor, where a blackboard and podium stood at the center. With the AC off, the humidity in the classroom was so intense I could see my reflection on the top of a desk and the erasers on the ledge of the chalkboard were mushy. When I saw the repairman working on the AC, I assumed class would be canceled. But to my chagrin, Germiny was at the podium, ready to go. And despite some muttering I heard about Germiny being out of his mind, everybody took their seats. Under normal circumstances, I wouldn't have joined them. But just as I was turning to go, Amy came in the door behind me. She was clutching a half-empty Diet Coke, and was dressed for the weather in cute shorts, a T-shirt and a neon runner's cap.

"It's downright disgusting in here, George," she said, as she slid past me and took her seat.

"Unbearable," I said. I was tempted to ask her to ditch with me, but from what I'd seen the first couple of weeks, Amy was a conscientious student. No matter how dull the topic Germiny was prattling on about, she took meticulous notes. How she could focus in the heat that day, I don't know. Fortunately, the way the desks were set up, I could pretend to be watching Germiny, while actually getting a side view of Amy. So we both concentrated—Amy on Germiny's inane lecture about the easiest way to establish a pedagogical union, and me on other, less wholesome, unions. Amy finished her pop quickly, so during the five-minute break I excused myself and went out into the hall, where I bought two Diet Cokes from a machine whose motor wheezed from the struggle to keep the soda chilled.

I handed Amy one of the bottles when I returned. "Thought you could use another," I said.

"Thanks, George" she said, as she twisted the cap off. "This is perfect, and the caffeine won't do me any harm. Have you noticed that Professor Germiny is a bit on the dry side?"

"You think?" I said, with a laugh.

I was so thirsty, I had already finished my drink when Germiny resumed his harangue.

"Can I have a sip?" I whispered to Amy. She nodded. There were only a few ounces left in her bottle. I unscrewed the cap, and tilted the rim back in my mouth. The Coke was fizzy, but warm and a tad salty. As I drank, Amy scribbled something on a scrap of paper.

Mouth full, I looked down at her note. "It's mostly spit," she had written. The residue of carbonation bubbled up into my nostrils, and a sputtering cough spilled out of me as I dribbled cola-brown saliva onto my desk.

The woman in front of me swung around to give me a sour glare, but Professor Germiny was oblivious, and he continued droning on about the theories of John Dewey. I peeked at Amy from the corner of my eye. She chuckled happily to herself, even as she kept on taking notes.

I picked up the stained paper. "Come to the zoo with me," I wrote.

Amy grabbed the note, read it, wrote a reply, and handed it back to me, all without breaking concentration or eye contact with the professor.

"The zoo?" was all she had written.

"Right now," I wrote back.

For the first time, she trained those luminous green eyes directly on me. They shone out of her face like a pair of flood-lit aquariums, and I froze, unblinking, until she turned away and wrote again on the scrap of paper. My eyes widened, as I looked down at her message. "I'm in," she'd written.

I wrote so fast my cursive was almost illegible, "Meet me in the hall in five minutes." I handed the note to Amy, grabbed my notebook, tucked my pen behind my ear and, without looking back, headed for the door.

Willing the clock above the soda machine to move faster, I stood just outside the door. But the clock was spitefully unco-operative, so I began pacing from one end of the hallway to the other, until the repairman, whose armpits were dripping, turned around to give me a hard look. And then she came through the door. "A bit hot for the zoo, don't you think?" she said.

"Tell that to the bears," I said. "The least we can do is give them a little moral support."

It was so stupid hot that the only other visitors to the zoo were school groups and day camps, unlucky enough to have scheduled their trip in advance. The school buses were lined up in the park-ing lot, like yellow loaves of bread, baking in an asphalt oven. Four or five of the drivers were huddled together under an elm tree, smoking, cursing and trading sections of a rumpled newspaper.

Inside the gate, the main plaza was empty, except for a cadre of surly teenage employees, manning deserted hot dog stands and souvenir shops. There was, however, a line for the animal tram. The heat and the whining children had no doubt convinced their underpaid teachers and camp counselors to fork over a few dollars for the ride. Though not air-conditioned, the tram's two animal-themed cars were, at least, open air. And a breezy ride must have seemed preferable to a forced march.

The ticket taker, drunk on power, herded little bodies onto cars with the officiousness of a fire marshal. "But we don't want to go on *this* car," a girl in a pink Barbie shirt said, as the ticket guy shoved her group through the safety gate, "We want to go on the zebra."

"The ticket says giraffe." He locked the gate behind her. "Giraffe it is."

Amy and I walked away from the tram, down the African safari trail, which took us by the rhino, hippo, lions, and ostriches. The hippo was in especially fine humor, splashing in his pool and batting a ball up onto the rocks above with his nose, and then hitting it again on the rebound.

At the end of the safari, someone had thought to place a mist machine in the middle of one of the paths, and it threw glorious pellets of water into the air. Amy raced for it, and I chased her. We soaked ourselves in a rainbow of drizzle, until Amy noticed a line of kids waiting for us to move. Next we stopped for a snow cone, in the Antarctic plaza. While we were having our snack, the tram pulled to a stop nearby. The group on the zebra car got off and went inside the penguin house.

"Are you up for sneaking aboard?" I said as the tram began to pull out of the station.

"Stow away?" Amy said, nodding approvingly. "Which car?"

"I don't think there's much question?"

"You're right. Meet you on the zebra."

We sidled up to the car and lifted ourselves aboard and into seats at the front of the car. Some of the kids in the giraffe car gave us puzzled stares, but they were mostly focused on the animals. Everybody except for the Barbie brat, who was in the back row, right across from us. "I *saw* you," she hissed.

"What's that one called?" the kid next to her asked a very bored chaperone. "Shhh," the lady said, "just listen to the man driving, he'll explain it." But the driver, who was steering from the front of the giraffe car, did not share the ticket taker's esprit de corp. A young guy, maybe twenty, he must have been near the end of his shift. When we reached a straightaway he gunned the engine, heedless of the kids clinging to the safety poles and window ledges. And his narration was somewhere on the border of perfunctory and unhelpful. "There's an elephant on the right," he muttered into his microphone. "They're from Africa."

Now the girl in the Barbie shirt looked at her chaperone, "Mrs. Drucker, why did that man and that lady jump on like that?"

"Who knows, Karen," the woman said.

"But shouldn't they have tickets?"

"Yes," Mrs. Drucker said with a sigh, "I suppose so."

"You're *bad* people," Karen said. "I'm going to tell the driver." She moved toward the front of the giraffe.

"You *are* bad," Amy said.

"Undeniably," I said, as I made full-frontal eye contact with her. "Hey, here comes the bears. Let's get off. We owe them a visit. Besides, I think we'd be foolish to tangle with this Karen."

"There's no tram stop," Amy said.

"True, but there's a patch of grass we could land on, if you're not afraid to jump."

"On three," Amy said.

I grabbed her hand and laced my fingers through hers. She counted and we leapt forward onto the grass. My ankles buckled as I hit the ground. As I fell, I saw Amy land on the balls of her feet—back straight and balanced. But I'd neglected to let go of her hand, and I pulled her down into me. We rolled together on the lawn, bodies flush against each other. For a long moment, neither of us moved. "That was one hell of a landing," I said.

"The vault was my best event," Amy said. "I'm a gymnast."

"You'd have stuck it, too, if I hadn't dragged you down."

"I'm glad you did," she said, aiming those green eyes at me.

We held hands the whole way home.

When I was done shoveling our parkway, I began clearing the driveway of Mrs. Lazich, our neighbor to the right. While I worked, she came out on to her porch to watch, but she didn't speak until I was finished. "Hello, George," she said, in her accented English.

"Hello there, Mrs. L. How have you been?"

"Bad," she said. "Very lonely."

That kind of a blunt answer was typical of Mrs. Lazich. I don't know if it was a Serbian thing, or because her English was limited, or maybe was just her personality—but whatever the reason, she was always very direct. Too direct, Amy said. Mrs. Lazich used to march right up to her, put her palm on Amy's stomach, and say, "When you have baby?" Which was especially painful for Amy, since we'd had fertility problems. Mrs. Lazich and her husband had moved to Chicago from Serbia after the war. Mr. Lazich had started as a construction foreman, but by the time I knew him he owned his own little remodeling company. He built porches and decks with his son and a nephew. In the forty years they'd been here, the neighborhood had changed from a street full of immigrant bakers and steel workers to a block of investment bankers and index fund managers. But then Mr. Lazich died of a heart attack two years ago. Now their son ran the family business, and Mrs. Lazich was the very last of the old timers on our block. No wonder she was lonely. Since Mr. Lazich had died, I'd made it a point to cut their grass and shovel their walk, whenever I did my own.

"Where you stay now, George?" she said.

"Over on Sangamon," I said. "By the L stop."

"Sangamon," she sniffed. "Not a nice street."

"It's not so bad," I said. "I grew up in the city. I've lived in worse."

"Yes, you good man, George," she said. "Like my husband." Mrs. Lazich had always liked me. I think it was because, unlike most of the people on our street, I came from a working class family. "You move home soon, George," she said. From her gruff tone, it was hard to tell if it was a question or an order. Either was possible.

"Yeah, I don't know about that," I said. "You know Amy and I haven't really worked through everything yet."

"Amy no let you," Mrs. Lazich said, shaking her head bitterly. "I know. I talk to her. I tell her take you back."

That was one conversation I was glad to have missed. "You know," I said, "it was actually my fault—"

"These women," Mrs. Lazich said, waving her hand contemptuously, up and down the block, "work and work and work, then they pay stranger to raise the baby. Never, they cook a meal. I watch—always they order food from deliver. If they deliver sex, they want to order it too." A tiny grin escaped her lips as she admired her own wit. But soon her face resumed its sour expression. "And now they cry when he leave."

Mrs. Lazich was wrong about Amy. Wrong on all counts. Amy taught elementary school, so she had loads of vacation. She was a phenomenal cook. She wanted kids desperately and would have loved being a stay home mom. And, finally, though it was true I'd cheated on Amy, it wasn't for a lack of sex. Not that we lived like porn stars or anything, but let's just say that with Amy's help I easily met the American Cancer Society's recommended quota of prostate usage.

But there was no point in arguing with Mrs. Lazich, so I tried to change the subject. "Yeah, times really have changed since you moved here, I guess."

Mrs. Lazich ignored me, though. "Mr. Lazich—you think he always perfect? Bah," she sneered at the thought. "But I no cry like baby. I tell Amy. I tell her take you back."

"What did she say?"

"She tell me mind my business. She don't like me."

Amy's car pulled into the driveway then, and I said, "That's her right there. I should go. But it was nice talking with you Mrs. Lazich."

"Thank you for the shovel. Next time, you tell me you come, George. I bake for you."

"Okay," I said, "I'll do that."

Amy was standing outside her car, watching me as I strode over, snowflakes swirling around her head. "You've always been a good neighbor," she said. But despite the kind words, her tone was more reproachful than complimentary, as though she was thinking, "but not a good husband." She said nothing else and walked toward the house, the light from the porch making a silhouette of her tiny frame. I suppressed an urge to bundle her from behind in a huge, weepy hug. Instead I said. "Did you have a good day?"

"Did I have a good day?" Amy put her key in the lock before answering. Then she turned and glared at me. "No. No, I did not have a good day," she said, the chill of her tone daring me to ask her why.

"Sorry," I said.

"Are you sorry?"

"I was just making small talk."

"Don't," she said. "We're not friends; we don't make small talk."

We were in the house now, and Amy moved around the living room, flipping light switches and sorting the mail, tossing about half of it, including a brand new *Sports Illustrated*, addressed to me, into the trash can.

She marched into the kitchen and I followed two paces behind her. "You didn't need to shovel the walk," she said. "I'm not helpless. I was going to do it as soon as I got home."

"I know you're not helpless," I said. "I enjoy it. There's no driveway at my apartment building, so it only takes like five minutes to clear the walk there. I can use the exercise."

Amy grabbed a watering can and turned on the faucet. "Well, you've got your exercise now, is there anything else you need here?" She moved back into the living room and began watering the plants. I followed her, peering around the house as we walked. Everything felt strange to me. Not that there was anything in particular I could point to that was so different. Amy had tweaked the arrangement of the furniture a bit, moving the TV over into the corner and repositioning the couches, but it was still the same house. When we bought it, it was in dire shape. It's a three-bedroom Chicago-style bungalow, and the previous owners were the same generation as the Lazich's, so everything had to be redone. The living room had a floor to ceiling mirror on one wall, and fake wood paneling on another. And the roof had leaked, rotting half the drywall. I'd done most of the rehabbing myself, over the summers, and all my work was still there. No, it wasn't the house that was different; it was me. I was a visitor here, and from the guarded look on Amy's face, an unwelcome one.

"Are you even listening?" Amy said. "I asked you a question."

"Oh, sorry," I said. "I just kind of spaced out. Yeah, I came over because I needed some things. You know just little things I forgot. Some extra razor blades, my set of barbells and weights, a few books for school."

"Fine, go upstairs and get your things, and I'll have your mail ready for you when you come down," she said.

"Okay." I took a long look at Amy, before I headed for the stairs. She'd always been petite, but she seemed smaller than I remembered. And it sounds stupid, but I guess I'd sort of forgotten just how pretty she was. She has an adorable bump of a nose, a cascade of raven curls and, even at thirty-six, her body is awesome. And when she smiles, there's a dimple on her right cheek that lights up a room. She wasn't smiling then, though. The expression on her face was as forbidding as the tone of her voice. So I turned away from her and trudged up the stairs.

When I came back down in a few minutes, with the razors and weights, Amy was waiting for me by the door. "There's your mail," she said, pointing to a shopping bag. And without another word, she headed back to the kitchen.

"Oh yeah, Amy, one other thing," I said. Her shoulders and neck tensed at the sound of her name, as though my even saying it were some kind of violation.

"What?" she said, without turning to look at me.

"Yeah, if it's all right with you, I was going to grab a couple of pieces of furniture for my apartment. Only if you don't want them."

"Fine," she said. "Take whatever you want."

That kind of carte blanche about the furniture was not what I expected. I figured she would fight for the things she wanted, especially the things she'd picked out. Somehow, though, her indifference actually made me less eager to take anything. It was obvious she'd offered me whatever I wanted so she could get rid of me quickly. And the thought that my presence repulsed her was almost too depressing to deal with.

"You know what," I said, "never mind. We can work the furniture out later. The only thing I might want anytime soon is the basketball hoop in the alley."

"Fine."

"All right," I said. "I guess I'll be going now. I'll probably come back in a week or so to get my mail."

Amy spun around to look at me. "From now on," she said, "I'll forward your mail once a week, so you won't have to come here. And if you do come back, I'd like to have a couple days notice. Then I can arrange to be somewhere else while you're here." The way she said it—frost in her voice, lips tightly pursed—it was like a different person than the Amy I'd been married to. She was a fighter, not an ice-queen.

I staggered out of the house, without even a goodbye, and made my way to the car, weak in the knees, weighed down less from the barbells than from the feeling of total failure that stung every bit as much as the snowflakes lashing my cheeks. There was no point denying it any longer; I'd lost her.

CHAPTER 7

PAT MCDONOUGH, the athletic director at Garrison called me later that night. "Hey, George," he said. "Glad I caught you."

"Oh, yeah. What's up?"

"Good news," he said in a buoyant voice. "I found some money in the budget for an assistant coach."

"Oh, that's nice of you," I said, "but I don't think I need any help. There's just a dozen guys, and I don't mind running the show myself."

"I've already hired him," McDonough said. "His name is Tom Fasso. Great guy. He's one of my gym teachers, and he'd be thrilled to help out. In fact, he wanted the head coach's job originally, but he couldn't take it because he had a church commitment on some of the game nights. But he'll come to the practices with you. I think he'll be a big help."

"I guess it's a done deal, then," I said without enthusiasm. I had some misgivings about having an assistant who wanted to be the head coach. And it seemed a bit odd, McDonough hiring this guy without even consulting me. But there was nothing I could do about it, so I called Fasso to introduce myself. He certainly did love the Lord. Or so I was led to believe by his answering machine, which said, "I'm not home, but please remember Jesus is always with you."

When I met Fasso at the gym the next day, he was cleaning up after his gym class, collecting some plastic bowling pins and a couple of hollow balls. The good news was he was definitely not, as I had been dreading, the stereotypical coach, clipboard in one hand, crotch in the other. With his dirty blond pony tail and a big gold cross flapping on top of a sheeny sweat suit, he looked a bit like a seventies lounge singer. He wiped his palms on his thighs before extending a hand to me.

"You must be Tom."

"Nice to meet you, Mr. Cavaliere," he said.

"Call me George," I said.

Despite his effort to dry himself, his hands were still clammy, and I wiped my own palms on the back of my shorts.

"Oh, yeah, right," he said in a nervous pitter-patter. "I'll be with you in just a minute. Let me finish cleaning up here. Actually why don't you follow me." He moved frenetically across the gym, loading up a wheeled cart with pins and balls. I followed him into the equipment room. Despite the intensity of his efforts, he was remarkably inefficient. It took him half a dozen tries to unlock the closet, and then when he had replaced the pins and balls on a shelf, he seemed dissatisfied with the arrangement and started all over at the beginning, though I couldn't see much difference in the result.

His office was a little cubicle of a room, really a closet, which he shared with another teacher. "Sorry to keep you waiting like that, Mr. Cavaliere. Here, have a seat," he said, moving a stack of papers off his chair. "Sorry the place is such a mess, I just haven't had time to clean it."

"Mr. Cavaliere," he said, abruptly, as though he'd been meaning to bring it up. "I hope you don't think I'm coming in here to keep an eye on you, because I told Mr. McDonough that I didn't think it sounded too bad."

My eyes narrowed. "Didn't think what sounded too bad?"

"Oh, don't get me wrong. I told Mr. McDonough I wouldn't work with anyone if I thought they were treating the kids wrong," he said. "You know how kids are. They'll complain about running sprints, but it's good for them. They could use a little more exercise."

What he said made me feel a little better. I didn't like the idea of parents complaining about me, but if they were just griping about too much running, it was no big deal. Though it did piss me off that some weasel was going over my head, directly to McDonough.

"Heck, we all could use a little more exercise," Fasso said. "Even us gym teachers. I've just been so darn busy, I never seem to get the chance. Anyway, they need more discipline, not less. The kids, I mean. You wouldn't believe how much of a hassle it is for us in gym class. The discipline takes up as much time as the teaching."

There's an old saying, "Those who can't do teach, and those who can't teach, teach gym." And Fasso's little monologue didn't do anything to convince me otherwise. I'd been with him for ten minutes and already he'd complained twice about being busy. Hearing a gym teacher whine like that drives me bananas. They are the least busy people I know. In fact, if I could stand the shame of having to tell people what I did for a living, I would happily teach phys-ed. There's no easier route to the middle class. Once, for fun, I looked through the course catalog at ISU to see what kinds of classes phys-ed teachers take. Believe it or not, you can actually get a master's degree by studying things like Indoor Racquet Sports, Dances of the Decades and Broomball. And don't get me going on the preparation gym teachers do. Once, I was sitting behind a gym teacher at a faculty meeting, and he "planned" a whole week in ten seconds, by writing the word "softball" in the Monday slot of his calendar and drawing an arrow across the rest of the days. An arrow! He was too lazy to write the word four more times. Oh yeah, there aren't any papers to grade or exams to write either, and you get to go to work in sweats and shorts. Not bad for sixty grand a year.

Having just met Fasso, I couldn't say any of this to him. Instead, I asked him if he'd done much coaching before.

"Oh, yeah," he said, "I coached the eighth grade team at my church the last couple of years."

"So do you know much about the conference we're in?"

"Some. The team I coached was in a church league, but we played some of these schools in tournaments."

"I'm glad to have you on board," I lied. "You ought to be able to give us some good scouting reports."

"Glad to be of help, Mr. Cavaliere," he said, shaking my hand again.

That day was our final practice before our first game against Altgeld, and I felt like we were starting to come together a bit. Our help-side defense was becoming coherent, and all of the guys, even Morris, knew at least six good plays. Even so, he still found plenty of ways to attract the ridicule of his teammates. Like right then, the day before the Altgeld game, when he showed up late for practice and came out of the locker room wearing his game uniform.

"What's the *matter* with you, Morris?" Dan Wexler said. One stare from me was enough to shut him up, but I had the same question.

"We've got a game today," Morris said, though his voice was less sure than his words.

"No we don't, Morris," I said as gently as I could. "Game's tomorrow. Go on and change your uniform and when you come back, you owe me some sprints for being late." Morris was mortified by his screw-up, but he didn't complain about the sprints. He was a tough kid.

For the most part, Fasso stayed out of my way during practice. Though he did pull a few guys out of the shooting drills and work with them on their form. Which was bizarre, since his own technique was horrendous.

After practice, I gave a little pep talk about how far we'd come and how we were ready to face Altgeld finally. Mitch sniggered audibly at that, so I blew my whistle and said, "Five suicides." The other guys glared at Mitch, but by then they knew it was best to just run and not complain aloud. For two weeks now, any time one of them expressed any doubt about what we were doing or whether we could win, the whole team ran sprints. If they complained about that, I added more.

When they returned to the huddle, huffing and wheezing, I said, "Anything to add, Coach Fasso?"

"Yeah," he said, "just one thing. Now these guys at Altgeld, they play a lot of street ball. They're athletic like crazy, but completely undisciplined. They're not students like you guys are, so they won't even really have plays. Just run and gun. So you've got to outthink them."

I wished I hadn't asked him to pipe in, because what he said jibed completely with the stereotypes our guys already had about black players. The last thing they needed was to be told they couldn't compete athletically.

On my way home, I spotted Morris about two blocks from our apartment building. He waved at me, and I pulled over. "You want a ride?" I said, as I rolled down the window.

"Uh, yeah," he said.

"You've been doing really well in practice," I said. "You're our best defensive player and you've got almost all the plays." This was a bit of an exaggeration. He actually did know most of the plays, when it was just him and me with a Nerf hoop or if he could draw it on a piece of paper. But when we ran them live, in practice, he still got flustered and went to the wrong spot.

"Thanks, coach."

"You know, to be honest," I said, "you're probably one of our top five guys, but I don't think I'm going to start you just yet. We'll let you get your feet wet for a few games, and if you keep playing well, then you can start."

"That's okay, coach. I don't really want to start anyway. I'd probably freak out." We pulled up to the building at that point, and when we were out of the car, Morris said "Hey, coach, do you think I need new shoes?"

"I don't know. Let me see them."

He held up his feet. The shoes were worn and gray, but not ripped or anything. Still, it was easy to see why he wanted new ones. They were plastic, not leather, and the styling was so gaudy you had to believe they'd been designed for the Chinese market. One thing about them was impressive, though. They were gigantic.

I whistled and said, "What size are those?"

"Fifteens. The shoe man said if my feet grow any bigger, I'll have to get them special ordered."

"Jesus," I said, looking him up and down. "You're hands are huge, too. How tall is your dad?"

"I don't know." Morris looked down at his enormous feet. "My mom doesn't talk about him. He used to duck his head under the doorway, though, before he ditched us." He met my gaze now. "I guess he must have been pretty tall."

By then, I'd opened the door and we were inside the building.

"I'd bet you're going to be tall, too," I said.

"Do you think so?"

"Definitely. You know, with your quickness and height, you've really got a lot of potential."

"Oh," Morris said. From his blank look, I was pretty sure he didn't understand the word potential. But it didn't seem to bother him. He must have been used to not knowing things. "What do you think about my shoes?"

"I don't know, Morris. I guess they're a little beat up," I said, as we started up the staircase. "It might be nice to have a new pair for the first game."

"Yeah, that's what I been saying. Can you talk to my ma? I been bugging her about it, but she says they cost too much."

"Sorry," I said, quickly. "You know what, I shouldn't have said anything. That's really between you and your mom. It's not any of my business."

But Morris had stopped listening long ago. "Talk to her, coach," he said. "She's right inside." We were at his door now, and he fumbled with his keys.

"Listen, Morris," I said, "I really can't—"

By then he had the door open. He popped his head inside and called "Hey, Ma, Coach Cava—" but he stopped short, and his head snapped back through the doorway like it was on a rubber band.

"Get the fuck out of here!" a voice yelled.

Morris leapt back, his face ashen.

"What's that about?" I said.

I stuck my own head through the door. Their apartment was a studio; the same layout as mine. They had hung a curtain from the ceiling to divide the room up. On one side there was a twin bed, a little TV and a Nintendo set. On the other there was a convertible couch, pulled out into a bed. Morris' mother was standing next to it, struggling to wrap a towel over her waist with one hand, while bending down to fish her panties from the floor with the other. A short man, with a barbed wire tattoo on one bicep, stood on the other side of the couch, wearing only his underwear. A huge erection bulged through the front of his white briefs. He marched right at me. "Who the fuck are you?"

"Sorry," I said, backing up. "I live upstairs."

"Yeah, why don't you go on upstairs and mind your business."

"Morris, come here," Mrs. Spicer said. By now she had put on her clothes, though her face was still flushed and her hair was a lawless pile of brown. "I didn't think you'd be home, Morris. You said you had a game."

"We don't," Morris said, looking miserable. "The game's tomorrow."

I started toward the staircase, while Morris and his mom were talking. But I paused when I got there. Though I didn't want to get in the middle of a family squabble, the boyfriend's aggressiveness scared me. Remembering what Fitzgerald had said about the bruises on Morris' leg, I was reluctant to leave until I was sure he was safe. I glanced back and saw that the boyfriend's erection was melting.

As I took a step up toward my apartment, though, he said, "Jesus fucking Christ. Dumb-ass doesn't even know what day it is. Fucking retard."

He smacked Morris across the face.

Without hesitation, I bounded back down the stairs and slammed the guy up against the wall. He shoved back at me, but other than his penis, which was now once again fully erect, he was a lot smaller than I was.

"Keep your hands off of him," I said.

"He's not your fucking kid," the guy snarled. "Mind your own business."

"He's not yours either."

"How do you know that?" Spit leapt from his mouth, spraying my forehead.

"I'm his basketball coach. I live upstairs. If I hear about you touching him again, I'll call the cops."

"I *am* a cop."

"All the more reason you don't want to get arrested." I waited for him to hit me, but he was a bully, I guess, and preferred hitting a little kid to a grown man.

"Fuck you, smart ass," he said, but he stayed where he was.

"Come with me, Morris," I said. "You can hang out upstairs as long as you want."

Morris didn't say anything. He looked at his mother. She was crying, and she spread her arms as though to hug him. "Oh, Morris," she said. "Come here, honey."

Morris turned and followed me up to my place. After I opened the door to the apartment and let Morris in, I peered between the railings to the landing below. The boyfriend had gone back inside the apartment, but Mrs. Spicer was still there in the hall, leaning against the stairwell, sobbing.

"Sit down," I said, pointing to the futon. Morris' expression was hard to read, and his face was turning red where the guy had hit him. "I'll get you some water."

"What's his name?" I said, as I handed him a cup and a bag of ice.

"Andy something. I don't know his last name." Morris didn't look at me as he spoke. I wasn't sure if he was feeling anger at being hit, or shame at seeing his mom having sex. Probably it was both.

"Is he really a cop?" I asked.

"Sort of."

"What do you mean?"

"He works in the projects, in the city," Morris said, still staring at his feet.

"But not for the Chicago police."

"He's got a weird uniform."

"Yeah," I said. "He must be a Housing Authority officer."

"He's got a gun," Morris said, looking up finally.

I met Morris' gaze. "I'm not afraid of him."

Morris was afraid, though. His lips quivered and he looked away again.

"How long has your mom been with him?"

"I dunno, maybe three months."

"Does he hit you lots?"

"Only when I do something stupid. He doesn't stay over too much. I think he has his own kids."

"Unlucky bastards," I said. As soon as the words were out of my mouth I wished I hadn't used the word bastard. But Morris didn't seem to take offense. In fact, his eyes were so glazed, I wasn't sure he'd heard me at all.

We sat there in silence for a few more minutes. "Are you hungry?" I said, finally. My own stomach was starting to rattle.

"No."

"I'm going to order a pizza, anyway," I said. "You might get hungry later."

We watched TV until the food came, and as I suspected, upset or not, the smell of hot pizza was too much for him to resist. He was, after all, a thirteen-year-old boy. When we'd finished eating, he seemed so much cheerier I challenged him to a game of Nerf hoops. But he didn't want to play.

"I should go downstairs and check on my mom," he said.

"How often does he hit her?" I said.

"I've never seen him hit her," Morris said, "but one time, last month, just before you moved in, she had a black eye."

"That's nice of you to worry about her," I said. "You're a good son."

"No, I'm not," he said, his voice wavering with conviction. "It's all my fault. I screwed up the schedule. I'm too stupid to even know what day it is."

"This is *not* your fault," I said. "Look at me, Morris. Did you hear what I said? This is not your fault. So you mixed up the days—big fucking deal. No matter what you did, you don't deserve to have some asshole hit you. And neither does your mom. This is all on Andy, or whatever that asshole's name is."

I don't think I got through to Morris. He wasn't a good listener. But I felt better for getting it off my chest. And though I didn't say so, I was pissed at his mom for letting someone like that near her son. But, then, she had obviously had a hard life herself. A no-good husband, shitty job, tiny apartment, no privacy. That's the thing about teaching that makes your head spin. A lot of people who go into education think of it as a way to help people lift themselves up, to rise. But that kind of rags to riches story is rare. Really rare. When you meet the parents of the troubled kids, they're always just as messed up as the kids themselves. And it doesn't take a lot of imagination to see that most of my deltas are going to be lousy parents. Of course, that's what I was saying to my AP kids the other day, when I debunked the "Great Man" theory. People don't shape their own fate. We're all subject to social forces we can't control, and in the case of my deltas, or Morris and his mother, forces we can barely even comprehend.

But none of that intellectual bullshit was any help for Morris, who was worried about his mom. Or for me for that matter, because I didn't want to send him back down there, if Andy was still around. So I suggested Morris call her from my phone, instead of going straight down there.

She was home, and she was so happy to hear from Morris that I could make out what she was saying from the other side of the room.

"Thanks, coach," Morris said as he left.

"If you ever need a place to crash for the night, just come by," I said.

He didn't answer.

"I mean it. Really," I said.

"Thanks, coach." Morris stopped, with the door half-open. "You know, I wish my ma would date somebody like you."

At first, I wondered if maybe Morris was joking. But after I thought about it for a minute, it didn't seem so crazy after all.

CHAPTER 8

WHEN I WAS TWELVE, I spent the Christmas holidays with my father. Also, on two occasions, he wrote me a letter. Aside from that, I've had no contact at all with him since I was four. His first letter arrived when I was eight. The highlights were that he had moved to Dallas, where he owned a swimming pool, and had started what he rather vaguely referred to as a "new family." Plus he drove a white Mustang.

My mother was very intelligent, but she was a victim of her times. If she'd been born twenty years later, she would have gone to college and become a professional. But in her day a working class Irish girl, no matter how bright, was expected to settle for an office job and a nice husband. But my dad turned out to be a jerk, and her job, working as a secretary at the University of Chicago's history department, was difficult. You might think being a secretary in a place like that would be more prestigious than the same job in an insurance office. But the truth is the bigger the social distance between the boss and the employee, the easier for the boss to treat his secretary like an alien species. That's the way it seemed to me, anyway. Most of the professors were arrogant pricks, who used her as their own personal ass-wiper. History was one of the biggest departments in the university, so it was a bit like having twenty-two bosses. Some of the professors would never ask her to do anything, but others treated her like a personal assistant and took total advantage. My mom had beautiful handwriting, sharp and straight, and one time, one of the professors made her hand write two hundred invitations to his daughter's wedding; he didn't get her anything to thank her for doing it. Not even a card.

The worst, though, was all the typing. This was in the days before word processors, and some of the profs liked to write the first drafts of their articles and books longhand. Then they would make her type them up. And if they had publishing deadlines they had to meet, she would sometimes take work home with her. Lots of weekends, she'd be hunched over the 3M electric typewriter she kept on the kitchen table, punching away until late in the night. Sometimes, on long projects, pain would flare up in her wrists, and I'd make ice packs for her. Looking back, it was obviously carpal tunnel syndrome, but I never heard my mom use that term. Today, you'd get workman's comp, but back then secretaries didn't complain about that kind of thing. If they did, they'd lose their jobs. Like I said, the professors were all pricks.

There was one grad student in the department, though—Scott Rudolph was his name—who turned out to be a decent guy. When my mom had to work late, there was nowhere for me to go after school, so sometimes she'd pick me up and take me back to the office with her, where I would read or do my homework. Well, this guy Rudolph did some kind of clerical work for the department, and he had a little cubicle near my mom's desk. He was about the same age as my mom, in his early thirties. Anyway, he was single, and he always seemed to be hanging out in the office. From his awkward small talk and the way he kept offering to buy my mom coffee, I could tell he had a big crush on her. This wasn't such a shock; lots of men liked my mom. What did surprise me was how slow he was to ask her out. I never could figure out what he was waiting for, but I guess he just wasn't a very confident guy. Maybe he had been teased too much when he was little. And you could see why bullies would pick on him. He had droopy posture, thick glasses and enormous earlobes. Anyway, he seemed to think he could make friends with her by being nice to me. We had loads of fun. Whenever I was there we would race up the hallway on wheeled desk chairs. And a bunch of times he even hustled me in with him, past the guards at the University's field house, which for me seemed impossibly huge and glamorous, with its floor to ceiling bleachers and gleaming basketball court. Shooting hoops there was like running the bases at Wrigley Field. After basketball, we would wrestle on the huge foam port-a-pit that the high-jumpers and pole vaulters used for landings.

When he finally did get up the nerve to ask my mom out, she said yes. They were together for about two months, until just before my twelfth birthday party.

The week before the party, my mom had told me to make a list of friends to invite, and when she saw it she said, "No girls, hmm. Not interested yet, I guess."

Actually, earlier that year, I had gone out with a girl in my class for three days. Her name was Maggie Coughlin, and I had dumped her because, as I had indelicately informed her in my breakup letter, she wouldn't let me feel her flat little chest when we made out. When Sister Helen confiscated the note and congratulated Maggie, in front of the class, for her chaste ways, Maggie became rather bitter. She turned to the form of vengeance most easily wielded by a twelve-year-old girl: gossip. Anyone at the playground who would listen learned I had a very small penis. This speculation, though true, and richly deserved, soured me (temporarily) on females in general and Maggie in particular. But it was hard to tell what purpose would be served by sharing that story with my mother, so all I said was, "I just don't want a big party is all, Mom. We're going trick-or-treating, and you can't have too many people. It messes up the group." My birthday is October 29th, and I always had Halloween theme birthday parties.

"If that's how you want it," my mom said.

"That's how I want it."

"All right, I'll call their mothers—" she broke off talking and glanced down at the list again. "Who is this Scott? A new boy?"

"Duh," I said, scrunching up my face. "He's your boyfriend."

"Don't be smart," my mother said. "And for your information, he's *not* my boyfriend. Not anymore."

"What?" I said, grabbing her wrist. "Why not?"

"We're not seeing each other anymore," she said. "That's all."

"Why not? What happened?"

"What's it to you?" she said. "You never like any of my boyfriends." This was true, I was always glad to get shut of them. They were an oily bunch, who spoke to me only in commands like "Get off the couch," or "Go to the fridge and get me another Schlitz."

"But I like Scott. He's, he's. . ." I stumbled for words.

"He's what?"

"He's nice."

"Yes," my mom said, softening her tone, "he is nice. But he's just not really my type."

Not until much later did I understand that his being nice and not her type was not coincidental. I doubt my mother ever understood this at all. She never did find a good man. To me, though, at twelve years old, nice seemed to be exactly what we both needed. And I could talk my mom into just about anything, so I was sure I could convince her to get back together with Scott.

"But you said I could invite whoever I wanted," I said.

"I meant *your* friends," she said.

"Scott *is* my friend."

She shot me a dangerous look, but I persisted. "He was my friend first. You stole him. He used to play with me all the time before you started dating him. And now that you're done with him, you don't want me to see him any more. It's not fair."

"He'll think it's weird," my mom said.

"What's weird about it?"

"I just broke up with him. Why would I invite him to our house? It's a mixed message."

"You're not the one inviting him," I said. "*I* am."

I waited for more resistance, but that seemed to seal the deal. My mom never held out for very long when we argued. She used to say I was the best arguer she knew, and I think she was secretly proud of me for it. "Well, if you're inviting him than you have to call him," she said.

"Fine," I said, struggling to keep the note of triumph out of my voice.

My friends and I were out on the sidewalk in front of the house, putting the finishing touches on our costumes, when Scott showed up. We must have made a lousy impression on him. I ran with the toughest crowd St. Jerome Academy had to offer, and we'd decided to dress as gangsters—the black street gang kind, not the Al Capone type. To help us achieve an authentic look, before the party, my friend Pat and I had set fire to a pile of cork on the side-walk. By the time Scott arrived, the cork had cooled, and we were dipping our hands into it, smearing our faces with the stuff.

"That you, George?" Scott said, stopping several feet away from my friends and me.

"Oh, hey Scott," I said.

"What are you guys doing there?"

"Getting our costumes on," I said.

"Costumes?"

"Yeah. We're going as the P'stone Rangers."

"The P'stone Rangers?" Scott frowned.

"Yeah, they're the biggest gang in—"

"I know who they are," Scott said. "Is your mom all right with this?"

"All right with what?"

"Your costumes?"

"Yeah, sure," I said.

Scott looked as though he was going to say something more, but he changed his mind and started walking toward the house.

"Wait up," I said, motioning my friends to follow. "We were just about to go inside."

Scott didn't look back, but he slowed as he entered our living room. My mom was sitting in the loveseat, smoking.

"Hello, Joanne," he said softly.

"Hello, Scott." She took a drag on her cigarette and didn't get up from her chair.

"Why don't you open your presents, George," my mom said. "Then you can go trick or treating."

It was a decent haul: a new basketball, an official Chicago Police Department cap from Tony—his dad was a cop—and a slingshot from Pat, but I was too preoccupied watching my mom and Scott to do more than mutter a quick thanks after opening each present. They were standing on opposite sides of the room and hadn't said anything to each other since hello. I opened Scott's present last.

"What is that, a book?" Tony asked incredulously.

"Duh, you dumbass," I said, pointing to the wrapping paper, which said 'University of Chicago Bookstore.' With care, I pulled the tape from the package and unfolded the creases in the wrapping paper.

"Would you open it already, braniac," Tony said.

I was taking extra care not to rip Scott's wrapping paper, because I wanted to show him how glad I was he'd come. But, even at age twelve, I could tell it was a futile gesture. Scott was standing there in the corner, hands stuffed into the pockets of his jeans, looking miserable. I wondered where my scheme to get Scott back together with my mother had gone so wrong. The first part, which consisted of getting Scott to come to my party, had gone really smoothly. So smoothly, in fact, it only now occurred to me that there was no second part of the plan. Somehow, I had assumed that once they were in the same room together, they would realize how much they needed each other, and everything would work out. Scott took one hand out of his pocket and shot a nervous glance in her direction. My mom gave him a chilly stare in return, as she snuffed her cigarette out in an ashtray.

I tore open the package, and cradled the book in my hands. The cover illustration was of a huge prairie schooner fording a river, as a cloud of arrows descended on it, from a very hostile looking group of Indians. The book was a classic, Francis Parkman's *Oregon Trail*. It was the first real history book I ever read, and the only one I grabbed on the night Amy kicked me out.

"Let me see that," Pat said, wrestling the book from me. "This is perfect for you, braniac," he said, giving a fake snore.

"Shut up, Pat," I said. "Just cause you don't know how to read doesn't mean nobody else has to."

"That's still one of my favorites," Scott said, softly. "I hope you like it."

"Thank you very much," I said, in my most polite voice. "I'll start it tonight."

After the presents, we wolfed down an ice cream cake from Baskin-Robbins. When the cake was gone, my friend Tony said, "Can we go trick or treating now? It's already getting dark."

I looked over at my mom, and she nodded. "But be back by ten," she said.

As my friends made their way to the door, Scott slouched over to me. "Well, thanks for inviting me to the party, George. But I think I should be getting going now."

"Can't you stay any longer?"

"Oh, well, you guys will be gone for a while, and I," he shot a sad little glance at my mom, "well, I've got loads of work to do. But don't worry, I'll see you again soon."

"You will?" I said, brightening.

"Yeah, you know, at the department office."

"Oh," I said. "Right."

The front door cracked open, and Pat stuck his head through. "Let's go, George."

"Go on, George," my mom said. "Have fun."

At age twelve, Halloween was our New Year's Eve, and we'd been planning our night for weeks. While we waited for the little kids and their parents to clear off the streets, we did some obligatory trick-or-treating. But we were too impatient to fill our bags, one Mr. Goodbar at a time, so when we saw some fourth graders out without their parents, we snatched their bags, and ran off, howling with laughter.

When it was sufficiently dark, we walked over to our favorite hangout, the white alley, and gathered our ammo. Earlier, Tony and I had stashed two cartons of eggs and a brick of firecrackers behind one of the trashcans.

"Who should we get first?" Tony asked.

"It's George's party," Pat said. "Let him decide."

I thought about it for a minute. I didn't have any enthusiasm for the obvious targets, St. Jerome Academy and Danny Connors, an old enemy of our group.

"Maggie Coughlin," I said.

"All right!" Tony said, laughing. "Now that's what I'm talking about."

By Beverly standards, Maggie was rich. Her father drove a Cadillac and the Coughlins lived in a large bungalow that extended all the way back from the sidewalk to the alley. We hunched there in the alley, peering over the lids of the dumpsters and trashcans, at the kitchen window. The whole house was dark.

"Here you go, George," Tony said, handing me an egg.

I breathed deeply as I eyed the house. The fall air felt sharp and cold in my lungs, and I stared hard at Maggie's kitchen window without blinking.

"Come on, Cavaliere," Tony whispered, "do it already."

Inhaling as I pulled my arm back, I lobbed the egg toward the kitchen window. To this point, the night's mischief had given me no pleasure. I'd been sunk in my own thoughts—mostly about my mom and Scott, and I hadn't even particularly enjoyed stealing the candy from the little kids. But the crunch of eggshell colliding with glass yanked me from my stupor, and as the yoke slid down the windowpane, I felt a strange emotion. I felt powerful.

"Give me another," I said to Tony.

He handed me the carton. I brushed the tops of the eggs with my fingertips, like a piano player, testing the keys. A giddy fury surged through me, and I fired egg after egg wildly at the house, until the carton was empty. Looking up, I saw that the window was more yolk than glass, and the back wall was a mosaic of red brick and white shell.

"Hey, Cavaliere, you need to chill out," Pat said, and the other guys frowned and nodded agreement.

My hands were covered in yolk. I'd evidently gripped one of the eggs so hard it had exploded in my hand. I didn't recall the egg breaking, but then I didn't remember much of anything since I'd asked Tony to pass me the carton. All my senses seemed to have been dampened. That sense of diminished self terrified me, but even before the fear receded, I wanted that feeling again. I inserted a trembling finger into my mouth. The taste of the egg, viscous and salty, mixed with the fumes of burnt cork. A bit of yolk slid to the back of my throat and refused to travel farther. Again and again, I swallowed, but I couldn't force it down. Soon the swallowing became a sputtering cough, but the egg stuck there, pressing against my throat like the back of a spoon. Nauseous, I choked down the egg and wiped my fingers on my shirt.

"You okay, George?" Pat said.

"Let's go," I said. But the rumble of an automobile drowned out my words.

"Car!" Tony yelled.

My friends scrambled for cover behind the trashcans and cardboard boxes that dotted the alley. All of the hiding spots were either taken or too far away for me to reach, so I crouched low, hoping the car would drive on past, but instead it aimed right at me, the headlights trapping me like a pair of luminous chains. I flung my arms over my head, bracing myself as the grille of the car bore down on me. But the driver must have seen me, because the car lurched to a halt, trapping me flush against the fence, with less than a foot between the front bumper of the car and my knees. I scrambled across the hood, but the driver sprang from the car. He yanked my jacket, and wrestled me up against a garbage can. The smell of rotting food almost made me heave.

"You picked the wrong house, punk," the driver said. Behind us the headlights lit up the yard, and, in the glow, you could still see the eggs dripping down the red brick.

I didn't say anything, so he shook me harder. "What's your name, punk?"

When I stayed silent, he said, "You little shit. You can tell it to the cops."

"It's all right, Maggie," he said, looking back toward the car. "Don't be afraid of this little punk."

When he said her name my stomach sank. My eyes hadn't adjusted from the glare of the headlights yet, so I hadn't seen her, standing on the far side of the car. But I looked over at her now, and somehow she recognized me through the burnt cork.

"Daddy," Maggie said, "that's a boy from my school."

Her dad tightened his grip on my wrist. "This boy goes to St. Jerome's? What's his name?"

"George Cavaliere," Maggie said, looking away from me.

"Are you sure?"

Maggie nodded.

"Go phone his mother, Annie," Mr. Coughlin said to his wife, who only now emerged from the car. "I'll make sure he doesn't go anywhere." While Mrs. Coughlin and Maggie went inside to call my mom, I stood there on the back porch, with Maggie's dad, waiting in silence. Mr. Coughlin positioned himself at the top of the back stairs, to block my only escape route. He didn't need to worry; I was sunk in humiliation so deep I couldn't even muster the will to lift my head, let alone make a run for it. Despite the night air, my face was flushed and hot from the total shame that comes from doing a bad thing and, worse, getting caught.

Mercifully, my mom was there in less than ten minutes. She came around the back way, and marched up the porch stairs, clutching a mop, a bucket, four or five sponges and a bottle of PineSol. After plunking down the cleaning supplies, she rolled onto the balls of her feet, reached up and slapped me in the face. "What is the matter with you?" she hissed. Without waiting for an answer, she turned to the Coughlins. "My son and I will make this right. Your home will be cleaner than it was before George got here."

"Mom, you don't have to stay," I said. "I can do it."

"George," she said, shaking her head, "there is no way I am going to trust you to do this by yourself. Not when you can't even keep your room clean. You've shamed us both. You realize that, don't you?"

"Yes."

"I promise we will have this done before you are ready for bed," she said to Mrs. Coughlin.

"Oh, really, Mrs. Cavaliere," Maggie's mother said, "you don't have to do this tonight. I'm sure it can wait until the morning."

"If it's just the same to you, Mrs. Coughlin, I'd prefer to do it now. I don't know if you've ever tried to clean eggs before, but it's much worse after they dry. Besides, I'm not going to be able to sleep until this has been put right."

"Well, if you insist. I'll leave the back light on for you and help yourself to the garden hose." With that, Mrs. Coughlin went inside and we set to work cleaning. We worked for two hours, with barely a word exchanged between us. At one point, we found ourselves hunched together around the bucket of suds, "I'm sorry, Mom," I said.

"We'll discuss it later," she said, as she wrung the mop through the rollers.

The ride home was silent, too. But as we pulled onto our street, she began weeping.

"I'm sorry, Mom," I said softly. I hadn't seen her cry since my grandmother had died.

She wiped her eyes and shook her head. "This is my fault."

"Stop it, Mom. It's not your fault. It's mine."

"I know that a boy needs a father," she said. "But I've been telling myself I could manage all these years, and now I feel so stupid."

"What are you talking about, Mom?" I said. "This doesn't have anything to do with Dad."

"You need a father," she said. "Don't think I don't know that's what this whole business with Scott has been about. And I'm sorry that he's not right for me, since he seems to be just what you need," she grabbed my hand. "I am sorry about that, George."

I didn't know what to say, so I leaned across the seat and hugged her.

When I woke up in the morning, my mom was out. She came back in a few hours, carrying a big blue envelope.

"What's that?" I said.

"A plane ticket."

"Are we going somewhere?"

"You are. You're going to spend the Christmas holidays with your father, in Texas."

"What?"

"That's right. I called him this morning and made the arrangements."

"You called him," I said. "I didn't know you even had his number."

"I looked it up."

"Dad's never invited me before," I said. "Why now?"

"He didn't invite you now either, if you must know. It was my idea, actually. I figure since I haven't been able to discipline you, it's his turn to try."

"Jeez, Mom, I know I screwed up and all, but it's not like I get in trouble all the time. You don't really think I'm bad, do you?"

"I love you, more than anything, George, but sometimes you're so—" she shook her head, "so willful."

"Aw, Mom, I'm going to be fine," I said. "I don't need to go to Texas."

"George, I don't want to discuss this. This time you're just going to have do what I say. No debating."

"But—"

"George, I mean it!"

"Mom, would you just listen. I was only going to ask what you were going to do at Christmas."

"I'll spend it with Aunt Mary, like always."

"Okay, Ma," I said. "I'll go."

I didn't want to make her feel any worse. Anyway, I was excited about seeing my dad for myself. Almost everything I'd heard about him came from my mom, and it was not pleasant. The way she told it, he was a deadbeat, a two-timer and an asshole. I did have a few warm, if hazy, memories of my own: riding his shoulders to the playground, tooling around the sidewalk after him on my tricycle, wrestling with him on his bed. But I didn't doubt my mom—there were too many frightening memories— doors slamming, the smells of tobacco and whiskey, my mom slumped on the floor, sobbing while she cuddled me—for me to dispute what she said. Still, I wanted to see for myself.

In the end, though, my dad proved to be a disappointment, neither as frightening nor as fun as the father memory had conjured. He had dark hair and eyes, a meaty face and a gristly layer of beard.

"What happened to your Mustang?" I said, as he grabbed my bag and we piled into his Dodge Dart.

"Had to trade it in, after we had the twins. They're really looking forward to meeting you. They think it's pretty neat, suddenly having this big brother from Chicago. You know," he said, as though the thought had just occurred to him for the first time, "we really should have done this before. Visiting, I mean."

"Yeah, sure," I said.

"Listen, George," he said, suddenly solemn, "when your mom called, she said something about you being in some trouble."

"Yeah."

He gripped the steering wheel tightly, as he glanced over at me. "So, I guess she wanted me to have this big talk with you. Now, I'm not trying to duck out of my responsibility or anything, but it does seem kind of ridiculous, you know, me giving you this big lecture and all. I mean what with how I haven't seen you for all this time. Right?"

"Right," I said, turning to stare out of the passenger window.

"So here's how I look at it," he said, "you know what kind of things you shouldn't be doing, right?"

He peered over at me again.

"Right," I said.

"And you're only here for two weeks, so I can't really see the point of getting all heavy with you or anything. Not when I see you so little."

"Okay," I said.

"But anyway, if your mom asks, you can tell her we did talk about it."

It was weird; I mean what kid wouldn't be psyched about getting totally off the hook like that. Still, I was disappointed.

"I'm glad that's out of the way," he said, the tension easing out of his voice. "You know, I really think you'll have a good time. Like I told you, the twins are real excited about meeting you."

He was right about that. They raced over to the car and hugged me, like they'd known me for years. Then they fought about who got to show me their favorite toys first. Vera had a collection of Barbie dolls, and Victor had a box full of baseball cards. For the rest of my stay, they glommed onto to me like a rash, which was kind of cool for the first few days, since I didn't have any siblings at home. But I got pretty sick of it by the end of the trip.

The house was kind of a dump. A ranch style three bedroom, with a weed covered backyard. And the pool my father had mentioned in his letter turned out to be an above ground wooden tub, barely big enough to take more than a stroke in. Anyway, it was dry, and from the looks of the moss on the walls, it hadn't been used in years. "We had to let that go when the twins got big enough to run around," he said. "Took too much time keep the chlorine levels right. But we'll probably get it back in shape one of these days."

My dad worked nights at a factory, so he had loads of time off during the day. But he didn't really have much interest in me, or in his other kids either. He didn't ask me a single question about my life. When he wasn't at work, he always seemed to be watching a football game or tinkering with something in the garage. He wasn't mean, and I never got the feeling it was personal or anything. It just seemed like he preferred his own company. So mostly I played with the kids and with Kimberly, my step mom, who turned out to be really sweet. Oh yeah, she was really hot, too. Maybe it was because it was Texas, or maybe because she was five or six years younger than my mom, but, whatever the reason, Kimberly wore really provocative clothing: hip hugging denim shorts and tube top shirts so tight you could see the shape of her nipples. New

Year's Eve, the end of my first week there, was the first time I ever masturbated. The twins were bunking up together in Vera's room, so I had Victor's little racecar-shaped bed to myself. While my dad and Kimberly got wasted on Cutty Sark, I holed myself up in Victor's bedroom and humped away on a pillow, picturing Kimberly the whole time. That moment when I came, my first orgasm, was absolutely shattering. I shook all the way down to my toes, jaw slack, saliva dribbling over my lips and onto my chin. The pores of my skin flickered and tingled, as though I was being massaged with a dozen sharp combs. When I finally emerged from my stupor and my eyesight refocused, I stared at the little pools of semen I'd left on the pillowcase and the middle of poor Victor's bed. I tried to mop it up with my shirt, but I only made the mess worse, spreading the cum all around the bed. When I checked back later, there were half a dozen brown stains on the pillowcase and sheets. Panicked, I smuggled some soap into the bedroom and tried to scrub it clean, but it wouldn't come out. Still, mortified though I was at the thought of Kimberly finding out, I couldn't stop myself from masturbating again. For the rest of the trip, two or three times each day, I slipped into Victor's room and pleasured myself, hoping to match the ecstasy of that first time. But I never did get back to the peak of that first orgasm.

On the last morning, the whole family piled into the Dart to take me to the airport. As we waited at the gate, my dad extended a flaccid handshake to me, lit a cigarette and jingled his car keys. Vera and Victor gave me a huge, twin-style hug and cried. After I'd pried them loose, Kimberly said, "Come back and see us soon, all right." She pulled me tight, and her breasts rubbed up against my chest. My hard-on didn't wane until we began our descent into O'Hare.

A few months later, my dad sent me the second letter. Kimberly and he had split up. He was moving out. I crumpled the letter up into a ball.

CHAPTER 9

ALTGELD SCHOOL WAS RIGHT DOWN the street from Edgemont High, and Cynthia and Eric had told me they were planning on coming to the game, so I scanned the crowd for them, while I waited for the seventh grade game to finish. They were over in the tiny visitors section, sitting with the parents of my team. To get there, I had to pass by a wooden bleacher that lined one side of the court. It was jammed with students wearing Red Flash shirts. In fact, the whole crowd was a sea of lightning-shaped pennants, waving behind a row of cheerleaders who shouted the virtues of the Red Flash, as their seventh graders roughed up the Garrison squad.

"Thanks for coming to the game," I said, slapping Goldstein on the shoulder and giving Cynthia a light hug.

"I'm really glad we did," she said, with a big smile. "This is so much fun."

"Yeah, how about this school spirit," I said, pointing to the cheerleaders. "We don't get a lot of that at the high school anymore."

"Oh, I know," she said. "It kind of makes me wish I taught middle school. They seem so, I don't know, so innocent." Normally that kind of Pollyanna claptrap drives me nuts, but Cynthia said it so sweetly it didn't bother me.

I had been kind of hoping Cynthia was going to come by herself, since that would make it easier to turn the game into a date.

But now that I saw Goldstein there, I was glad he'd tagged along. After all, there was no reason to think Cynthia was any kind of a basketball fan, so it was good she had someone to talk to during the game.

"Hey," I said, looking at Cynthia, but not at Goldstein. "I've got to get my guys back to their school after the game. But it's only a few minutes away. Why don't we meet up for a drink? Eight o'clock or so."

"Oh," she said, her cheeks flushing. "Oh, I'm sorry, I've already got plans for tonight."

"Hey, yeah," I said. "No problem. We'll do it another time then. What about you, Goldstein? You are legal, right? Wanna grab a beer?"

"Maybe another night," he said.

A buzzer sounded, ending the third quarter of the seventh grade game. "I better get to the locker room," I said. "But thanks for coming to the game. Really, it means a lot to me."

"Good luck," Goldstein said. "I saw the Altgeld team on their way to the locker room. Those are some big kids."

Altgeld's coach, Charlie Macintosh, showed us to the visitors locker room, which was really just a utility closet with a couple of benches. "How have you guys done this year?" he asked, as he jiggled the lock. He was an older black guy, maybe fifty, with white hair and a lined face.

"Haven't played yet," I said.

"This is our fifth game already." He paused, waiting for me to say something, but I didn't, so he said, "Been coaching long?"

"No," I said. "Actually this is my first year coaching and, like I said, this is our first game of the year. How 'bout you?"

"Let's see," he looked up at the wall as though he were calculating the years, but the effort was a pretense; this guy knew how many years he'd been coaching with as much certainty as I know the number of women I've had sex with. "I guess this is my twenty-third year. We played in a tournament last weekend. Got four games out of it."

He was dying for me to ask him how they'd fared, but I was determined not to give him the satisfaction. If he wanted to brag, he was going to have to do it without any solicitation.

"We did pretty well," he said.

"Yeah, that's great," I said.

"We won the tourney."

While we were talking, his team filed by, wearing their bright red uniforms. Goldstein was right, they looked more like a high school team than an eighth grade squad. At least three of them were over six feet. My guys stared up at them silently as they passed. But if they were intimidated, they hid it well. I had run them to the point that they knew better than to show fear.

"Thanks for the key," I said, closing the door to the locker room behind me.

My team changed into their uniforms and chatted nervously for a few minutes. When everybody was dressed, I stood up on the end of one of the benches. But I didn't say anything. Instead, to increase the effect, I waited for them, in ones and twos, to notice me and stop their conversations.

Pretty soon, only Morris was talking—about girls, if the phrase, "You see her tits?" was any indication.

"Shut up, guys," Colin said. "Coach is giving his pre-game talk."

"I'm incredibly proud of this group," I said. "You have worked extremely hard these last two weeks. I looked over my practice plans on the bus ride over here, and I did a little addition; you've run 60 suicides, learned 4 offensive sets and 8 special plays. You've mastered help-side defense and become experts at checking out under the boards. But most of all, you've become a team.

"Now, I know last year the Red Flash destroyed the Tornadoes. But you know what, that doesn't mean anything. Not a thing, because you may be the same group of players, but we are a completely different team. And you guys know it, too. The first day of practice, there was a lot of talk of how we couldn't beat the Red Flash. Well, I sure hope we've run all of that negativity out of your systems. Bottom line is this: I believe in this team. If you do, too, we can win this game."

I put my hand out, and the team huddled around me. "One, two, three, WIN!" we shouted.

The final score of the game was Altgeld 73, Garrison 11. But those numbers are misleading; the game wasn't nearly as close as the score would indicate. At halftime, it was 42-0.

My kids, it turned out, were right. Garrison had to be one of the best eighth grade teams in the history of the world. First of all, their court was a tiny little bandbox, with the half-court line only about five feet above the top of the key, and there was so little width that the three-point arc and the sideline converged at the baseline. Using the cramped space and their size for everything they were worth, they ran a merciless 1-3-1 trap. As soon as Colin brought the ball over half court, they squeezed him between two of their six-footers. I'd heard about the trap, and we'd worked on it all week. I told Colin to throw it to Mitch in the middle, who was supposed to hit Colin cutting off of a back screen. We'd got the timing down pretty well, but we don't have the size to simulate that kind of a trap in practice, and the real thing was completely different. Now Colin is a nice player, but he's only 5'2", so he couldn't see over the top. And Mitch was supposed to come to the ball and meet the pass, but he didn't move. He just stood there, frozen. With nobody moving, Colin had no hope. For the first ten plays—the first *ten*—he brought the ball up, got trapped, and then either had it ripped out of his arms or threw a wild pass over the fingertips of one of their huge forwards, which was stolen by their defender on the weak side. They raced in for ten straight uncontested lay-ups. With the score 20-0, I called a time out.

I paced the sidelines for a moment before talking, struggling for composure. The guys on the bench had given up their seats to the starters for the timeout. "What are you doing?" I screamed. "These guys don't deserve seats. What the hell for? They can't be tired. They've been watching the game, just like you!" Now I turned to the starters. "You guys are pissing straight up in the air. Yeah, they're good. Okay, really good. But they've already got their own cheerleaders. If that's what you want to be, you can trade in your uniform at halftime, and I'll see if I can find you a red fucking skirt."

I stalked away from the bench, breathing hard, my eyes bulging. When I felt a little more under control I glanced over at Cynthia and Goldstein. They were laughing about something, and seemed to be paying no attention at all to the game. For some reason that made me angrier. But I bit my lip and came back to the huddle. "We've worked on how to break the 1-3-1," I said, talking a little slower now. "Mitch, you've got to move to the ball. And Colin, if nobody moves, you're better off dribbling than throwing the ball up in the air like that."

"Sorry, coach," Colin said. He and Morris were the only ones looking at me. The referee blew the whistle, indicating the timeout was over.

"Morris go in for Mitch," I said. "Colin dump it into Morris, and run that cut, like we talked about."

The guys gathered around for the team huddle and handshake, like I'd taught them, but I was still too angry to do it, so Coach Fasso ran it without me. He said, "Now remember guys, they want to play street ball, so try to stay disciplined. Outsmart them."

After the huddle broke, Morris just stood there, quivering. "Coach," he said. "I don't know if I can remember the play."

"Sure you can," I said. "Give and go. It's simple, give and go."

Morris staggered onto the court, like a drunk, and the referee formed his hands into the shape of a T and blew his whistle. A technical foul.

I lost it. "What the hell are you doing!" I screamed, marching onto the court and jutting my face up into the ref's jawbox.

"He forgot to check in at the scorer's table."

"Oh come on! This is his first game."

The ref shrugged. "Got to know the rules."

"This is eighth grade," I said. "Eighth grade! Where the hell do you think you are? The NBA Finals?"

He cocked his head to the side and said, "Sit down and shut up or you'll get your own tech."

While I was jawing with the ref, the Red Flash point guard sank a pair of free throws to make the score 22-0. When we inbounded the ball, Colin did a better job of staying out of the corner, and Morris seemed to have calmed down during the technical free throws. He moved strongly to the ball, giving Colin a big target hand, just as I'd taught him. Then as Colin cut to the hoop, Morris hit him with a bounce pass, pretty as a picture. Colin went up for the lay-up, straight and true. But the Red Flash center was waiting for him under the hoop. He was so much taller than Colin that he blocked the shot with his *elbow*. The ball caromed off of Colin's chest and out of bounds. When the Red Flash came down-court, they ran a set play for their center, and he laid an easy one in from four feet.

The rest of the half wasn't much better. At the end of the first quarter, it was 28-0. After that first timeout, we ran our plays fine, but the facts on the court were stark. Their guards were as big as my center, and their center was four inches taller than either Morris or Mitch, our biggest guys. Every single one of their starters could shoot from the outside. They moved with fluidity and grace, shooting and passing with skill. When we had the ball, they either stole it or blocked our shot almost every time. Under no circumstances could we ever have beaten them.

Between the quarters, I paced over to Red Flash bench. "Hey, you wanna take your starters out now?" I yelled at Macintosh.

"It's only the end of the first quarter," he said innocently.

"I don't give a damn. It's not a fair fight and you know it."

"Back to your bench, coach," the ref said, pointing a long finger at me.

Macintosh kept his starters in for a few more minutes, but at least he took off the 1-3-1 trap. Now our guys could get a few shots in the air. But they were so jittery and demoralized that they fired a series of bricks. When he did finally put in the second team, they were noticeably worse than his starters; still, they would have been our five best players. Their third team was a fair match for our starters, but by then we were down nearly forty and I had our subs in, and they couldn't have scored that many points if they were being guarded by chairs.

When the half finally ended, my team filed into the locker room, grim as a funeral procession. But I stayed out on the court pacing the sidelines, pissed off. I was pissed at Fasso for calling their system street ball. He was blind as a bat if he couldn't see Altgeld was more disciplined and organized than we were. And I was mad at Altgeld's coach for running that 1-3-1 trap. Sure, it was effective and Macintosh coached it well, but it defied the whole point of eighth grade hoops, which is to let the kids improve by playing. I mean really playing. Instead, he was scripting their every move, over-coaching them so that they never took any chances. I mean, if this was a high school championship game, then you do whatever you have to in order to win. But with 13-year-olds, you ought to let them play. The other thing that bothered me was the 1-3-1 trap was dependent on the small size of their court. In a bigger gym like Garrison's, we would have been able to spread the Red Flash out and reverse the ball, and they wouldn't have gotten so many steals.

And I was pissed at my players, too, for panicking. They were scared of Altgeld, because most of their guys were black, and Fasso's comments about street ball had obviously gotten in their heads. Mostly, though, I was furious at myself for giving that ridiculous pre-game speech and for thinking I knew better than the kids did, when I told them we could win. My confidence was based entirely on my own sense that I could out-coach the other guy, who, it turned out, was pretty damn good. I had simply been in denial about our talent. In basketball, coaches matter, a little, but players play the game. And Bobby Knight couldn't have beaten Altgeld with my guys. Now that I had seen another team, our squad's deficiencies were obvious. Other than Mitch, we weren't particularly good shooters, but more importantly my guys were short, slow and physically weak. None of this, though, was their fault. In fact they had tried to explain it to me. But I hadn't listened and had forced them to shut up by running them half to death. The irony was that my own overconfidence contradicted my most basic history lesson, about how individuals are powerless when stacked up against large social forces. Even if I was a great coach, an idea pretty hard to swallow with my team down 42-0, my rich white kids had about the same chance of beating Altgeld at basketball as Macintosh's guys did of beating my kids on the SATs.

The locker room was silent, and all thirteen heads were hung. "Huddle up, men," I said. They trickled over toward me at a pace that under normal conditions would buy them extra sprints. "Basketball is a fun game, boys. Let's go out and try to enjoy this second half. Here's a new rule: if you don't look like you're having a good time, I'll take you out of the game." We broke the huddle and headed back out to the court.

The second half was much better. I'm sure most of it was because Altgeld played their second and third string, but still, we moved the ball well, showed decent help-side defense and, best of all, played without fear. Oh, and Morris scored our first hoop of the season. It was a nice one, too. A little turnaround jumper, just like we've been working on.

CHAPTER 10

THERE WAS A PLEASANT SURPRISE in my email box, when I checked my computer between classes. A note from Alyssa Taukeuchi, a former student. *"Hey, Mr. C,"* she wrote. *"Or George I guess I should call you, now that I'm out of college. I'm back home, living in an apartment in Lincoln Park, and I just got together with some old friends from your class. Do you remember Sarah Snyder and Mia Kleps? They say hey. Anyway we were talking about you, and, believe it or not, we all agreed your AP class was the best class we took in high school. I didn't even know if you were still at Edgemont, so I decided to look you up on the web and see. I sure hope this is your address— how embarrassing if it isn't :) Anyway, I'm just taking a year and having some fun, bartending at O'Sullivan's, in the city, until I get a real job next year. Good times! You should come by some time when I'm working—any weeknight except Monday. First one's on me :)*
    Love, Alyssa

The first chance I had to reply was during delta World History, while the kids were filling out their worksheets. *"Great to hear from you,"* I wrote. *"Of course I remember you. You might be surprised if you knew how often I thought about you. I love hearing from former students, especially when they're adults :) I'm glad to hear you're taking some time to have a little fun after college. Good move! I'd love it if you bought me a drink. Second one's on me.*
    George C

Computer smiley faces. Makes you want to puke, right? Yeah, I'm going to hell, I know it. The only thing I can say in my defense is that Alyssa is stunningly attractive. Her dad is Japanese and her mom is Swedish, a spicy combination. Even back six years ago, when she was in my class, I knew she kind of had a thing for me. She never made much effort to hide it. In fact, she used to stop by my room after school and chat me up about how high school boys are so lame. A couple of times she bugged me enough that I gave her a ride home. I never crossed the line, though, not with her or anyone else. I'm not saying I deserve a medal or anything. Anyway, it was hard to see what exactly was wrong with dating her. After all, she seemed like a bright, fun adult. And it was her idea to get together.

So, yeah, I went to O'Sullivan's on Thursday, after practice. O'Sullivan's is a big hangout for DePaul University, a typical sports bar, with a college emphasis. Lots of big TVs, a couple of pool tables, pennants for DePaul and all the local pro teams. But it was pretty empty when I got there. I found a stool at the end of the bar, and waved at Alyssa. She was wearing a tight half-shirt, that revealed a pierced belly button on her sculpted midriff. With her ivory skin, black hair and green eyes, she was even better looking than I remembered.

"Hey," she said, when she spotted me, "how's it going, Ge-or-ge? I'm glad you came." She leaned across the bar to hug me, and her breasts brushed against the inside of my arm— 22-year old breasts—it makes my knees weak, thinking about it.

"I've never been here before," I said, looking around the room. "Pretty cool place. Are you enjoying bartending?"

"It's not too bad," she said, as she sprayed some tonic into a glass of ice. "I don't know, I guess I should get going on my career and all—my parents sure want me to—but I am so not ready to face reality yet. Anyway, this job keeps me in rent. Solid tips."

"I bet," I said. "Someone like you must clean up."

She leaned over the bar, so that her mouth was just inches from mine. "Someone like me?"

"You know," I said, lowering my voice, "someone as gorgeous as you."

She tilted her head to the side, as though thinking over her response. Then she batted her eyelashes and said, "You don't look so bad yourself."

"A bit grayer maybe," I said.

"You were starting to go a little salt and pepper, back when I was in school. But I always liked it. You were definitely the hottest teacher at Edgemont. Do you have any idea how many girls had a crush on you?"

"There's no accounting for some people's taste," I said.

She laughed at that, and I said, "What about you? Remember back in high school, how you used to complain that the boys were so immature. Did you find things any better in college?"

"Not so much," she said, shrugging. "I dated a couple of decent guys. But I haven't found the right one yet, I guess."

"Yeah, well, I thought I'd found the right person, but it didn't work out for me. So I guess you just never know."

"Are you, uh, did you—"

"Yeah, I got married, let's see, you must have been in college by then. But we split up this past summer."

The grin disappeared from Alyssa's face and her eyes seemed to deepen in her head. I guess she had supposed I had been single all this time. She nodded to herself, and then her lips spread into a smile again. "Oh, that's too bad."

"For the best," I said firmly.

"Hey, I've got to take some orders here," she said. The place was starting to fill up. "There's a DePaul basketball game coming on TV in about half an hour, and it's going to be a little nuts in here. But let me buy you that drink."

"Bourbon on the rocks," I said.

By the time she came back, someone had turned the volume all the way up on the big screen TV, and you had to shout to be heard over the din. Two jockish-looking guys in baseball caps sandwiched me at the bar, yapping past me from either side.

"It's going to be crazy until after the game," Alyssa said, handing me my drink. "How long can you hang out?"

The prospect of watching a whole game by myself, amidst a sea of frat boys, did not appeal. "You know what," I lied, "I'm supposed to meet a friend in a little bit, but maybe we can get together this weekend or something, and really catch up, when you're not working."

"That sounds great. Give me a call. Believe it or not," she said with a wink, "I'm the only Alyssa Taukeuchi in the Chicago book."

I reached for my wallet to pay for the bourbon, but she put her hand on top of mine. "First one's on me, remember." She tickled my palm with her fingertips before releasing my hand.

I am not exactly a perfect person, so it might seem unfair that women tend to fall in my lap. It's kind of hard to explain. People sometimes tell me I'm handsome. And for a long time, I thought that was why I've had such an easy time of it. (Ever since the seventh grade, the first time Mary Margaret Kennedy stuck her hand down my pants in the basement of St. Jerome's church, I've never gone more than a few weeks at a stretch without getting some action.) But lately I've started to wonder if success with women has anything much to do with looks. After all, I'm in my late thirties. My hair is turning gray and I've even started to grow a bit of a potbelly. And still, I *know* there are a half dozen bars I could go to on any given night, and if I stay 'til last call, when the genuine hoe-bags separate themselves from the flirts, I'd wind up getting my dick wet. I guess I'm just one of those guys—you know the type. Not that it's fair. I mean, Lord knows I would never let a sister date somebody like me. But the thing of it is, women have no one to blame but themselves.

I mean, take Amy for Chrissakes. She's good-looking. I mean, *very* good-looking. When we were in graduate school, it seemed like half of the men in our program asked her out. And most of these guys were really sweet, too. But none of them did it for her. They all bored her to tears, with their earnest manners and sweet tempers. Women have used a lot of names to describe me, especially Amy, but I can't ever remember being called boring.

I met Alyssa for coffee late on Saturday afternoon, at a European-style cafe. It was Alyssa's idea, "I'm really sick of bars, actually," she'd said.

For some reason, though, it didn't go well. I think it was partly the way she was dressed. She had on a sleek designer blouse and black slacks. Though she looked great, it was a little disconcerting because I was just wearing old jeans and a rugby top. I guess she thought of it as a real date, between adults. But after seeing her the other night at the bar, exposed belly ring and all, I had a hard time letting go of the fantasy Alyssa. And the daylight and lack of alcohol sure didn't help any. We found it hard just to get the conversation going.

"Now remind me what you majored in."

"Chemistry."

"Yeah, how was that?"

"Boring," she said, making an ugh face. "I don't know; it was all right I guess. My parents really want me to go to medical school, and every single other person who was a chem major seems to be doing that, but I just can't see going to school for that long. I don't know what to do."

I didn't really have that much to say about chemistry, so I asked her what her friends from high school were up to.

"I don't keep in touch with too many of them anymore. Mostly just Sarah Snyder and Mia Kleps. Sarah is going to law school down at U of I, and Mia is working for a consulting company. She's going to be traveling four days a week. That sounds really cool and perfect for Mia. Well, you remember Mia. She's always been ready for a little adventure."

"Yeah," I said, "she's a good egg."

The truth was I didn't exactly remember either Mia or Sarah. I mean the names were kind of familiar, but it was six years ago, and I must have had 700 new students since then. Unless there's something special about them, like Alyssa, they all kind of blur together.

"What about you?" she said. "How have things been for you?"

"I don't know," I said, "pretty good. I mean my wife and I separated, but that probably isn't the best topic to get into. And school, you know school is just school."

There was an awkward silence, and I tried to fill it by telling a story about my days as a high school basketball player. One of our regular games was against a deaf boarding school. Even though nobody could hear at the deaf school, not even the staff, they played the national anthem before each game. But this time, there was a mix-up. Somebody must have hit the wrong button on the tape player and recorded over the *Star Spangled Banner*, replacing it with our coach's profane pre-game talk (he was especially angry because we'd lost to them at our court a couple of weeks before). Well, believe it or not, the refs and the guys on our team were the only ones aware of the mix-up. The other team and their whole crowd, hundreds of people, sang the words aloud, with their slightly off pronunciation, keeping time with a fellow at center court who signed the words. And the big finish came just at the part of the tape when our coach said, "Let's go out and kick some deaf ass."

Not a bad story. Unfortunately, Alyssa had already heard it. I started to get suspicious when she only gave a polite chuckle at one of the best laugh lines, and her nod of recognition when I got to the part about the tape clinched it. "I told you this story when you were in my class, didn't I?" I said.

"Don't worry about it," she said. "It's a great story."

"Oh, sorry," I said. "That was a long time ago. I have a hard time remembering which stories I told to which classes."

"Keep going," she said, adding more sugar to her coffee. "It's hysterical."

So I pressed on, but the air had seeped out of the balloon, and I tried to finish the story as quickly as possible. We muddled through another ten minutes of conversation, until, mercifully, the check came. I gave the waitress my debit card. She took a long time getting back to us, and while we sat there, waiting, neither of us said anything. I suppose we were both trying to think of a polite way to extricate ourselves from what had become a fairly dull date. In the end, it all felt too real. Which kind of defeated the purpose. After all, I suppose part of the appeal for both of us lay in breaking the student-teacher taboo.

The waitress came back to our table. "I'm sorry," she said, in a hushed voice, "but your debit card didn't clear."

"Didn't clear?" I said. "Did your machine break?"

"No, sir." She gave me an embarrassed smile, holding out my debit card toward me. "I guess—well, it said your account doesn't have sufficient funds."

"That's not right," I said. "The school puts my direct deposit statement in every other Friday."

The waitress hunched her shoulders and bit her upper lip, but didn't say anything.

"Did you try it a second time?" I said.

"Three times," the waitress said, looking miserable.

"Oh, let me pay, George," Alyssa said, reaching for her purse.

"No, no, I got it," I said, snatching the card from the waitress and giving her another. "Put it on this. It'll go through. Sorry about that," I said to Alyssa, "I don't know what happened. My check goes through automatically on direct deposit. I've never had a problem, before this. The only thing I can think of..."

"The only thing you can think of is what?" Alyssa said, when I didn't finish my sentence.

"Nothing," I said. "It's nothing." But it wasn't nothing; it was Dara. I remembered what she'd said when I asked her how she gotten my address. From Susie in payroll. Dara really was crazy; I mean messing up my lunches and screwing up the delivery of my videos was one thing, but tampering with my finances was no game.

"Hey, this was really fun," Alyssa said, fidgeting with the clasp on her purse.

"Yeah, let's have coffee again sometime."

"Yeah, definitely," she said, looking relieved that I was ready to call it an evening.

I didn't feel like going back to my little apartment yet, and it was still early, so I took a cab to a bar near my house. But the prospects for hooking up there were pretty dire; none of the women were even close to as good-looking as Alyssa. So I went home, smelling of smoke, my head tingling from five or six whiskeys.

There was a message from Dara on my voicemail. She'd tried every form of communication, but ever since that night when I'd thrown her out, I had been really good about ignoring her. Ripping up her notes, deleting her emails without reading them and screening her phone calls. Maybe it was the scotch or maybe I was feeling shitty about myself, after striking out with Alyssa, but tonight I actually listened.

"Oh, George," she said, "since we saw each other last, I've been so depressed. I have just been trying to get through this thing one day at a time. I know you've suffered, too. I know you're in trouble at school. But I can help you. You need me to help you. We've both had a lot of pain from this. But you know what? Life is short, and we can't live in the past. I hope you realize that before it's too late and you miss out on something special! I really believe we can repair what's been broken. Please call me. I love you."

Her smug, self-satisfied tone pushed all my buttons. And then there was the bit about my troubles at school. Did she mean just the stuff I already knew about, like the bad food Betty served me and the videos and copies that weren't getting delivered and the direct deposit thing, or was she somehow involved in the investigation about my comments, too? I played the message again, and even after a second listen I still couldn't tell. But either way, I couldn't just let that go without calling her back and bitching her out. It was too late to try her on her cell, what with her husband around. So I called her extension at the school, and got her voicemail. As soon as I heard the beep I launched into her.

"Dara," I said, "you're not really this dense, are you? I don't know how else to explain your inability to see that I want nothing to do with you? Is there something hard to understand about the way I've been treating you. In case you haven't noticed, I'm trying to ignore you. Since you seem to need more explanation, please believe me when I say you are incredibly stupid, and I never, ever want to talk to you again.

"Oh, and since you seem to think I owe you some sort of an apology, well; here you go: I'm sorry I ever slept with you and I never would have done it if I'd known you'd wind up being such a whore. I know about your little scheme to get me. I know you've got all your bitch friends plotting against me at school. It's not bothering me, so you may as well give it up, and, for the last time, leave me the fuck alone."

I hung up the phone and went to bed.

CHAPTER 11

On Monday, I got a message on my voicemail from Frank Brewer, the head of the local teacher's union. "What the hell happened today, Cavaliere?" he said. "Ted Asbury drove all the way in from regional headquarters to meet with you, and then you stand us up. This is a busy guy. And I had to get a sub for my class, which comes out of the union budget." Asbury was the union lawyer for our region, but I had as little use for him as I did for Brewer.

You might think a guy like me, from a blue-collar background, would be in tight with the union. But I'm not a joiner. The truth is, some of what the Republicans say about teacher's unions is dead on. Unions are there to help the lowest common denominator. Take the tenure policy. It's absurd. You work four years at a school, manage not to get fired, and you've basically got a job for life. Even if you can't teach a lick. So most of Brewer's time is spent trying to protect burnouts, who quit teaching years ago, and idiots like Doug Feeny, who lack even a rudimentary knowledge of their subject. And then there's the union salary schedule, which is based on seniority, not on skill or department. So a driver's ed or PE teacher who's been here twenty-five years makes more than I do. Which, when you think about it, means the better teachers, like me, are subsidizing the crackpots and cranks.

So, out of principle, I didn't join the union for my first few years. But eventually they wore me down. Not because I bought into the idea, but because Brewer negotiated this ridiculous thing called Fair-Share, which basically means you have to pay 70 percent of the normal dues, even if you don't join the union, because you supposedly benefit from the work the local does. So when Fair-Share took effect, I figured I might as well join.

Still, I'd never taken an active role in the food drives, regional caucusing, or voter registration campaigns Brewer's always got going on. But if I wasn't the world's best union member, I'd never got much from them either. To be honest, though, Elaine's talk of the board and their lawyers and Mrs. West, with her legalese, had gotten to me a little bit. So after my meeting with Elaine and the Wests, I had let Brewer know about my situation.

But that didn't mean I was going to kiss his ass. I called him back and said, "I don't know what you're talking about, Brewer. You never told me about any meeting."

"I sent you a note, yesterday," he said. "I told you to meet us in the private dining room at one o'clock. We scheduled it for your prep period. If you were busy, you should have told me, and we could have worked out another time."

"Yeah, that's a great point," I said. "Except this is the first I've heard about it."

Brewer exhaled before answering. "Not only did I send you a note, George, but I walked down to your room, and your student-teacher didn't know where you were. So we went back to the dining room and waited for you, until Asbury had to leave."

"Listen," I said, "I don't know how to make this any more clear. This is the first I've heard about it. So stop griping and call Asbury back to reschedule."

"I'll see what I can do," Brewer said, gruffly, "but let's be honest here, the guy isn't exactly your biggest fan."

"Believe me," I said, "the feeling is mutual. Don't think I've forgotten how the guy lied to me about that sexual harassment sensitivity training bullshit."

Four years ago, I took a sexual harassment sensitivity course at a YMCA in the city. The Y was in a rundown area of town, sandwiched between an all-night coffee shop and a furniture liquidation store, whose sign promised easy credit in English, Spanish and Polish.

Inside the place, the decor wasn't much nicer; the room we used for our class was apparently an aerobics studio most of the time. The air was moist and hot, and smelled like sweat. My classmates were seated already when I arrived. There were just three of them and they were a sorry bunch—all of them profoundly disfigured. One had a cleft palate, the second a huge birthmark on his cheek in the shape of Kentucky, and the last guy, Smitty, had a wandering eye.

Our instructor, Walt, was about forty, with a puff of curly hair and huge biceps. "We're used to thinking from our own point of view, aren't we?" he said at the start of class.

"Yes, sir," said Smitty, the trick eye guy.

Walt's rhythm seemed a bit thrown off by Smitty's answer to what had clearly been a rhetorical question, but he pressed on. "Of course we're familiar with our own personal histories, and we may think it's crazy for someone else to be afraid of us, since we've never harmed a soul. And we know that we don't intend to hurt other people. But sometimes we don't stop to consider the personal experiences of the other person, and of ladies in particular, do we?" Walt said.

"No, sir," Smitty said.

"Does anybody here know what the percentage is of ladies over age twenty who have been sexually assaulted?"

"No, sir, I do not," Smitty said.

"Fifty," I said.

"Uh, yeah, it is fifty," Walt said. He sounded bummed, like I'd stolen his thunder by knowing the answer.

"Think about that," Walt said. "One out of every two. That can help us to understand the other person's point of view. You may mean no harm, but half of the female population has had a bad experience, and every lady knows some other lady who has been a victim. And we don't want them to feel that way. We don't want them to fear us, do we?"

"No, sir," Smitty said.

"After all," Walt said, solemnly, "these ladies are our sisters, our mothers, and our daughters, aren't they?" The other guys in the class nodded as though this was a profound nugget of wisdom. And Smitty tried to give Walt more affirmation, but Walt seemed to be getting tired of his toady act, and he cut him off. "So today we're going to learn how to let those sisters, mothers and daughters know we have good intentions. We're going to start with a multimedia presentation on how we can decide what kinds of things are appropriate and which are not."

The multimedia presentation turned out to be one of those old filmstrips, with the soundtrack on a cassette recorder. The kind that beeps, when it's time to advance to the next slide. Walt played it on a projector from the pre-plastic age that hummed so loud, you could barely hear the narrator's voice, but what you did hear was as dated as the equipment. The film was called "*No Means No!*" and the narrator talked in that super earnest style, whose grave Letterman's been pissing on for three decades. And the unsubtle language was straight from the dawn of the date-rape age. "Many fellows think when a girl says stop, she is just playing hard to get," the announcer said. "After all, what could be more beguiling than to have your beloved tantalize you with a romantic game of hide and seek." It went on like that for forty minutes. When, at last, it ended Walt passed out some paper and pencils.

"What's this for?" I said.

"We're going to take a quiz," Walt said.

"A quiz?"

"Well this *is* a class, and you have to do well enough to get credit."

"What happens if we fail?" Bobby, the guy with Kentucky on his face, said nervously.

"You can take it again at the end of class," Walt said, "and if you fail that, you can always sign up for the course again."

But they must not have wanted any repeat business, because the quiz seemed designed to ensure everyone would pass. It was true-false, only five questions long, and ridiculously easy. It went like this:

True or False
1. Girls who hitchhike are expecting to trade sex for a ride.
2. If you take a girl out to dinner and spend a lot of money, she has to reward you with sex.
3. Girls who wear sexy clothing are "asking for it."
4. It's not rape if the girl is sleeping or unconscious and doesn't say no.
5. A girl can't be raped by her boyfriend.

We exchanged papers at the end of the quiz and I got blue-grass Bobby's. Walt read out the answers—one by one, instead of just saying they're all false—and Smitty gave a happy grunt after each one, as he saw that he got it right. But poor Bobby seemed not to remember what he'd answered, because when I handed him his paper back, he asked me how he did. "Two out of five," I said, softly.

He hung his head. I felt bad for him. I mean he didn't look like a rapist or anything, just a sad sack, and the only explanation I could come up with for his futility was that he was illiterate.

The last activity of the day was this horrendous role-play. "Let's imagine we are at work, and there is a female co-worker you are interested in," Walt said. "We are going to simulate a conversation you might have with her at the water cooler. When it's your turn, one of you will be yourself and since we don't happen to have any ladies in the class this time, one of your classmates will have to pretend to be the female."

"Are there *ever* women in this class?" I said.

"Well, no," Walt said. "Not yet. Anyway, why don't you and Smitty start, George?"

We cleared a couple of exercise bikes out of the way, and Smitty and I stood up on the stage, underneath a poster that said, *"Boundaries Protect Everyone."* I was the female first, and Smitty tried to chat me up, using these little cue cards, while the rest of the class evaluated his conversation to see if what he said was appropriate. Smitty turned out to have a zest for the theatre, and he bellowed his lines like he was auditioning for *Cats*. "Did you see *ER* last night, ma'am?" he began. "That's one of my favorite programs. I seldom miss it."

I was supposed to read my own lines back, but I found it almost impossible to concentrate on what he was saying. For one thing, Smitty had moved all up into my personal space, and his breath smelled like burnt grease. And contending with his wandering eye was brutal. I couldn't tell which eye was watching me and which one was over checking out the audience's reaction. It was like being courtside at a tennis match. My neck got sore from glancing back and forth so much. Finally I gave up and studied the Lexington-Louisville corridor on Bobby's face while I spoke. "No, I didn't get a chance to see it." I said.

"It was a very special episode," Smitty thundered. "Dr. Green bedded a new nurse."

"Wait a minute," Walt said, stepping up toward the stage. "Wait just a minute. Who can tell us what Smitty said that was wrong here?"

After a minute, Bobby raised his hand. "He shouldn't talk about sex with someone he barely knows."

"Excellent," Walt said. "Why not?"

"Well, like they said in the filmstrip, the lady may not feel comfortable discussing such things at work. If you talk about doing it, she may think you want to do it with her. And maybe she just wants to talk about work."

"That makes sense, Smitty, doesn't it?" Walt said.

"Yes, sir," Smitty said.

It was my turn next. "Thank God it's Friday," I said, mumbling my lines at the speed of a traffic report.

"Yes, indeed," Smitty boomed, "we can all be glad the weekend is here."

"What kind of plans do you have you tonight?" I said.

"Wait, George," Walt said. "Wait just a minute, we can't hear you. And you're not even making eye contact with your co-worker. That's not very realistic, is it?"

Gritting my teeth I looked straight at one of Smitty's eyes, and barked out my lines, in a staccato voice. "WHAT KIND OF PLANS DO YOU HAVE FOR THE WEEKEND?"

"George," Walt said, "I want you to do it right."

"You could hear me, couldn't you?"

"Now, George," Walt said in a warning voice.

"That's how Smitty talks and you didn't say anything to him."

"Your performance isn't as sincere as Smitty's."

"Yeah," I said, "maybe that's because sincerity is a hard thing to fake."

Walt didn't think that was funny, but he finally let Smitty and me sit down. Then it was Kentucky Bobby and the cleft palate guy's turn. My suspicions about Bobby being illiterate were confirmed when it was his turn to read from the cue cards. He stood at the front of the room, miserable, forehead beading with sweat.

"You can begin, Bobby," Walt said to him.

"Oh, sorry," Bobby said. He glanced down at his card for a second, then looked back at Walt. "The print is so small. I can't read this without my glasses."

So Smitty offered to read the cues for him, and Bobby acted out his scene pretty effectively. He seemed to have a good memory. Mercifully, that was the final activity of the day, and Walt dismissed us. All of us except for poor Bobby, who had to take his quiz again. I fiddled with my backpack, before leaving, until Walt turned around to find more copies of the quiz. Then I sidled up to Bobby and whispered in his ear, "Write F for each one."

Going to the sexual harassment seminar was actually not my idea. I was forced to do it because of this bogus charge one of my student-teachers, Sandy, brought against me. Sandy was a little speck of a girl, maybe 5'2" and a hundred pounds. Her size was actually a problem for her in the classroom. She didn't have the presence to command the kids' attention, not even the AP kids. Not that little people can't be good teachers. But they've got to have a big personality. And this Sandy just didn't. She was too contemplative, too soft spoken. Anyway, I had to give her a lot of help, and we were working late in my classroom one night, when she shot me this really sexual vibe. It wasn't anything she said, just the way she paused and looked at me as we went over her lesson plan. So—spur of the moment—I leaned over and brushed her lips with mine. She kissed me back. No big deal; just a test kiss, short and soft, mostly lips. Make no mistake, though, she did kiss me. But then her body went stiff, and she got up to leave. "I can't do this," was all she said.

She didn't come in to teach the next day, and I had to cover for her class. Then, after school, her supervisor called me and said he was filing a sexual harassment complaint with the school.

So I talked to Brewer, and he called Asbury, and the three of us got together for a war council. I told them what had happened. In my favor, I hadn't stalked her, threatened her, or even told any Clarence Thomas style jokes. Plus it was just one kiss, and she admitted she'd kissed me back. Case closed, right? Think again. She said she felt "pressure" to kiss me, because I was her supervisor and was supposed to write her a recommendation. Which was total bullshit, because, like I said, she kissed me back. And anyway it's not like I'd been plotting it for weeks, pestering her to go on a date with me. It was just a spontaneous thing, and she felt it, too. Not that I'm defending what I did. We never should have kissed. I knew it as soon as she stood up to leave. But calling it harassment was a crock. So I told Brewer and Asbury that I wanted to stand up for myself and fight it out in the hearing.

But they just wanted the whole thing to go away, and they talked me into settling with the board. Since the girl didn't have much of a case, Asbury struck a deal that he assured me was fair. All I had to do was attend these sensitivity training courses and agree to have a letter put in my file, which meant I was on probation until my next tenure review, in five years. That was it, they said, no other penalties.

Well, I was still on probation four years later, when we finally met to discuss the charges the Wests were trying to pin on me. The mood was tense right from the start of the meeting. Of course, my guard was up because of the way they'd sold me out four years ago. For his part, Brewer still seemed miffed about me missing the first meeting, and Asbury looked as though he didn't have especially fond memories of me. "I'm in a hurry," he said. "I had to squeeze you in today, because of the mix-up last time. So why don't you just tell me what happened." He was a rumpled guy for a lawyer, with shaggy hair and a day's growth of facial hair.

I gave him the story, and he listened without commenting. Then he said, "All right, so this is a basic hostile environment case."

"There wasn't a hostile environment," I said. "That's a load of crap."

"The standard for hostile environment on a race-based claim is fairly easy to meet," Asbury said. "Especially in a classroom."

My muscles had been twitching since I'd sat down, so I got out of the chair and paced across the room. I hate chairs. I'd pretty much always rather be standing or walking. That's one of the things I like about teaching. I can get up and move around whenever I want. "Doesn't a hostile environment have to be more than one incident?" I said.

"Usually it does," Asbury said. "But these things are very subjective, and the threshold is lower with kids. Did you single out the girl at all, when you did the Native American thing?"

"No. There was no hostile environment."

"Well what about this incident with African Americans?" Asbury said.

"It's got nothing to do with the case. It was a different day, the girl isn't African-American, and she wasn't upset when I said it."

"How do you know she wasn't upset?"

"Because she laughed."

"Really?" Asbury said. He stopped taking notes and gnawed on the cap of his pen. "She laughed?"

"Laughed, smirked, whatever. Let's just say she looked happy about it. Then she wrote down what I said. She was trying to catch me."

"She may have succeeded," Asbury said, frowning. "Two separate incidents make the case much more compelling."

"Are you saying I can't win?"

"It's tempting to view these situations as win or lose," Asbury said. "But 'us versus the school board' is not the optimal way to think about it. I prefer another negotiating dynamic; it's called 'Mutual Interest' or 'Win-Win.' The objective is to meet the other side halfway, to satisfy their needs, and they meet us halfway to help us achieve our goals."

"What are their needs?" I said.

"To prevent this from becoming public. To make sure they don't have parents breathing down their neck, accusing them of employing a racist faculty member. And, if possible, to save themselves expensive litigation costs."

I paced across the room, while I chewed over what he'd said. "And what are our interests?" I said, after a minute.

"To save your job."

"That's it?" I said, glancing at Brewer. "You're not concerned about avoiding litigation costs?"

"Of course we are," Brewer said. "The union has a limited budget for trials, but our priority is to keep your job."

He was lying. He didn't give a damn if I got fired, but I let it go. "So what's your plan then?" I said.

"We offer them a deal: They keep you on staff, and you will have to make some sort of apology to the kid—maybe a letter of contrition or something. And, George," Asbury looked at me somberly, "I'm sure they'll want you to have some kind of, some..." He fumbled for the right word, "some remediation. They'll probably insist your tenure be revoked pending completion of some program or workshop to show you had changed."

"*Workshop?*" I said.

"It's standard in cases like this." Asbury said. "You'd take some workshops on the history of racism and how prejudice perpetuates poverty and discrimination."

I raised my eyebrows at that. "A workshop on the history of racism? That doesn't sound like something I would enjoy."

"What's that supposed to mean?" Brewer said.

"It means the last one was the single most humiliating experience of my life."

"You can save the outrage for somebody who cares, George," Brewer said. "We didn't get you into this mess."

"Also," Asbury said, "you'll need to have a mentor, here at school, to supervise you for the next tenure cycle."

"This is *our* proposal?"

"That's right," Asbury said, as he put the cap back on the pen. "And there's no guarantee they'll accept. The pressure from parents may be so great that they vote to dismiss you anyway."

"Look, George," Brewer said, "we have to give something to get something."

"Who's we?"

"That's unfair," Brewer said.

"No, it's not," I said. "I can see what I'm giving, but I'd like to know what exactly the union's giving?" They exchanged a conspiratorial glance and then Brewer nodded. That was one thing I didn't like about the two of them; they were too chummy. "I mean it," I said. "What's the union giving up? Aren't you supposed to fight this out for me? In court, if you've got to. Why have I been paying dues all these years, if not to have you working for me, now that my tail is in a crack."

"Think about what you're saying, George?" Asbury said. "Do you want to gamble your career on this thing, all or nothing? Don't you think it makes more sense to take a deal?"

"It makes more sense for you," I said. "Win-Win. Sure. Win for you; hoard your precious litigation budget. And win for the board; they get to deal with this quietly—the whole thing goes away. But I don't see how I win."

"If you play hardball with the board, George," Asbury said, "they will fire you. It's their right. That doesn't mean you're without recourse. But it does mean we can't help you until after the firing, and by then it may be too late."

"Why would it be too late?"

"Let's assume that the board votes to dismiss you, and then you appeal." Asbury took the cap off his pen again, and put the stem in his mouth. "While the case is adjudicated, the presumption is that the decision holds. In other words, you won't be allowed to work while the case is being fought. That would be an unpleasant situation. You might find it embarrassing to be out of the classroom, and then force your way back with a court order. I've seen that happen, and these things never stay quiet. You'd have parents flooding the school with requests to have their kids taken out of your classes and rumors running wild. Believe me, it would be ugly."

"You know," I said, "if I weren't already on probation, they wouldn't be talking about firing me. I never should have listened to your advice last time and agreed to a deal. I should have fought it out."

Brewer bit his lip, as if to stifle a thought, but then he blurted out, "If you could keep your hands to yourself and your mouth shut, then *none* of us would be here."

"That's what I thought," I said, nodding, "this is bullshit. You guys would rather cover your own asses than fight for me. You know what, Brewer, you're right. I got myself into this mess. I'll get myself out of it. You guys are off the hook." I grabbed my notebook and pen and strode out of the room.

CHAPTER 12

PEOPLE HAVE TOO MUCH TIME on their hands. Or so I concluded when I peeked into the Garrison gym, during the seventh grade game, and saw the size of the crowd. There had to be 200 people in the stands for our home opener, mostly middle-schoolers, but dozens of adults, too, including a smattering of teachers and at least one parent of every kid on our team, except Morris. My guys were changing in the locker room, and I had a few minutes, so I slipped along the bleachers toward the far end of the gym.

When I got level with the far hoop, the ball changed hands and the two teams rushed toward me, so I waited before moving on. While I was frozen there, a lanky man of about forty, wearing a starchy business suit, came bounding down the bleachers, two rows at a time. "Hello," he said, grabbing my hand. "They tell me you're the new coach. I'm Dan Wexler's father. You'll be seeing me at most of the games this year, so I wanted to connect with you."

"Yeah, nice to meet you," I said, giving him a light shake, before pulling my hand back. "George Cavaliere."

"Hold on just a second," he said, pulling his BlackBerry from the inside pocket of his suit. "George Cavaliere," he said, tapping on his screen with two fingers. "Is that two R's?"

"Whatever," I said.

He punched the screen a few more times and said, "Listen, George, I was just talking to some of the other parents, and they told me you don't work at the school here—and I think it's just great that you're willing to volunteer your time with the kids."

"I'm not volunteering," I said. "They're paying me."

He nodded at me, as if he thought that were swell. "But you know, nobody seems to have contact info for you," he said. "So why don't you give me a number—maybe a work number or something—in case I need to reach you." He treaded cautiously around the word 'work,' as if he suspected I didn't have another job, or, if I did, my job must really suck.

"I don't like to get calls at work," I said, "so if there's something you want to discuss, you might as well bring it up now."

Dan's dad fumbled with the BlackBerry for another few seconds before turning it off. "No, it's not anything specific. It's just I heard about the game against Altgeld the other day." He smiled sympathetically. "Tough loss. And, well, it sounds like you could use a little help."

"Help?"

"You know, diagramming plays and that sort of thing."

"I don't need any help."

"Are you sure? Listen, think about it and if you change your mind, let me know." He pulled a business card from his wallet and extended his hand. "I actually played some JV ball at Yale, and we had great coaches. I can fax you some of our materials."

I let the card dangle there in his hand. "Who'd you say your kid was?"

"Uh, Dan," he said, his face darkening.

"Right, Dan," I said and stalked off toward the locker room.

Despite that little shot across the bow, my hands were shaking. The truth is, seeing all the parents there made me a little jittery. After all, I'd known for some time that they'd been bitching about me running the kids too much in practice. And I was okay with being known as a hard-ass coach, if there were results, but it wasn't so easy to defend, given the way we'd got hammered by Altgeld. I mean, if we sucked anyway, what was the point of all those sprints?

Back in the locker room, the guys were goofing around, snapping towels at each other's asses and play fighting.

Morris had his shirt off. "Let me get some of that deodorant," he said to Colin.

"No way, man," Colin said, turning his back. "I don't want you stinking it up."

Colin had a point. I could smell Morris' ripeness from halfway across the locker room. But Morris strong-armed Colin and grabbed the deodorant from him. Then he took a huge swipe under each armpit, leaving streaks on the side of his torso. Morris handed it back to Colin, but Colin took a look at it and said, "Dude! You left a hair on it. Just keep it."

"Sweet," Morris said, and then he reached inside his shorts and swiped the inside of his thighs.

"Disgusting," Colin said, shaking his head.

"What?" Morris protested.

Just then Mitch and Dan came into the locker room. "Hey, have you guys seen the cheerleaders? They got new uniforms and they're over in the adaptive gym warming up."

"How do they look in them?" Colin said.

"It sucks," Mitch said. "You can't see anything. The old ones were awesome, because they were all shrunken up. You could see the bottom of their asses, when they jumped."

"How did Ashley and Jenny look?" Ben asked.

Mitch smacked his lips and flashed a dirty smile.

"Which one looked better?" Colin said.

"Ashley," Mitch said. "Oh, man, I can't wait for the dance tomorrow. I'm gonna grind with her." He held a towel against his groin and gyrated across the locker room.

"I don't know," Colin said. "Jenny's got a better face."

"Who cares about faces in the dark," Mitch said.

"Hey, coach," Morris said, looking at me, "which one of the cheerleaders do you think is hottest?"

"All right, settle down," I said. I'm not exactly the world's biggest prude, but listening to thirteen-year-old boys talk about sex was starting to gross me out. Anyway, the guys were a little too loose, in my opinion, considering we had a game in a few minutes. But I was reluctant to crack down on them. Since the Altgeld fiasco, I had been trying to keep a lighter atmosphere in the locker room.

"Come on, coach, only two of them are hot at all," Morris said. "The rest are all fat pigs. You've seen them. Ashley's the blond one with the huge tits—sorry, I mean huge—" Morris stopped himself, grasping for an adult-friendly euphemism. But after a moment, he gave up and resumed his description, "And Jenny is the dark-haired one with the tight—"

Coach Fasso had come in the locker room now, and he frowned as he cut Morris off. "I don't even want to know what you are talking about, Morris. How would you like it if somebody talked about your sister like that?"

"I don't have a sister," Morris said.

"Don't be smart, Morris."

"I'm never smart, coach," Morris said.

The guys laughed at that, but Fasso said, "You know what I mean. You ought to be ashamed of yourself. That is sick. Really sick."

"Why are you picking on me, man?" Morris said. "Mitch started it and I was just—"

"That's enough, Morris," I said, "We've got a game in like five minutes. Get focused." I walked over to the chalkboard, to diagram a play, and as I was drawing, Fasso followed me. "I don't know where a boy that age gets those attitudes from," he said.

"Where doesn't he get it from?" I said, as I drew up the outline of the court, "Internet, movies, TV, friends, his mom's boyfriend."

"You're right," Fasso said. "That's what's so scary. The whole country's headed for trouble. Real trouble. It scares me. Really, it *scares* me when I think about young people today. I mean, kids today—" he shook his head. "It's not like it was when we were growing up."

I've learned to stomach stupidity from my students, but it drives me insane with adults. "No, you're wrong," I said. "Kids today have it easy compared to the 70's and 80's. Graduation rates are higher, college attendance is better, teen pregnancy, crime, drug abuse—it's all better than when we were their age."

"Oh," Fasso said, stumped. "Maybe it just seems that way. But that's why I work with kids, you know, because they're the future."

I turned my head, so he wouldn't see me gag.

"Hey, I don't know if it's my place, Mr. Cavaliere," he said, "but I was thinking maybe we should post some team rules about how to talk in the locker room. You know, so Morris will know exactly what kind of stuff is out of bounds. I keep a list on my computer that my buddy from church forwarded me. I could just print out a couple copies."

"You know, you missed most of it," I said.

"Most of what?"

"Most of that exchange about the girls. Morris was right. He wasn't the only one talking about the cheerleaders. He was just chiming in with the others. The only difference is he didn't have the sense to tone it down when you came in the room."

"The rules have apply to everybody. Sure, of course," Fasso said. "But don't you think it would send a good message if we sat Morris for today's game?"

"Benched him?" I stopped drawing and turned to look at him. He was serious. "No, I don't think it's a good idea," I said. "Not at all. In the first place, I'm not a big rule guy, and, frankly, if the guys want to talk about girls, I don't really see the harm. I mean, we are actually in a locker room. If they can't do it here, I mean for Chrissakes." I shook my head.

"With all respect, Mr. Cavaliere," Fasso said, "I can't agree with you there. When I hear a kid talking like that, it scares me, really scares me. Makes me think he's headed for some serious trouble. But I guess you're the boss."

The game started poorly, with three quick turnovers on our side. Stevenson came down and dumped the ball into their big guy, a real lard ass, who was six-feet and maybe 220 pounds. In his green and red uniform, he looked like a Christmas ornament come to life. But he was surprisingly nimble underneath the hoop, and he scored twice, putting them ahead, 4-0. I was afraid we were in for another Altgeld-like drubbing. Ben, the big guy we had in there, wasn't strong enough to handle him, so I sent Morris in to play center, reminding him first that he had to check in at the scorer's table. Fasso, sitting next to me, shook his head when he saw me send Morris in.

"Do you still got a problem?" I said, keeping one eye on the action.

"No, coach," he said, but then a roar from the crowd drowned him out.

Morris had blocked the big guy's shot into the stands, and as Colin high-fived him, Morris gave an exuberant squawk that got the crowd shouting again. The ref whispered something into Morris' ear, and then came over to me and said, "Coach, I warned him about taunting. Next time is a technical." Fasso shot me an I-told-you-so look, which I ignored.

Colin stole the in-bounds pass and finally got our guys to settle down and run the offense. The other coach had his guys playing a lame 2-3 zone, with everybody keeping one foot in the lane. With all of his guys packed in there like that, he was daring us to shoot, figuring we were likely to miss anything from more than fifteen feet. This was exactly the kind of defense that made me nuts, because it doesn't teach the kids anything about how to play the game. But we had prepared for it, and my guys knew they should reverse the ball against the zone, while our big forwards set screens on the weak side. We ran the play for Mitch five times in a row, and each time he got a wide-open look from ten or twelve feet, which was an easy shot for him. He made four of them, putting us up by four points, and the other coach called a timeout.

My guys came cruising into the huddle, smiling and slapping fives with each other. "Good work, guys," I said. "Watch for them to extend that zone. So Mitch, if they send Big Jelly out to guard you, give him a shot fake and drop the ball into Morris. Now, when we're on defense, they're going to keep trying to dump it into the fat kid, so Colin I want you to really pressure the point and take away that easy angle on the pass. And Morris, that was a great block, but watch the taunting; we can't afford to get a tech. Anyway, I don't want you trying to block him like that every play. If you do it too often, you'll get in foul trouble. Instead, make him put the ball on the floor." The horn from the scorer's table sounded, so we put our hands together and yelled "Hustle!"

As I'd predicted, the other team tried to adjust to our offense by extending the zone. So Mitch got the ball to Morris in the middle like I'd asked, but Morris missed a couple of foul line jumpers and we had trouble scoring for a while. On the other end, Morris ignored what I'd said. Instead of pushing the big kid off balance and further away from the hoop, he let him establish a base on the block, while Morris lay back and tried to swat his shot as he had earlier. But the big guy was crafty, and now he gave a couple of pump fakes before he went up with the ball. Morris fell for it and wound up drawing two quick fouls. Soon the game was tied again.

I took Morris out of the game and sat him down on the bench. He was panting and heaving, more from excitement than exertion, since he'd only been in there a couple of minutes.

"Morris," I said, evenly, "didn't you catch what I said during the last time out?"

He looked at me as if I'd asked him to calculate the square root of a three digit number. But I was getting better at figuring him out. Instead of yelling, I said, "Okay, what I said was if you sit back and try and block this guy's shot all day, you're going to get in foul trouble pretty quick. So what I want you to do is to move him away from the hoop, like we talked about this week in practice."

He nodded, but I still wasn't sure he understood. But I couldn't worry about him right then, because the game was still going on and we were down six points now.

"Coach, are you sure you don't want to go zone?" Fasso said. "Their guards can't shoot and we could keep the ball away from the big guy."

"These guys will learn how to play man-to-man, if we have to lose every game this season. If we had more help-side down low, the guy wouldn't be able to get a shot off, anyway."

Unfortunately, with Morris out of the game, I didn't have any good options for guarding their big kid. I didn't want to put Mitch on him, because I couldn't afford to have him get in foul trouble. So I sent Ben back in, but he was about half the size of Big Jelly, and with no help-side support, Jelly got an easy shot nearly every time down. But at least we were getting open looks on the other end, in the middle of their zone. We basically traded baskets with them until halftime, and we went into the locker room down by only six, which wasn't bad considering Morris had sat out the rest of the half with foul trouble.

Back in the locker room, I said, "The offense is working fine. Let's keep dissecting that zone. Mitch already has ten points at halftime." He smiled at that, but I scowled down at him, "Don't get big on yourself, Mitch, because you're playing a lousy game. You're not helping on the big guy. You have got to come over when he gets the ball and double team him. And, Morris, remember, I don't want you to try to block his shot. Move him off the blocks instead." Morris stared back at me, stupidly, and I had to bite my lip to stop myself from snapping at him. "All right, let's get some shooting practice before the buzzer sounds. Everybody but Morris."

"What did I do?" Morris said, as the other guys scurried out of the locker room.

"Nothing," I said. "I just want to show you what I mean about moving the guy off the block. Let's pretend the blackboard is the hoop, and I'm you and you're him. Okay, now try to establish position." We jostled for a second, and I used my knee to drive him back across the locker room until we reached the bench.

"Now, you do it to me."

"Good," I said. "That's exactly how you should play him."

"Okay, I got it, coach."

He did finally get it. From the second half tip-off, he fought Big Jelly on every possession. And with some help from Mitch, the big kid was forced to take eight-foot turnarounds, which was out of his range. But Morris picked up two more silly fouls, when he tried to block Big Jelly's shot. That gave him four, and meant he could foul out at any time. But I kept him in there, because there were only a couple minutes left in the game, and we didn't have anyone else who could guard the big guy. On the other end, their defense didn't improve any, and we clawed our way back into the contest.

With a minute-thirty to go, we took the lead by two points on an offensive rebound and put-back by Morris. And then on the next play Colin picked the pocket of the other team's point guard and hit a lay-up to put us up four. That's where it stood with thirty seconds left, and we were looking pretty good, when the ref called Morris for shoving Big Jelly off the block. It was a lousy call, because Morris didn't do anything different on that play than he had been doing all game. I gave the ref a hard look, but didn't say anything because we couldn't afford a tech at this point in the game. Since it was Morris' fifth foul, he had to come out of the game. But Morris didn't realize that until the ref marched over to him and pointed him to the bench. From there it was a train wreck.

"What?" Morris said. You could just see the total shock in his eyes. "But I didn't even do nothing!"

"Yeah you did," the ref said, "five things."

"Morris," I yelled, marching out onto the court, "get over here! I'll explain it to you later." But Morris didn't hear me. So I went to go fetch him. By this time, Colin was tugging on Morris' arm, trying to drag him to the bench. But Morris was fifty pounds heavier than Colin, and it was slow going. I grabbed his other arm and said, "I'll explain it to you on the bench, Morris."

"But that's bullshit," Morris said, way too loud, as he swung one arm free from Colin's grasp.

The ref took his time, pulling his hands out wide before sweeping them together in a T. "Technical foul," he said.

Now our whole team was furious, but at Morris, not the ref. A tech was the absolute worst case scenario. Big Jelly was going to get two free throws for the original foul plus the two for the tech, which, if he made them all, would tie the game. And the worst part was they would get the ball back after the free throws. We finally got Morris over to the bench. He sat at the end, his head in his arms, not even watching as Big Jelly stepped up to the line for his free throws. The fat fuck hit all four shots. Stevenson took the ball out and ran the clock down to ten seconds, before starting their play. Sure enough, they went into the big kid. Poor Ben wasn't able to keep him away from the hoop, and Big Jelly did a nice duck-under move and put the ball in as time expired. The Stevenson bench emptied onto the floor and mobbed Big Jelly, as my whole team filed silently into the locker room. Everybody ignored Morris, except for Mitch who said, "Fucking retard. You cost us the game." I'd warned him about talking to Morris like that, but I couldn't bring myself to punish him, or even disagree. In fact, if I hadn't seen a tear sliding down Morris' cheek, I would have added my own two cents. Instead, I went into the locker room and said, "No speech today. We've got another game Monday. See you then."

After the game I drove straight home, without giving Morris a ride. He must have left right from the gym floor, without bothering to shower or even change his clothes. I saw him about a block from home, slumping down the street, still wearing his uniform. He didn't look up, and I didn't slow down. I felt bad for him, but I was exhausted and didn't have the heart for a long talk with him right then. Besides, there wasn't any reason to believe he would listen.

Anyway I'd decided that tonight I was going to ask Cynthia out, and I didn't need Morris hanging out in my place, mucking it up. I had meant to call her sooner, but I'd got temporarily distracted by that little episode with Alyssa. It had been a good while since Cynthia had come to the game at Altgeld, and I was a little worried it would seem weird, me waiting this long to call her. But I'd poked around at school and nobody seemed to think she had a boyfriend.

Cynthia Juniper was exactly one listing above Dara Jurevicius in the staff directory, which was not the best omen. But I picked up the phone and punched in her number, slowing down with each digit. The last number was an eight, and I put my finger on the pad, but instead of hitting it, I took a deep breath and hung up the phone.

I sank onto the futon and aimed the phone's antenna straight at my temple. "What the hell is wrong with you?" I said out loud. Never in my life, not even in junior high, had I done that. Not once had I called a girl and bailed before she answered.

Cursing myself as I moved, I paced across the apartment in three big steps and back again. On my second circuit I snatched the mail from the kitchen counter. Sitting down, I flipped through it, tossing the junk into the trash can. And it was all junk, not even a bill, just mailers and ads. But then I had a change of heart and retrieved a Chinese menu from the trash. Trying my best not to dwell on just exactly what I had been reduced to, I jotted an emergency list of talking points on the menu, in case the conversation stalled out.

This time I punched out the number as fast I could. It rang once, twice. On the third ring the line crackled. "Hello, Cynthia?"

It must have just been static on the line, because the phone rang again. I exhaled as it rang a fifth time. Still no answer. The line crackled again and her voicemail picked up. I left no message.

I stared down at Cynthia's entry in the staff directory, clutching the phone and wondering why I could neither shit nor get off the pot. According to the directory, Cynthia lived in Lombard, a dreary suburb with more Olive Gardens than sidewalks. Why a single woman in her twenties would live there, and not in the city, I had no idea. But then she wasn't the liveliest person I'd ever met. Yeah, she was sweet and all that, but I couldn't remember anything she'd said that'd made me laugh. Her shortcomings didn't explain why I couldn't muster the stones to call her, though. If I had a dollar for every attractive, but boring, woman I'd ever hit on, that'd be one fat wad of dollars. No, the truth was ugly, I was going soft, afraid she'd turn me down. I'd about run out of epithets to hurl at myself when the phone rang. I dropped it, as if it had bit me, and it clattered to the floor, still ringing.

"Hi, is this George?" It was Cynthia's voice.

"Oh, yeah," I said, "hi, how are you doing?"

"It's Cynthia Juniper."

"Oh yeah, great. Yeah, how's it going? What are you up to tonight?"

"Not so much. Grading papers, mostly. I was just on the other line." She paused for a second, and there was a long silence. "Anyway, I saw you called," her voice kind of trailed up at the end, making her sentence into a question.

I grabbed the Chinese menu. "Oh, yeah," I said, unfolding it as I spoke. I'd already squandered the first precious talking point, which was me asking her what she was doing tonight. "Yeah," I said, reading out number two. "I was just calling to thank you, actually, for coming to the game. It meant a lot to me. I'm just sorry we didn't play better."

"You shouldn't thank me," she said. "It was a lot of fun. Eric was saying maybe we should go to another one later in the season."

"Yeah, well, anyway, like I said, it was nice of you to come. Also I was uh," point three was to ask her how her classes were going, but I didn't see any smooth way to get there from where we were. And according to number four, I was supposed to ask her out for coffee this Friday, but the way things were going, that seemed wildly ambitious. "Anyway, I just was calling mostly to thank you for coming to the game. I'll see you at lunch, I guess."

"Oh, sure," she said sounding half-relieved and half-surprised. "Have a good night, George." I balled up the menu and chucked it at the trash can. It missed by a solid three feet.

CHAPTER 13

MONDAY MORNING GOLDSTEIN and I were on our way to the cafeteria when we saw Sean Robbins at his locker. The floor all around him was covered in old worksheets and musty gym clothes. He was rummaging through the locker, saving a few items and stuffing them into his backpack. Everything else, papers, burger wrappers and ripped spiral notebooks, he was dumping onto the floor.

"Hey, are you all right, Sean?" I asked. He hadn't been back to class even once since his fight with Billy.

"I'm straight," Sean said, without looking up.

"What are you doing?"

"Clearing out of this mug." He turned around to look at me. His neck still had red bumps, where Billy had choked him.

"What did they give you, ten days?"

"Yup."

"But you don't need to clean out your locker for that."

"I am *out* of this mug," Sean said, "and I *ain't* coming back."

"What, 'cause of this whole thing with Billy?"

"No, that ain't it." He turned back to his locker. "I'm just through with all this bullshit."

"Come on in my room and talk about it for a minute," I said.

He looked back at me skeptically. "Talk about what?"

"Just to talk. I like you, Sean," I said. "If you're dropping out, then this might be the last time I see you. Anyway, I feel bad about what happened. I mean, it was in my class and if that had something to do with you leaving—"

"No, that ain't it. I'm just through, that's all."

"Just talk to me for a minute, anyway. Come on, my room's right here. I promise I won't try to talk you into staying." I walked toward the room without looking back to see if he followed.

He did follow, and as I opened the door to let him and Goldstein in, I said, "So tell me, what made you decide to do this?"

"Man, school ain't for me," Sean said, leaning against the wall as he spoke. "I can do it, but it just ain't my thing."

"You know what," I said, "I'd probably get in trouble if the principal heard me say this, but you're right. This is a waste of your time. You're not going to college—not with your grades—and if you did, you'd fail out by Christmas anyway." Sean nodded as if this made sense to him.

"So what are you going to do?" I said.

"Get a job. Make some money."

"Do you think you can handle that?" I said. "Working some shit job, for six or seven bucks an hour."

"I work part time already. It's enough to get by."

"Now it is," I said. "You're living at home with your mom, right? Your old man is out of the picture?"

"I ain't even ever met him," he shook his head. "Not since I can remember anyway."

"But you're not gonna want to stay home for long. Not when all your buddies are moving out and doing stuff. So what happens when you get some girl pregnant? Are you using protection?"

He didn't answer.

"I know you don't want to be the type of man that leaves his kid high and dry, like your father did? You're a better guy than that."

He nodded.

"So what's it gonna be like with no high school diploma? Are you the sort of guy who's happy washing cars with the *cholos* from Pilsen, for minimum wage? Some folks don't mind living like that. Like your boy Luther. As long as he got paid, and didn't have to work too hard, he'd be fine. But you? I don't think so. After a while, you'll get tired of it. You might jack a few cars, here and there, for some extra cash. Maybe on the ninth time, maybe the tenth, you'll get caught. After parole, you'll get busted again, and do some real time, get yourself sent to Joliet for a while. And they'd love to have you there. Good looking guy like you, you'll be real popular at Joliet."

He looked at me like I was crazy and then laughed. "I ain't gonna be nobody's bitch."

"You talk tough," Sean, I said, "but I know better. If it weren't for Mr. Goldstein and me, Billy Jackson would have his foot so deep in your ass, you could floss with his shoelaces. You know what the girls call Sean?" I said, turning to Goldstein.

"What?" Goldstein said.

"Pretty eyes."

Sean smiled at that.

"You like that, huh?" I said.

"Nah, man," he laughed.

"Don't laugh. You're too pretty to go to jail, and that's not a compliment. Handsome is a compliment. Pretty? That's the fast lane to a sore ass."

"Man, Mr. Cavaliere," Sean said, "you're tweaking." He shook his head. "You said you weren't going to try to talk me into staying."

"I'm not trying to talk you into anything," I said. "I already told you, you're right. School is a waste of your time. You're not a good student; you never, ever do your homework, and even when you pay attention, you still fail my tests. How many credits do you have now?"

"Twelve," he said.

"Twelve." I shook my head. "You're a junior and you've only got twelve credits. At that rate, you're going to be 20 or 21 before you finish up here. I'll be honest; I don't think there's any way you're going to make it that long. Not when all of your friends have either graduated or dropped out."

"Wait. What are you saying?" he said. "You told me I'm not going to make it if I drop out, and now you're saying I shouldn't bother staying in school."

"That's right, I'm saying both things, because they're both true. Your future at school looks shitty, but you're not going to be happy working a low wage, no skill job. The way things are going right now, I would *not* want to be you. Your future sucks. It might be hard to hear, but I'm just being honest with you."

He scowled at me for a minute, and I thought he might be getting angry. But then he said, "So what should I do?"

"I don't know, Sean," I said. "I really don't. But you know what. It doesn't matter what I say. I'm not going to give you advice. I've made this same speech to enough kids to know better than that. It never helps. You've got to figure it out on your own." I stood up and reached for his hand, "Good luck."

"Thanks, Mr. Cavaliere" he said. "Thanks for being straight."

"So, are you horrified?" I asked Goldstein, when Sean had left.

"No, actually," Goldstein said. "I think he appreciated your honesty. You don't often hear teachers tell their students that they're likely to be buggered. Or that they ought to drop out. It's kind of refreshing."

"Yeah, Sean is a very contrary person. If you tell him he should do something, his instinct is to rebel."

"It takes one to know one, I guess," Goldstein said. But he laughed as he said it, and he spoke without that tone of disapproval I'd sensed when he first came here. "Do you really think he's better off, though, dropping out?"

"I don't know," I said, "I really don't. But I guess I think a kid like Sean needs to get beaten up by the world a little before he'll figure it out. The problem is these kids hear so much crap, from the time they're in elementary school, about how they can be anything they want and do anything they want, that they believe it. Even, no *especially*, the delta kids. I asked them at the beginning of the year what they wanted to do for a living when they grow up, and you wouldn't believe the kinds of jobs they said."

"Like what?"

"Journalist, computer programmer, neurologist. I mean these are kids who read at fourth grade levels. The neurologist, that was Luther. I asked him if he was any good at science. He has a D in biology, *delta* biology. When I told him neurologists go to school for nine or ten more years *after* high school, he thought I was joking."

"But how can you tell a kid he can't be successful, just because he comes from a disadvantaged background?"

"Maybe with little kids, I can see why you want to encourage them to dream, but these guys are juniors. They're seventeen years old. If they don't read well now, it's too late."

"Too late?" Goldstein said, his face somber. "I guess you're right, but too late in high school, that just makes me so sad."

I felt sorry for Goldstein. He really had some angst.

* * *

That day Billy Jackson spoke up as soon as the bell rang. "Yo," he said, "what did the Puerto Ricans do?" This was Goldstein's day to teach, and he peered at Billy over the frames of his glasses, but didn't say anything.

"Huh, Mr. Goldstein? What did they do?" Goldstein hadn't called on him, but Billy kept talking anyway. He left his hand up, though, to mitigate the offense.

Goldstein shot me a perplexed look.

I shrugged my shoulders. I didn't have a clue what he was talking about either.

"Hold on, Billy," Goldstein said, "let me do the announcements before we start class."

"Man, can we skip the announcements, Joe?" Luther said. "It's the most boringest part of class." Since Sean had left, Luther had tried, in his own pathetic way, to be the class cut-up.

"Don't be so negative, Luther," Goldstein said. "There might be some nice opportunities there that you could take advantage of."

"Like what?"

Goldstein glanced down at the sheet. "Well, let's see. There's the Student Council. They always need more good people."

"How much do you get paid for that?" Luther asked.

"Well, no, you don't get paid at all," Goldstein said. "It's a volunteer activity, but it would look good on your college applications. Besides you could try to improve the school."

"Man, some people are suckers," Luther said.

Goldstein was undeterred by this pronouncement and proceeded to read every single item in the bulletin. Most of them had to do with after-school activities, including an information session about the French Club field trip, an SAT preparation class and a volunteer group that works with a women's shelter. He looked up hopefully after each announcement, to see if there was any interest.

"What else is going on?" he said, looking back down at the sheet. "Oh, yeah, Bulls Win! Fifty-Cent Hot Dogs!" He read it with genuine enthusiasm, exclamation points and all.

"You hear that, Luther?" Billy Jackson said, smiling wickedly.

"Hmm?" Luther mumbled.

"Fifty-cent hot dogs, Luther."

"Shut up, Billy," Luther said, certain he was being mocked, but less clear why.

Billy did his Luther impression. A raspy baritone. "Fifty cent hot dogs? I got me five dollars. Them's ten hot dogs. Let's eat!"

The whole class howled with laughter, and I got up out of my seat and walked toward the door, to hide my smile.

"All right, Billy, that's enough," Goldstein said as Billy cackled on.

"Mr. Cavaliere?" Federico Alvarado said, as I walked past his desk, his intonation rolling up and down with each syllable of my name. His eyes moved around while he spoke, as though he feared I might scream at him at any moment.

"Yeah, Federico? What's wrong?" I looked down at him, wondering if he was going to cry.

"Good morning, Mr. Cavaliere," he said. Each word rose and fell as though he was short of breath.

"Good morning, Freddie."

He tugged on my shirt. "I don't like nicknames."

"Oh, yeah," I said, "I forgot." He'd told me that on the first day. Kind of pathetic, but I guess he must have had some nasty ones back in middle school.

"Here, Mr. Cavaliere," Federico said. He held out a sheet of paper toward me. A drawing of a man in a suit of armor, holding a sword. It was good, surprisingly good. The knight was drawn in crisp lines, and the colors were vivid. But I wasn't sure if he wanted me to take the picture from him or just admire it.

"It's nice," I said, walking away from him. "I like it."

Federico was maybe the saddest of the sacks in that class. He had terrible body odor and a hunched back. When Sean had still been around, he and Luther had made him the most frequent target of their jokes. Sean in particular liked to ask Federico if he had taken, "One of those Puerto Rican showers?"

by which he meant a couple of swipes with a bar of deodorant, but no scrubbing.

Federico is the type of student you want to feel sorry for, but I've learned, over the years, bullies mostly have pretty good taste. When they torment other kids the victim usually is, in fact, pretty unlikable. Much as I would have liked to help Federico, he was just too depressing to be around. Even his cap bummed me out. It was an old Cubs hat with a soggy brim, a foam facade and a mesh back.

"Here's my homework, Mr. Cavaliere," Federico said, handing me a sheet of paper. He was the one kid in the class who reliably did his assignments.

"Don't give it to me," I said. "Mr. Goldstein is teaching today."

"Oh yeah," Goldstein said, overhearing our exchange. "Yeah, everybody pass up your homework?"

"Man, you're blowing me, Joe," Luther hissed at Federico. "Why you gonna go and remind him to collect the homework?"

"Like he wasn't gonna remember anyway," Billy said.

If Federico was grateful to Billy for his intervention, he didn't show it. He stared straight ahead, like he did when any of the students spoke to him.

Despite the general shuffling of notebooks, it didn't take Goldstein long to realize that only two or three students had their homework. I'd tried to warn him the assignment was too hard for these kids. Instead of the usual worksheets they got from me, Goldstein had asked them to do something creative. He'd given them a bunch of sources that described Ancient Rome and asked them to imagine they were time-travelers. They were supposed to keep a journal of what they saw as they traveled through the empire. It was a cool assignment, actually, but it was more appropriate for a higher level class.

"All right," Goldstein said. "Where are they? Billy, where's your homework?"

"It's right there," Billy said, pointing to the little pile in Goldstein's hand.

"Oh, right, sorry," Goldstein said. "How about you, Anisha?" She shook her head no. "And Luther, I gather you don't have it."

"Man that homework was so gay," Luther said. "Mr. Cavaliere's is easier."

"Luther, do *not* use gay as an adjective in my class," Goldstein said, his eyes flashing. I'd never heard Goldstein refer to it as "my class" before. Though it was good to hear him assert himself, I doubted this issue was worth taking a stand over.

"Don't use gay for what?" Luther said.

"What I mean," Goldstein said, "is don't call something you don't like gay. It's prejudice, like racial bigotry."

"Nah, it ain't like that," Luther said. "It's got nothing to do with being homo. That's just what people call stuff they don't like."

"Yes it does. You say gay because you're homophobic."

"Are you calling me a fag?" Luther said, his eyes bulging.

"No, homophobic means fear of homosexuals."

"No way," Luther said, a little calmer now. "I ain't afraid of no faggot. If some fairy came all up on me, man, I'd bust him in the ass."

"You'd do what?" Goldstein said, his eyes twinkling.

"I'd bust him..." Luther trailed off, as the other kids burst into laughter. Goldstein scored some points on that one. Kids love to see a teacher embarrass a student—as long as it's not them. Luther seemed to think it was a cheap shot, though. You could see from his snarled face that he knew Goldstein had taken his words out of context, but he was completely unable to articulate why that was wrong.

"What's up with that," he said, when the laughter had died down. "Are *you* some kind of homo?"

"No, I have a girlfriend," Goldstein said. "But I hate all kinds of discrimination. I'm not black, but I won't let anybody use the N word." Most of the kids seemed to be impressed with this answer.

"It ain't the same thing," Luther said. "God made Adam and Eve, not Adam and Steve."

"Man that line is so *old*," Billy said. "You need to update your material."

"Anyway," Goldstein said, "let's just make it a rule that we won't use gay as an adjective in this classroom. You know studies show one in ten persons are gay. So if we call each other names, we are insulting our own classmates."

This, as it turned out, was a big mistake. Luther surveyed the room, counting off students on his fat fingers. Then he began scribbling in his notebook, a long and evidently painful series of calculations. Conceding defeat in his unsuccessful battle against the laws of arithmetic, he pulled a calculator from his backpack. "Wait a minute," he said, interrupting Goldstein, who by this time had turned to the chalkboard, "that means there's two fags in here."

The class howled at this, and another student yelled out, "Who are they?"

Luther looked around the room, his gaze resting briefly on Billy, but then he came to his senses and settled on Federico. "Here," he said, "this Puerto Rican dude is a homo. He talks all sweet like the fags do." Luther's revelation caused the two boys nearest to Federico to scoot their desk-chairs away from him.

Federico kept staring straight ahead, refusing to acknowledge the ruckus going on around him. But as the laughter grew louder, he finally said, "I'm not ga-ay," still without turning around. Unfortunately, his voice cracked as he said the word gay.

"Gay boy!" Luther responded cheerfully.

"I'm not ga-ay," Federico insisted, a tear falling down his cheek.

I rose from my chair. Up until now, I had resisted the temptation to intervene. I knew that once I did, the students would consider it a tacit admission on my part that Goldstein was incapable of managing the class. But the mayhem had reached such a pitch that I was ready to assert control, whatever the consequences. Before I could say anything, though, Goldstein took over.

"You know!" he said, shouting down the class. "You know, what psychologists say about homophobic people, don't you?"

They didn't know.

"They say," he stared at Luther, "they say that people who are obsessed with gays behave that way because they are unsure about their own sexuality."

This worked—kind of. The class howled with laughter again, momentarily forgetting about Federico. But Luther glared at Goldstein with undisguised hatred, and poor Federico stared at his shoes.

"All right," Goldstein said when it was quiet again. "Let's take out our notebooks and pick up with," he paused looking down at his notes. "I think we left off with the split of the empire into two parts, with two capitals, one at Constantinople and one at Rome."

He'd lost them already. The polite ones cupped their brows so he couldn't see them sleep. Luther, though, was more brazen. His head hung forward, as if he were there for a scalp exam.

Billy was the only alert student; he raised his hand up again. "Hey, Mr. Goldstein, you forgot about my question."

"What question?"

"What did the Puerto Ricans do?"

"I don't understand your question, Billy," Goldstein said, looking near the end of his rope. "What do you mean, what did they do?"

"You know," Billy said, grinning, "the Egyptians had pyramids, and the Greeks did the Olympics, the Romans—"

Goldstein cut him off. "That's a good question, Billy. We'll get to Latin America later in the semester."

I glanced over at Federico, hoping he didn't see where Billy was going. Federico just looked confused. He perked up when he heard Puerto Rico, but he hadn't figured out Billy's question yet.

"Mr. Goldstein," Billy said, "they never did anything good, did they?"

Now Federico was upset. He glared—at Goldstein though—not at Billy. Even his anger was pathetic. He couldn't sustain the scowl. His upper lip sagged pitifully and he gripped his shabby cap. Goldstein should have told him to put it away, school rules.

Billy still had his hand up, still grinning. It was hard to say if he was messing with Federico or being serious. It didn't seem like him to pick on someone as helpless as Federico, and his smile didn't necessarily mean he was trying to instigate something. He pretty much always grinned like that. He was a happy kid. The only time I ever saw him in a bad mood was when he choked Sean.

"Well," Goldstein said, turning to me with a desperate glance, "why don't we ask Mr. Cavaliere for help here."

All eyes in the room turned to me. Shit, I thought. What *did* the Puerto Ricans do? I didn't have a clue. Roberto Clemente, the baseball player, popped into my head. Not a sufficient answer. I tried to change the subject.

"Actually—"

"That's racial," Federico said, interrupting me. He meant racist. I was impressed he spoke up, though. I didn't think he'd challenge Billy.

"No, man," Billy said, "I'm not racist. I got a cousin who's Mexican-Puerto Rican. Besides, my mother used to date a Colombian-Puerto Rican."

Aha. Billy thought Puerto Rican meant Hispanic. I went to the map and circled Puerto Rico with an erasable marker.

"See here, Billy. Puerto Rico is just one place where they speak Spanish." I pointed to Mexico, Peru, Honduras. "If you're talking about a Spanish speaker, you call them Hispanic."

"All right," Billy said, still not satisfied. "Then what did the... the Hispanish do?"

"Hydraulics, the Hispanics invented hydraulics." Federico again.

Luther looked up abruptly. "Uh-uh," he shook his head. "Africans invented hydraulics."

Billy looked back and forth between Federico and Luther. Then he grinned at me. "Well Mr. Cavaliere, which is it? The Africans or the Puerto Ricans?"

I chuckled a little before answering. "Well, Billy," I said, "I'm really not too sure who invented hydraulics. But I think that would be a great extra credit assignment for anybody who needs a few points. Now, though, you need to give Mr. Goldstein your attention so you can finish learning about the fall of Rome."

When the kids were gone, Goldstein's body slumped and his eyes drooped in defeat.

"Feeling humbled yet?" I said.

"Yes," Goldstein said. "Yes, I am." He sighed and looked up at me. "What went wrong?"

"You've read Machiavelli?" I asked him.

"Yeah."

"It's better to be feared than loved."

"But I don't want the kids to fear me," he said. "I want them—" he stopped himself in mid-sentence.

"You want them to like you," I said, finishing his thought.

He nodded. He didn't need me to explain why that was a mistake.

"You're right," he said. "I know it's stupid to want them to like me. But isn't there a happy medium I can find. I mean what about respect? Can't they respect me without fearing me?"

"Sure, some of them can, some of them do already, like Billy. But Luther? A kid like that—for him niceness and weakness are exactly the same thing, and he'll never respect either. If you don't scare him, he'll run wild over you. Look, you can always be harsh now and ease up when you feel more comfortable. But it's almost impossible to be soft early and demand control back later."

"Yeah, I guess I may as well forget about getting along with Luther now. He hates me."

"At least you shut him up there at the end," I said.

"I can't believe I sank to that level. I'm no better than he is. I basically teased him for being sexually insecure." Goldstein looked truly disgusted with himself.

"It is a language he understands," I said.

"But I even lied to them," he said.

"Oh yeah?"

"Yeah, I told them I have a girlfriend."

"You don't?"

"Not really. Well, kind of. It's complicated. But do you know why I said that?"

"Because you didn't want them to think you're gay."

"Exactly. How *awful*, how, how weak is that? I mean, here I am, making a big stink about how we ought to not discriminate against gays, and I'm so afraid a bunch of teenagers might think *I'm* gay, that I lie to them."

"You did the right thing," I said.

"No, I didn't," he said firmly.

"Yes, you did. Listen, this was one of your first days in front of a tough group. And make no mistake here; some of these kids are homophobic. The sad fact is the most prejudiced kids in the school when it comes to sexual orientation are the deltas. If they really thought you were gay, you'd lose them and you'd never get them back."

"That's so disappointing," he said. "I mean, you'd think if anyone would be tolerant of other people, it would be, it would be—"

"It would be poor blacks?" I interrupted, laughing. "Come on, you're smarter than that. Poor blacks are probably as bigoted against gays as anybody else in the country. They get it in rap and hip-hop; they even get it in church. You heard that line about Adam and Steve. Luther goes to church three nights a week. Did you know he sings in a touring gospel choir?"

"Really?"

"Yeah. I think he thinks being fat helps his voice. And remember, delta is not representative of the school. Most of the blacks at Edgemont are in the beta track, and they come from middle class, educated families. Delta is a different world. You're getting a really weird view of teenagers. Most kids are not like Luther Watkins. Don't let him sour you on teens."

"You're right," he said, with a sigh, "but those kids, the tough kids, those are exactly the ones who I want to reach. But the way things are going, I'm not reaching anybody. I've only barely started, and already I feel like I was naive to think I could have an impact. The deltas think I'm some kind of hippie weirdo, who they can run roughshod over." He shook his head. "I suppose the AP kids like me well enough. But what do they need me for. I mean, take Anne Burch. She's more politically knowledgeable and more of an activist than I am. What's she going to learn from me? The whole thing is so discouraging, I wonder if I should just forget about teaching and go to law school."

"You want my advice?" I said. "Here you go. Don't force your politics on them. Teach them stuff. Interesting stuff about history and let the politics come out of it naturally. Then they can make up their own minds about what's right and wrong."

He nodded but didn't say anything.

"And, Eric," I said, "do me a favor."

"Sure," he said, "what is it?"

"Don't go to law school. Don't give up on teaching just because you're having a rough start. You can do this. I don't know if you can make a difference, but you've got what it takes to be a pretty damn decent teacher."

I'm not really sure where that little speech came from. After all, I'm usually pretty skeptical when it comes to idealism. When I first met Goldstein, I was initially hoping he'd get humbled a bit. Not out of malice, but because that's what he needed before he could learn anything important. That's just how people are wired. Well, Goldstein had been humbled, no doubt. But this was almost too much. There's a difference between humility and humiliation.

* * *

We had another home game after school. The crowd was a lot smaller than at the first one. In fact, when I got there, at the start of the seventh grade game, the only people there were a few parents and my team. Everybody except for Morris. "Have you seen, Spicer?" I said to Coach Fasso, when he came into the gym.

"Oh, gosh," he said, turning pale as he spoke, "you didn't you hear about Morris?"

"What, is he all right?"

"No. He's in trouble. Real trouble this time. Suspended."

"What did he do?"

"Mrs. Towson caught him in the girls bathroom next to the adaptive gym last night, during the dance. He was with a girl, and they were necking."

"Necking?" I said.

"Well, that wasn't all they were doing."

"Oh yeah?"

"Well I don't know exactly what it was, and I didn't ask. It's none of my business," Fasso said, blushing, "but it must have been bad."

"I guess that's pretty serious stuff in a middle school," I said.

"But it's worse than that," Fasso said. "A lot worse. The girl's a real sweetheart. But she's, well, I'm not sure how to put it, but she's a little different. You know, special."

"Retarded?"

"I wouldn't want to use that term, you know," Fasso said. "Something's not quite right, if you know what I mean. Anyway, a lot of people are saying she might not have known what she was doing."

"Jesus fucking Christ," I said, exhaling, "what is the matter with Morris?"

Fasso looked like he was going to cry, and I was truly baffled for a minute as to why, but then it hit me. "Oh, sorry," I said. "I'll try to watch my language."

"I do appreciate it, Mr. Cavaliere."

"Well what are they going to do to him? They can't expel him, can they?"

"Oh, I couldn't really say," Fasso said, "you know, that's for the principal to decide. But at least we don't have to worry about Morris anymore."

"How do you mean?"

"Well, we can't have a guy like that on the team."

"Is that what the principal said?"

"Well, no. Not yet. But it goes without saying, don't you think?"

"No. I don't get why that follows," I said. "The school's going to punish him however they've got to punish him, but it's not like he did anything bad as a part of the team. When he gets back from suspension, if they don't expel him, I don't see why we wouldn't let him play."

Fasso was so flabbergasted by the suggestion that he didn't even reply.

In any case, it turned out we didn't need Morris that day. The other team was truly awful. They were from a tiny Catholic school, and their coach came up to me before the game and apologized in advance for their performance. "I'm afraid we won't be able to give you much of a game," he said. "St. Andros is a really small school and we don't even have a gym. We've only had three practices." He was so sure they were going to lose, I thought he might be trying to psych me out before the game, but when I watched his guys warming up it was obvious he was serious. Their guys looked like midgets out there, and they couldn't even do a proper lay up line.

Mitch was a man among boys against them, driving to the hoop at will and getting nearly every rebound. I was glad to get a win under our belts, even though the game itself wasn't really all that satisfying, considering how bad the other team was. Anyway, I found myself kind of preoccupied with Morris. I actually spaced out a couple of times during the game and didn't even use any of my timeouts. Not that I needed them. Our guys really ran their stuff well, and we wound up winning by twenty-five.

As soon as I got back to the apartment building, I knocked on Morris' door. The TV was blaring in the background and he didn't answer for a moment. "We won our first game today," I yelled, staring through the wrong end of the peephole.

That piqued Morris's curiosity enough to get him off the couch. "Probably because I wasn't there," he said, opening the door.

"No, this team was pretty miserable," I said. "You could have had ten blocks."

"Did you hear I got suspended?" Morris said.

"I heard," I said. "Sounds like a mess. Is it all right if I come in and you can tell me what happened?"

"I guess so," Morris said, opening the door. "My mom is at work." I'd seen glimpses of their apartment that other time, when Andy the asshole was there, but I'd never been inside. The layout was pretty much the same as my studio, but it was cleaner than I'd expected. Since there were two of them living there, but no walls, they had put up a sheet as a divider. Morris' bed was on one side and his mom must have slept on the couch. The only other piece of furniture was a TV, which was tuned to one of those talk shows where they've got some trashy, fat chick and her baby on stage, and they give her three "boyfriends" DNA tests, right there on the set.

"Everybody was at the dance last night," Morris said.

"Hang on," I interrupted, turning the volume off. "All right, I can concentrate now. What's the girl's name?"

"Cassie," Morris said, looking down at his feet as he spoke.

"And how did you figure out that she likes you?"

He furrowed his brow. "Jeez, coach, she put her hand in my—"

"Okay, okay," I said, holding up my hand. "No, I didn't mean that. I guess what I meant is how do you know her?"

"From school."

"You're very literal minded, Morris."

"Is that good?"

"Good question," I said. "I'm not sure, actually. But what I mean is, how did you guys get together?"

"But I was just telling you," Morris said.

"No, how do you know her? From class, from friends? Did you kiss her first, or did she kiss you? Did you guys start talking at the school dance last night or what?"

"I dunno, she's in my class and we goof around in there."

"What class?"

"With Mr. Fitzgerald."

"That's your special-ed. class?"

"Yeah."

"Have you guys ever made out before?"

"We've never made out. Not last night either."

"But I thought this whole thing was about you getting caught with her in the bathroom."

"Yeah, but we didn't make out."

"I don't follow," I said.

"Okay," Morris said. "They were playing such *garbage* music, so nobody was dancing. And Mitch started a game of double dare."

"Dare?"

"Yeah, like truth or dare, but in double dare the dares are really like, you know, for real."

"You hang out with Mitch?" I said. "I thought you hated him."

"He's really conceited, but you know, we're both on the basketball team. Anyway, we were playing dare with these girls, and for a while it was just normal stuff, like daring people to slow dance and grab each other's butts. But then Mitch asked Cassie if she wanted a truth or a dare. And she said truth, but then she didn't answer his question so he gave her a double dare."

"What was the truth thing he asked her about?"

"He wanted to know what her IQ was."

I shook my head.

"I guess it was kind of mean," Morris continued, "because she's not real smart. Actually, I'm smarter than she is, if you can believe it. So she said she would do the double dare, and that's when he dared her to give me head. So we snuck out of the cafeteria and went to the girl's bathroom at the end of hall, 'cause it's usually pretty quiet over there. That's where Mrs. Towson found us."

"Had you guys, well, you know, were you pretty far into it?"

Morris looked puzzled.

"You know, were you kissing, or had you got to the point where... where your pants were down?"

"I told you, coach, I didn't kiss her," Morris said, grimacing as though tasting sour milk. "Have you seen her?"

"No," I said.

"Well, she's kind of ugly."

"Morris," I said, frowning, "you can't do that to somebody. You can't use people like that."

"I didn't make her do anything," Morris said. "She wanted to do it."

"No, she didn't," I said. "I'm not saying you raped her. But it's not as simple as saying she chose to do it. Think about what you did, Morris. You say this poor girl is dumb and ugly. Well, Mitch is cool, right?"

"Yeah."

"First he humiliates her by trying to get her to admit she's stupid, and then when she won't, he dares her to give you a blow job. How easy do you think it would have been for her to stand up to Mitch and say, no I don't want to play this game?"

"Not very, I guess," he said.

"Then you go off with her, and you let her service you, and you don't even kiss her. So she doesn't even get to feel like you like her. You treated her like you'd treat the plumber, who came to your house. She's a person, Morris. Not a jerk-off machine." I spoke bluntly because I knew with Morris, if you didn't, there was no hope he would understand. But I tried to keep my tone from being too harsh, because I didn't really blame him. Sure, he'd acted like a pig, but knowing what I did about his life, it was hard to see how he would know better. I mean where was his model for a stable relationship? But as I watched his eyes cloud up, I realized it didn't much matter what I said or how I said it. Words were never going to get through to Morris. No, the only way he was ever going to learn how to behave was if somebody showed him. Unfortunately, it was clear as could be I was the wrong man for the job.

CHAPTER 14

WE GET A RIDICULOUS AMOUNT of mail everyday: announce-ments, lists of absences, memos about upgrades for the school's computer network, promotions for universities, and catalogs for maps and teaching aids. But then suddenly for two weeks, my mailbox had been empty. Almost all of the mail is crap, so I hadn't exactly treated it as an emergency or anything. I did try to complain about it once or twice, to Gwen, the mail lady, but she always seemed to be out of her office when I knocked on her door. And today, when I checked my box it was still empty, except just as I was about to shut the door, I saw a hand enter my mailbox. The fingers were long and pale, with gaudy, red polish on the nails and a tiny diamond on the ring finger. Then the hand was gone, and a note was there in its place.

The mailboxes are stacked on top of each other, in a bank that runs from the floor up to about six feet high, the whole length of the mailroom's rear wall. My box is in the top row, and I can see into it only because of my height. But from the angle of the hand, I knew its owner couldn't see me. I grabbed the note.

"*I need you to call me,*" it said. "*You're in big trouble and I can help.*"

That last sentence set me off. I marched straight to the door that led to mail sorting area. Behind the door is a room, where Gwen works all day. You have to have a key to get back there, and

I guess they close it off so she can stuff mailboxes without getting in the way of the staff on the other side. The door was just opening, and sure enough, Dara was coming out of the room. I nearly barreled into her, and she stepped back into the mailroom, flinging an arm in front of her face, as though I might hit her.

Gwen got up from behind her desk and glared up at me with hateful eyes. I'd never been in Gwen's work area before. There wasn't much in the way of decoration, just a desk, a wooden stool and an old radio that was crackling out a Sinatra tune.

"Can I help you, George?" Gwen hissed. I wasn't surprised at her hostility, since she was one of Dara's little cronies. And it hit me then, she must have been throwing out my mail, which was why I'd missed the meeting with Brewer and Asbury. I had to give it to Dara. She had loads of friends, and they were a loyal bunch. It was probably her best quality, but it sure had come back to bite me in the ass.

"Yeah, Gwen," I said. "You can help me. Both of you can help me. Just stop it."

"Stop what," Dara said defiantly.

"Both of you, all of you, just stop messing with me."

"All of who?" Gwen said.

"You and all your friends, Dara," I said. "You've been mucking things up for me around here, trying to sabotage everything I do. Stop it and let me do my job in peace."

"No one's trying to sabotage you," Dara said.

"Yeah, you are," I said. "And you know what, you got me. You win. So I hope you're happy. You and your friends have screwed me up big time: Susie in payroll made sure I didn't get my checks, I can't get a video delivered or a copy made, Betty, in the lunch room, is trying to give me salmonella, and now Gwen here won't give me my mail. All right, it's pretty funny. Freaking hysterical. But don't you think it's time we all started behaving like adults?"

"I don't know what you're talking about," Gwen said. "I haven't thrown out any mail."

"You can deny what you and your friends are doing, if you're too embarrassed to own up to it. All I'm saying is stop it. You're not the only one who can play these games."

"Did you hear that, Gwen?" Dara said. "He's threatening me."

"Oh, I heard it," Gwen said, nodding righteously.

"As long as we're on the subject of threatening," I said, "what exactly did you mean when you said you know I'm in big trouble?"

"It's not exactly a secret that you're being investigated, George," Dara said.

"Right, your network of spies. And how exactly do you propose to help me?"

"I know a lot of people, George," she said, smiling coyly. "Important people in this school, and they can either help you or make things difficult for you. Very difficult."

"You mean Wentworth. You put him up to this, didn't you? You got him to rat me out to Elaine, about that thing I said to Colleen."

Dara's smile disappeared and her lips puckered into a sour frown. She hadn't wanted me to know it was Wentworth.

"I didn't say that."

"You're sleeping with the little bastard, aren't you?"

"It's none of your business what I'm doing with who," Dara said backpedaling as fast as she could. "Think about it, George. Why would I try to get you in trouble if I was trying to get back together with you?"

"That's funny," I said, "because I was going to ask you the exact same thing." I slammed the door so hard I heard the frame rattle, as I marched out of the mailroom.

* * *

That day was Morris's first back on the team, after being on suspension. I was demonstrating the up-and-under move to him and the other big men, when I felt a pop on the outer edge of my left knee. The next thing I knew, I was on the floor, rolling and screaming.

"Mr. Cavaliere! Hey, you wanna watch your language?"

I didn't realize I'd been swearing, and my eyes were shut, so I wasn't sure who'd said that. When I opened my eyes, everything was blurry, but as my vision focused I could make out Fasso peering down at me, with that pole-up-his-ass frown he gets when I do something un-Christian.

"Get me some fucking ice!" I screamed. "Ahh, fuck! It hurts."

It really did. I felt so much pain I couldn't even lie still. Instead I rolled around on the floor, clutching my knee, the muted sound of bouncing basketballs echoing in my head. Soon, though, the gym went silent, and I realized the whole team had gathered around me. They were quiet and frightened. Especially Morris. He bit his lip and muttered to himself, "Shit. Shit. Shit."

"I'll be all right," I said through clenched teeth. "I'll be okay."

Wexler burst through the crowd with an ice bag a minute later, and I put it on the knee. The pain was still so intense, though, it was about all I could do to keep the ice balanced on my knee. Gradually, the burning faded and there was just a throbbing in my leg.

"Okay," I said finally to Fasso, "give me a hand up."

He bent down to help me, and I stood up stiffly. When I was in the air, I dipped my bad leg onto the ground with great care. It felt stiff and weak but there was no pain.

"Maybe it's just a sprain," Morris said.

"Yeah, probably," I said, though I wasn't sure of that at all. I've sprained my knee plenty of times. This was different. I'd never felt a pop like that before, and it scared me. "You know what," I said to Fasso, "it's starting to swell, and just to be on the safe side, I think I'd better go home now, while I can still drive. Why don't you just run practice without me today?"

"Are you sure?" Fasso said.

"Yeah," I said. "See you guys tomorrow."

The kids looked at each other nervously and I heard some grumbling about "Coach Jesus." This was not the first time the kids had made fun of Fasso. His goody-two-shoes act didn't play well with eighth graders, who were obsessed with sex, even if they weren't having any. And with his muddled instructions, even Morris could see he was an incompetent coach. Still, I normally wouldn't have tolerated that kind of disrespect. Fasso may have been a buzz kill, but, like it or not, he was part of our team. There was nothing I could do about it then, though. I barely had the energy to limp out of the gym, let alone discipline the team.

"See how the knee cap moves freely like that?" Dr. Bowen asked. I was sitting on a table in Bowen's office, three days after the injury, my legs dangling off the end as he hunched over my knee.

"Yeah," I said, my stomach tightening.

"The cap—it shouldn't move like that." Bowen stood up and walked over to the wall. He was a big guy, with a barrel chest and wisps of brown hair that ringed his balding head. On the wall was a poster with the title, *The Amazing Knee*. "See this," he pointed to a white line on the side of the knee. "This is called the anterior cruciate ligament. Its job is to stabilize the knee, when you jump and turn."

"Yeah, the ACL," I said.

"Yours is torn. If it weren't, your kneecap wouldn't move like that. You said your knee collapsed when you fell on it. That's why."

"So are you saying with a torn ACL I could fall down at any minute?"

"Not exactly. Not just walking down the street. The ACL only comes into play when you turn, or run, or jump. But if you ever want to play sports again—with a torn ACL, your knee will give out when you make a movement that requires lateral stability."

"So I could play without getting it fixed," I said, frowning as I remembered the pain I'd felt when I hurt it, "but every so often, I'll just collapse to the floor again."

"Exactly, but that's not the only problem. If you exercise without one, you'll also damage the cartilage, and that will lead to arthritis later on."

"Shit," I said.

"This is a serious injury," Bowen said.

"Surgery?"

"Yup. This is what I'll do," he pointed to the area just below the kneecap on his chart. "I'll make an incision on the patella tendon—that's what connects the kneecap to the joint—then I'll extract a small piece of that tendon. Next, using an arthroscopic needle, I'll take the extracted tendon and knit the two loose parts of the ACL back together. It's really pretty amazing," he said, smiling. "Like a transplant, only you're the donor and the recipient. Twenty years ago, this operation didn't even exist, and people in your condition lived the rest of their lives with what they used to call a 'trick knee.' Now, I do four of these operations in a morning." If it hadn't been my knee he was talking about, I would have thought he was cute, the way he was all psyched about it.

A nurse had come in the room, and Dr. Bowen said, "Evelyn will tell you how to prepare for the operation."

Evelyn was very attractive. German accent, blond hair and fairish skin.

"Have you ever had general anesthesia before?" she said.

"No."

"Here is a metaphor that may be of help in understanding the process." Her English was excellent, but overly formal, in the way educated immigrants sometimes speak. "General anesthesia is, perhaps, like having your car battery die and then when the car is turned back on, everything becomes haywire. You will not feel normal for several days, perhaps."

There's nothing less sexy than a hospital, so I've never understood the old cliche about hot nurses. Or airline stewardesses, for that matter. I don't know if it's all that re-circulated air or maybe it's because I tend to fly the discount carriers, but most of the flight attendants I've come across are kind of haggard. But anyway, Evelyn was almost ridiculously sexy with her chesty figure and tight rear. So I scrambled for something to chat her up about. "Several days," I said. "How long is that?"

"It is different for everyone."

"I'm a quick healer," I said. "If I have surgery on a Friday, is it possible I could be back at work on Tuesday?"

"I do not believe this is realistic," she said. "The first night after the surgery is a painful night. We will medicate you as much as may be permitted, and you will start to feel better the next day. But you can not drive for a week, and many people do not return to work for perhaps ten days."

"Ten days? Really?"

"Yes. Some people return to normal faster, but there is considerable swelling for the first few days. It is a good idea to keep the leg up in the air. This is not something which most of us are permitted to do at work." She hadn't cracked a smile yet; she was cute, but a real dour frau.

"Yeah, I'm a teacher," I said. "But I don't like to miss work. I've missed like three days in fifteen years."

"This is an impressive record of attendance."

"I'm kind of the Cal Ripken of my school," I said.

"I am not familiar with Cal Ripken," she said as she continued to check off boxes on her chart.

"Oh he's, well, it doesn't really matter who he is. Anyway, I kind of pride myself on my attendance."

"Yes, but I fear this record is unlikely to continue. It may be very difficult to teach with the swelling you will have."

"Yeah, I guess so," I said.

"Are you married?" she said.

"Uh, not really," I said, surprised by the question. With as cold as she had been, that was the last thing I'd expected to hear her say.

"Many people do not have such trouble with this question," she said, a glint of humor finally sneaking out of her stalag-like face.

"I'm separated," I said. "Will I see you after the operation, for rehab?"

"Perhaps you misunderstand the purpose of my question," she said with devastating calmness. "Whether you are in a relationship is none of my concern, but you will need to have someone to help you get home from the hospital. You cannot check out, if you are by yourself."

"Oh, really?"

"Yes," she said. "You will not be able to drive, and you will need someone to help you the first day. This person will be needed to get ice and to provide meals and to help you to the bathroom."

"Okay," I said. "That will not be a problem."

Actually, it was a problem. I honestly didn't know who to ask. I don't have much family. It was always just my mom and me. And she died of breast cancer, the year after Amy and I got married. I'm kind of glad I never had to tell her that Amy and I had split up. She loved Amy like crazy. But I figured it couldn't be as bad as Evelyn was making it sound. I've always been able to take care of myself.

The morning of the surgery, I arrived at the hospital at five a.m., and found, to my surprise, that the operating room was already a hive of activity. I met with the anesthesiologist, Dr. Kapadia, first. He was tall and thin, with chocolate skin. "The general anesthesia is administered by a mask, on the operating table," he said.

"Really?" I said. "A mask? Nobody told me that. Is there some other way to do it? I have this thing about breathing. I tried to scuba dive once and—Hey, what's that?"

"I'm going to give you a little shot in the arm," Dr. Kapadia said. He watched, holding a syringe in one hand, while the nurse swabbed my arm with a white cloth.

"What's in the needle?" I said.

"Just a little concoction to take the edge off. Lots of people are squeamish about having a gas mask on their face, so we give them this to help them relax." While he was talking, he stuck me in the area just below my right bicep and pushed down on the plunger. "When it hits, you'll feel like you've had a few cocktails."

Immediately is when it hit. I've never tried anything harder than weed, but for the first time, I think I understood the appeal of intravenous drugs, like heroin or cocaine. My mood changed like somebody flicking a light switch. Gone was all the anxiety about the mask and the needle and the surgery.

"That's not like any cocktail I've ever had," I mumbled. Dr. Kapadia chuckled as my bed was wheeled away.

Soon I was in the OR and Dr. Bowen was examining me. "That's funny," he said, pointing to my leg. I had written "Wrong Knee," in big black marker on my right knee.

"Oh, yeah," I said. "I heard about someone who once got the operation done on the wrong knee, so I thought it would be a good idea, just to make sure. Not that I don't trust you. And the thing is, I almost put 'Right Knee' on my left knee, because I wasn't sure if you would even look at both knees, but I didn't want you to think I was stupid, putting 'Right Knee' on my left knee. So I thought about writing 'Correct Knee,' but there wasn't room."

I looked over at Dr. Bowen and saw that he wasn't paying much attention to what I was saying. Nobody was. All the nurses and med students were scurrying around the room, filling out charts and reading monitors at what seemed to me an absurdly fast pace. "Is it always so busy—" I started to say, but before I could finish my sentence, someone put a mask over my face.

I took two breaths, and then I woke up in a different room. Nurse Evelyn from Dr. Bowen's office was fiddling with some kind of monitor that was attached to my bed. "Good morning," she said. "How are you feeling?"

My head was foggy, and I felt like I'd been pummeled with a sack of dumbbells. "I didn't know you'd be here," I said.

"Always when Dr. Bowen does an operation, I work in the hospital," she said. "If there is any problem, I can take notice of it and make a report back to him. And how do you feel?"

"Okay," I said, my voice creaking.

"The throat hurts, yes?" she said. "It is the mask they used when the anesthesia was administered."

It sounds stupid, but only then did I remember that the reason I was in the hospital was for a knee operation. I looked down at my feet, but the knee was covered by a blanket. Though I wanted to see what it looked like, pulling the blanket off was way beyond my capabilities.

Evelyn seemed to read my thoughts. "You won't be able to take the bandages off for five days," she said. "There will be a scar on the patella tendon and a smaller one on the outside of the knee. Can you feel the knee yet?"

"I can't feel it at all."

"Good. You'll have more sensation when the general anesthesia wears off, perhaps this afternoon. There will be pain. When you feel it, push the red button to give yourself morphine." She handed me a remote control type console that was connected, by a wire, to a beeping LCD display on wheels.

I pushed it and felt an immediate surge of pleasantness rush through my body.

"You feel it already," she said, a smile peeking out. "Save some. The machine only permits four doses per hour, and you will want more later, when the general anesthesia fades."

"How bad will it get?" I said.

"It's different for each person," she said. "Some people say it is not so bad, others complain more. But it will be the worst sometime after midnight, so if you can, perhaps, sleep through it, you should. Sleep as much as you can today. I have to go now, but there's one additional instruction. You may have difficulty getting to the bathroom." She held up a plastic container. "Use this bottle. It is very important that you produce some urine by six o'clock."

"Important?" I said. "What happens if I don't?"

"Try to," she said, smiling cryptically as she left the room.

"Where are you going?"

"There are other patients," she said. "But I will be back to check on you later."

When she left, I turned on the TV and tried to watch SportsCenter, but I was too groggy to follow it. Soon I was drifting in and out of dreary, slow dreams about hospitals and blond nurses. Occasionally the staccato echo of a TV jingle jolted me into frightened alertness, but I would soon fade out again. When I finally woke up, my head felt clearer, but that wasn't entirely a good thing, since the pain in my knee was beginning to build. At first it just felt stiff and swollen, but the more I woke up the more the pain sharpened. Soon, a parade of hospital employees—med students checking my chart; orderlies with hairnets, dumping my trash into a rolling garbage bin; nurses reloading the IV—came through the room. One of the nurses, not Evelyn, who seemed to have disappeared, asked me how I was doing.

"Not too bad," I said. "My knee is starting to hurt a bit, though."

"Have you been using the morphine?"

"Yeah," I said, "a little bit."

"How about urination?" She pointed to the bottle Evelyn had left on my bedside table.

"What's the big deal about that?" I said. "Evelyn made a stink about it, too."

"So you haven't been able to?"

"No," I said. "I'll give it a try right now." I grabbed the quart bottle, and pulled it under my blanket. But I couldn't pee one drop. In fact, the whole groin area just felt numb.

"Is this going to be a problem?" I said.

"We'd just like you to have all of your faculties back by the time the next shift comes in, at six. If you do, you can go home tonight."

"I've still got three hours," I said. "But what happens if I can't pee by then?"

"Just try to," she said.

One of the orderlies had left a pitcher of ice water on the table while I was sleeping, and I figured drinking fluids might make me have to go. After chugging the pitcher, I felt full, but not that tense feeling you get in the diaphragm, when you have to pee.

Later an orderly came in with my dinner, and as he set it on the bedside table, he did a double take. "Yo, that you Mr. Cavaliere?"

"Yeah," I said. "You were in my class." I knew the kid's face, but I couldn't summon his name. But you get that a lot as a teacher; it's a bit like being a minor celebrity. You have so many students—after fifteen years of teaching, I must have had close to two thousand—that it's pretty common for people to stop you on the street or in the grocery store to say hello. Unless they were somehow really special, like Alyssa, I tend to forget. And I was drawing a total blank on this guy. Normally I try to fake my way out of it by calling them "kiddo" or avoiding any name altogether.

But in this case I just didn't have the energy. "I'm sorry," I said. "I don't remember your name."

"Sean," he said, pointing to the red lettering, knitted onto his hospital-issue shirt. "Sean Robbins."

"Oh, Jesus!" I said. "The fight with Billy."

"Yeah, that's it," he said.

"Sorry," I said, "I'm totally out of it. I didn't even see your nametag. This morphine is serious stuff. Of course I remember you. Well it looks like you're doing okay here. A job in the hospital isn't too bad."

"Yeah, it's all right," he said. "They give me benefits. I'll tell you though, we see some pretty messed-up things. No offense, Joe, but sick people are depressing." He flung a plastic brown tray down on my table and said, "You know, I wasn't the best student in school, but you were all right, Mr. Cavaliere."

"Oh, yeah, thanks," I said. "Now that you've worked for a bit, does it make you think twice about leaving school?"

"To be honest," Sean said, shaking his head, "not really. It's just not my thing. Do you got any bed pans that need cleaning?"

"No," I said, "what's up with that anyway? The nurses keep bugging me about whether I've peed. What are they going to do to me, if I can't?"

"Oh, man," Sean shook his head, "you better give them some piss or they're going to put a catheter in you? You ever have one of those?" He pursed his lips and his eyes went wide.

"No."

"They take a needle this big," he held his hands about six inches apart, "and stick it in your dick."

"Shit," I said.

"How long did they give you?"

"Two more hours," I said.

"You got any visitors coming?"

"No," I said. "I don't think so."

"Hey, I'll tell you what," he said. "I get off duty in about an hour, but I'll come back as soon as my shift ends and help out."

"Help me out how?" I said. But before he could answer, a nurse came in the room and started fiddling with the equipment.

An hour later, I still couldn't pee, but the area just above my groin was starting to tighten. With nothing further to show for my efforts, I decided I might have better luck standing up. But it was no easy trick to get out of bed. I had to lower the guardrail and then swing my legs over the side, which took some doing, since my body was weak. And when I'd done it, and was sitting up in bed, I got head spins and had to sit still for a few minutes. Finally, I pushed off the bed and dipped my bad leg onto the ground, like you would if you wanted to test the temperature in a pool. The leg didn't hurt, at least not any more than it had lying down, but it was so weak I couldn't let go of the guardrail. I decided to try my luck urinating, right there by the bed. But since I was holding onto the guardrail with one hand, and I had to hold the receptacle with the other, I was nervous I might miss the jar. I didn't need to worry. When I got my gown off, I saw my penis for the first time that day. Gray and unhealthy, it looked like a stale, mini-bratwurst. I jiggled and squeezed, but came up dry. If there was no life in my penis, though, there was plenty going on in my bladder. It bulged over my waist, throbbing and pulsing so much it looked like somebody had implanted an egg at the bottom of my torso.

"How's it going, man?" I covered myself and turned around. It was Sean. He was still wearing the dark blue uniform all the non-medical staff wore, and he had a gym bag on his shoulder.

"Not too good," I said. "No luck."

"You want some of mine?"

"Uh," I looked up at the clock. Only ten minutes before six. "Well, I don't want a catheter." I handed him the pitcher.

"Nah, man," Sean held up his hand. "I brought my own." He reached into his bag and produced a plastic container that was half full of urine.

"Thanks, I really appreciate it," I said, grabbing it from him.

"No problem," he said.

"Hey," I said as he turned to go, "check this out." I lifted my gown and showed him the bulge above my waist. "Do you think that's bad? I mean, maybe I should just get the catheter."

"Wow." His eyebrow cocked on the right side of his face. "How much water did you drink?"

"Two pitchers. I thought it might make me have to go. Do you think a bladder can burst?"

"I don't know, Joe," he shook his head. "That don't look good."

Now I didn't know what to do. I sure didn't want a needle in my dick, but I was starting to get scared. I had time to give it one more try before six, so I stood up and pulled back the gown and pushed. One gleaming yellow drop squirted out. I've never been so pleased to see urine in all my life. On the next push the flood-gates opened. My whole body relaxed as a broad and deep river of pee streamed out of me. After two minutes the quart container was well over half full, and I didn't feel at all close to being done. Worried that I might run out of room in the container, I hit the nurse's call button.

"Congratulations," Evelyn said, when she arrived moments later. "This is a lot of urine."

"Yeah," I said, "I think it's going to spill over. Can you get me another pitcher?"

When she returned—just in time, as the quart container was nearly full—she put the empty pitcher on the side of the bed where I was peeing. With one motion, I grabbed the new one and moved the old onto the table. Or I tried to. Focused on catching the stream with the empty jug, I could only look at the table out of the corner of my eye. I misjudged it, and the container, a full quart, tumbled onto the floor. I heard it crash, but since I was still peeing, I couldn't reach down to pick up the overturned jug. By the time Evelyn got there it was too late.

A quart is a whole lot of urine. The entire floor, from the bathroom to the window was covered in it, and, injured like I was, I could only stand there in horror as it flowed through my slippers and between my toes. The warmth of the pee on my toes and the stench in the room caused me to lose concentration, and my aim— yes, I was still peeing—and now I sprayed some onto the bed.

They had to switch me into a new room so they could clean the old one. And since my gown, which had been around my ankles, was soaked, Evelyn had to change my clothes *and* bathe my feet. No easy task, considering my knee had to remain bandaged.

"I'm really sorry," I said, over and over to her as she mopped my feet with a cloth. "I was trying to grab the bottle—"

"Perhaps we might not discuss it further," Evelyn said without looking up at me. "This is not the most pleasant duty."

I guess I couldn't blame her, but it pretty much took the wind out of my sails as far as asking her out. Which was probably just as well, because she didn't seem like much fun. When she finished, I was so embarrassed that I wanted to go home, even though it was hard to see how I was going to take care of myself. But since I had peed and didn't need a catheter, they let me check out. They just made me sign a piece of paper, swearing there was somebody at my house to take care of me that night. I signed it and got in a cab.

"You sure you don't need no help," the cab driver asked when we got to the apartment.

"I'm fine," I said. "My wife is coming home real soon."

I made it up the stairs without too much trouble. Before I'd left, the discharge nurse had taught me how to walk stairs, by leading with my good leg when going up, and my bad leg when going down. "Just remember, good boys go to heaven," she'd said, "and bad boys go to hell."

After I turned on the TV, I hobbled over to the freezer and made myself an ice pack. Then I lay back on the futon and elevated my knee with several pillows. By then the leg was so swollen that the knee had lost its shape, and it was hard to tell where it ended and where the calf began. But at least the pain subsided a little.

I had been lying down for only a few minutes when I decided I wanted a whiskey. I'd read somewhere that alcohol thins the blood, so it probably wasn't a good idea to drink before the swelling stopped. Plus it said on the bottle of painkillers that the pills shouldn't be mixed with alcohol. Still, I wanted a whiskey. I hobbled over to the fridge and poured some ice into the glass. The bottle was below the sink, and I reached down, fumbling with the handle of the cabinet. I got it open, but the pain in my knee forced me back up into a standing position. Since the bottle was pretty far inside the cabinet, I didn't see how I could get low enough to reach it. Stepping back, I swung my hand low and deep, like a wrecking ball on a crane. The glass of the bottle brushed against my fingers, smooth and cool. But then the bottle clattered to the kitchen floor, way out of my reach. Desperation is the mother of invention, so after a moment of deep depression, I had an idea. I'd bought a pair of tongs to go with the little hibachi grill I had moved onto the fire escape. I fished them from the drawer and pulled a chair to the middle of the kitchen floor, a few feet away from the bottle. Leaning back, off the side of the chair, so that my torso went parallel to the floor, I reached for the bottle with the tongs.

After a few tries, I managed to slide the handle of the bottle between the arms of the tongs, and lifted. By now, I was sweating profusely, but I had the bottle. Without bothering to wipe the sweat from my brow, I poured myself a drink. Maybe, I thought, as I looked down at my shaking hands, I'm an alcoholic. There was a knock on the door. I stared down at the brown swirl of whiskey, considering whether I should drag myself to the door or drink my whiskey and pretend not to be home. After a second knock, I hauled myself to the door, and peered through the eye-hole. Morris and his mother were just turning to leave. She was carrying a pot of some kind.

I opened the door.

"Oh, Mr. Cavaliere," Mrs. Spicer said, "that is you. We heard some noise upstairs, and we didn't know if you had got home yet from the hospital."

"Yeah, I just got home an hour ago," I said.

"Well, we don't mean to bother you," Mrs. Spicer said. "We just brought you some dinner." She took the lid off of the casserole she was holding. It smelled like mac and cheese. "Morris told me what happened to you. I figured that you'd have a hard time cooking, living alone and all."

"That's awfully nice of you," I said, "but I'm all right. Maybe it's the anesthesia, but I'm just not that hungry."

"We've got plenty of extra," she said. "It would mean an awful lot to Morris, if we could do something for you. I mean, what with how you done so much for him."

Morris was beaming proudly at his mother, looking away from me, the way kids do when they've done a good deed, but don't know how to handle praise.

"Oh, okay," I said. "Why not? If I don't eat it now, I'll save it for the morning." I reached out my hand for the dish.

"Oh, careful, it's still hot," she said. "I'll just put it on your stove to cool."

She moved toward the door, and I backed up to let her in.

Maybe it was the exertion from the whiskey or the lingering effects of the anesthesia, but I felt really dizzy. "I'm supposed to keep the leg elevated," I said. "I'm just going to sit down on the couch, if you don't mind."

Morris walked with me as I lumbered over to the futon. Even under normal circumstances, he wasn't all that talkative, and now he didn't say anything at all.

"I'm limping pretty bad, aren't I?" I said, once I was settled and had taken a few good breaths.

Morris nodded.

"Yeah," I said, gritting my teeth. "Yeah, it hurts a good bit." I lay back on the couch and put my legs up.

"How was the game last night?" I said.

"I played pretty good," Morris said. "But we lost."

"We played Parker, right? How was it?"

"We should've won. Parker sucks."

"And how," I considered how to phrase it. "How did Coach—" I was in too much pain to be subtle, "how did Coach Fasso do?"

"Uh, everybody wants you back," Morris said.

I guess you can chalk up another sin to my slate, because the truth is it made me happy to hear that the kids preferred me.

Neither of us said anything for a moment, so I pointed to the TV. It was tuned to CNN, which I knew wouldn't interest Morris. "You can turn to whatever you want. The remote's on the table."

Morris didn't change the channel, though. He seemed just happy to be there.

I'm a talker, and I tend to get uncomfortable when a room goes silent. So I'd been working pretty hard to make conversation, but it occurred to me that Morris was perfectly content just being in the same room. I suppose he just wanted to see that I was okay.

"Come on, Morris," Mrs. Spicer called from the doorway. "Let's leave Mr. Cavaliere alone."

For the next week, Mrs. Spicer sent Morris up with at least one meal a day. Usually, I hate it when people do nice things for me. The idea of somebody pitying me makes me cringe. For some reason, though, having Morris and his mother look out for me was different. Maybe it was because I had seen their dirty laundry, and there was no possibility they felt pity for me. My life was a disaster, but at least I had company.

CHAPTER 16

SINCE MY SURGERY, getting going in the morning had become a major production. Nurse Evelyn had ordered me not to get the scar on my knee wet for two weeks. Which made showering a major pain in the ass. I had to rig this plastic bag around my knee with a rubber band, and then be extra careful while drying it off. Getting dressed was no picnic either. Monday, five days after the surgery, I decided to go back to school. But I still could barely bend the knee, so it took me like ten minutes and a boatload of pain just to put on my pants, some socks and a pair of shoes. Fortunately, I didn't have to teach, since Goldstein was taking all my classes. He smiled when he saw me limp into my classroom, using a crutch and wearing a brace, just minutes before AP began.

"Hey," he said, "good to see you. The kids are going to be so psyched. They ask about you everyday. How are you feeling?"

"Uh, I've felt better," I said. "I'm off of the pain killers now. I didn't want to come to school all drugged up. But I'm kind of weak. If it's okay with you, I'll just ease back into it a bit, and let you do your thing."

"Sure, of course."

The bell rang then, and as Goldstein headed to the front of the room, I said, "I'll just grab a seat." I picked a desk in the far corner, where I'd be out of the way. The desk in front of me belonged to Dennis Toshiro. He nodded at me as he sat down, and said, "Yo, Mr. C."

"You don't mind if I prop my leg on the back of your desk, do you Dennis?" I said.

"Nah, go for it," he said. Dennis was a mellow kid. Lazy, but good-natured.

Most of the kids seemed really pleased to see me. "Welcome back, Mr. Cavaliere," they said, or "How was the operation?" And just before the bell rang, Anne Burch said, "Hey, Mr. Goldstein, we should give Mr. Cavaliere his card."

"Oh, right," Goldstein said, scurrying over to the bookcase and retrieving a huge poster. All the kids' names were scrawled along the edges in magic marker. In bright gold letters, it read, *"We're glad to have you back, Mr. Cavaliere. We really Kneed you here!"*

"Ouch," I said grimacing. "Your sense of humor, Goldstein?"

"Nope. It was Anne's idea, actually."

"Well that's awfully nice of you, Anne," I said, dropping my biting tone. "It's a lovely poster." Next to their names, most of them had written generic little get-well messages. There was even one from Louis, which made me glad, though all he said was "Come back soon."

"We did really miss you, Mr. Cavaliere," Anne said. "Not that Mr. Goldstein isn't doing well. I think you'll be very impressed with his progress."

I laughed at that, and Anne said, "No really, Mr. Cavaliere, he's going to be an excellent teacher."

"Oh, I believe you," I said. "It's just such a, I don't know, such an adult thing to say."

The second bell rang, and Goldstein passed out a sheet of directions and jotted the dates of Reconstruction on the board.

"What are they working on?" I said to Goldstein.

"Oh, it's this little problem-solving activity I came up with."

"Problem solving?" I said. "That's the hot fad in grad school these days, right?"

"Yeah, I suppose so," he said. "But it seems like a good idea to me. Put them in a historical situation—one where there's a crisis or dilemma, and you ask them to formulate a policy. It should force them to really come to grips with the issues."

"What problem are they solving?" I said, putting finger quotes around the word "solving."

"Well it's Reconstruction, right after the Civil War, and I told them that they are advisers to the president, and they are supposed to figure out how to help the newly freed slaves. So they have to identify the problems faced by the freedmen and then come up with a list of proposals to fix them." He threw a quick dart of a glance at me. "What do you think?"

"You know I'm not the biggest fan of group work," I said. "All that touchy-feely, 'learn from each other' crap gives me the creeps. Whatever happened to the idea of teachers just teaching?" He looked a little glum at my assessment, so I threw him a bone. "But having said that, it sounds pretty solid for what it is."

"Louis' got his hand up. I better go help him," Goldstein said.

"Mr. Goldstein," Louis said, as he paged through one of the articles, "what kind of protection did the government give the freedmen against the Klan and the White Leagues?"

"Not nearly enough, I'm afraid," Goldstein said. "There was the Ku Klux Klan Act of 1871, which was supposed to protect them, but the Supreme Court ruled it unconstitutional. They said it was an overreach of federal government power."

There were other hands up, and Goldstein circulated around the room, making little jokes here and there, but mostly answering questions on the history of Reconstruction, and I had to admit he really did know his history. I was impressed with the kids, too; they were really working hard, and I wondered if maybe I had been too harsh about the project.

But when Goldstein called all the little groups back together to report their solutions to the rest of the class, I decided I had been right all along. The kids started out okay, when they diagnosed why Reconstruction was a failure. All the groups were able to regurgitate the standard story, which is basically that after Lincoln was shot, the new president, southerner Andrew Johnson, sold out the freedmen by letting the unrepentant racist elite of the South reestablish control. The freedmen were given no land, little education, no compensation and limited rights, through the brutal "black codes." To make things worse, the rise of the Klan soon symbolized southern determination to defy the North, through violence if need be. All this was fine; the kids had done their reading, and they knew the material. But when it was their turn to offer solutions, they stumbled. Over and over, they said things like, "We should break up the old plantations and divide the land up among the former slaves. Each freedman would get 40 acres and a mule." Or they insisted, if they were in charge, "The federal government would arrest the Klan and stop the terrorism." And they would make sure "the freedmen have just as good schooling as the whites do." Goldstein nodded enthusiastically after each comment. There was this genial quality to the way he stroked them that the kids found reassuring. Which was fine when the kids were right, but sometimes they're wrong, and they need to be called on it. Goldstein hadn't learned to do that yet, but I got my chance at the end of class.

Like most new teachers, Goldstein's timing was off. He had a tendency to rush through a lesson, and today there was a full six minutes left at the end of the class, and Goldstein had nothing else planned. So he turned to me and said, "Is there anything you want to add about Reconstruction, Mr. Cavaliere?"

"Actually, yeah," I said. "You guys did a nice job on the problems of Reconstruction. And you've got the right villain. Everybody's blaming old Andy Johnson. Why not? He's about as good a whipping boy as you're going to find; a racist, a Southerner, a slaveholder. But the real question is could anyone have done better in his situation? Could Lincoln have done better?"

I let the question hang over the class for a long moment before continuing. Nobody answered. "John Wilkes Booth was the best thing that ever happened to Lincoln." That drew a laugh, but I kept talking, "No, I'm serious. Semi-serious, anyway. Getting assassinated was the best thing for his historical reputation. The war was the easy part. But what then? Could Lincoln have persuaded most Americans to support full citizenship for blacks, even when the North was still segregated? Could he have got Southerners to live peacefully with blacks, to break up plantations and redistribute the land? In America, in 1865? That's pretty radical stuff. And even if you gave every black family 40 acres and a mule, so what? Does that solve the problem for African-Americans in this period? Remember what we've talked about all year; there are huge social forces at work here, and great men, even great governments, are powerless to fight them. What's the biggest economic issue in the South, in the post-Civil War period?"

The class was quiet, but I just sat there watching the clock as the awkwardness grew with each tick. This was a tactic Goldstein hadn't mastered. He was afraid of the silence, afraid to make them squirm. Sometimes silence is a teacher's strongest ally. People don't really start thinking, don't really start learning, until they're uncomfortable.

Finally, after forty-five seconds, a hand went up, and you could feel the relief in the room.

"Yeah, Louis, go ahead," I said.

"Declining cotton prices," he said. "That's why all the New South advocates were pushing for industrialization. Cotton prices peaked in 1860, and they went down every year after that."

"You got it," I said, giving him a wink. "Excellent answer. So how much would 40 acres of cotton land and a mule have helped?

Answer, not so much. All Southerners were poor after the Civil War, and there was nothing the government could have done about it. And that, children," I said as the bell rang, "is the last word."

I came into practice that afternoon with a chip on my shoulder. The team had gone 0-2 in my absence. One of the losses was respectable, to a decent opponent, but losing to Bryan School by eight points was inexcusable. We had way more talent and size than they did, and we'd beaten them by five the first time we played. And our opening drill did nothing to assuage my anger. Our lay-up line, the most basic of drills, was horrible. The guys were all over the place, slow to rebound lay-ups, out of formation, walking not running between stations, and joking way too much. Fasso was at church, which was good, because he wouldn't get his feelings hurt when I lit into them.

I took three long pulls on the whistle. "Okay, huddle up," I said after they had raced over. "Time to get serious." The guys leant in, and just as I was set to rip into them, I noticed that Ben and Morris had bowed their heads.

"What are you doing, Ben?" I said.

"Oh yeah, sorry," he said, lifting his head.

"Do we only do the prayer when Coach Fasso is here?" Morris said.

"Prayer?" I said. "Jesus Christ! This is a freaking public school. All right, that's it. Let's run the God right out of you. Five suicides."

Not a single guy complained about the sprints, which was a sign they knew they'd lost discipline. When they finished running, I called them together and said, "What the hell happened here while I was gone?" All of the guys looked at Colin, and he squirmed a little before saying anything.

"Coach Fasso doesn't know what he's doing," Colin said softly.

"Yeah," Mitch chimed in, "He doesn't even know our plays. He would call like two at once during the game, and he made us run our man offense against the zone. The other team was laughing at us."

"Stop your whining," I spat. "That's bullshit. Don't blame Coach Fasso. I don't care who is coaching you. Coach Fasso may or may not have been calling the right plays, but that is out of your control. Everybody on this team needs to worry about what *they* can do. And one thing you damn sure can control is your effort. And I ain't seen any effort today. Run five more."

When they were done, I said, "Now lets try that lay-up line again, boys, and this time with some energy."

They did hustle for the rest of the day, but when we ran through our offensive sets, they were all out of synch, and it was clear they'd been telling the truth about Fasso. Still, with two more practices before our next game, I had time to get them back in shape. And sure enough we got back on the winning track against Grant, with a two-point thriller.

CHAPTER 17

HERE'S A FACT you might not know: At the Chicago Fertility Institute, the instruction sheet—the one that explains where to put the canister that holds your semen—is laminated.

Another fact: The Chicago Fertility Institute keeps an impressive selection of porn magazines in a three-ring binder in the masturbation cubicle. And whoever was in charge of acquiring the clinic's collection made an effort to be sensitive to infertile couples of all creeds and colors; in addition to *Playboy* and *Penthouse*, there's smut featuring Asian, black and Latino women. Though I suspect if the office managers were more sophisticated consumers of porn (or had bothered to examine the magazines), they would've known that trying to square jack-off material with the dictates of political correctness was a waste of their time. The Asian magazine, for example, seems not to have been intended for Asian men, but was rather designed for (and almost certainly by) fetishistic white men. Or so I was led to believe by the dozen or so advertisements for Filipino mail-order brides and by the "Yellow Sluts" photo-spread, in which all of the men, posed in domineering positions, are Caucasian.

I know all this because Amy and I had fertility problems. We tried to have kids for several months before we saw a specialist. It turns out my boys can't swim, but if they're thrown into the deep end of the pool, they might conceivably get the job done.

So the doctor told us our only hope was through in-vitro fertilization. That's the process in which they take the eggs and fertilize them in a test tube and then implant them in the woman's uterus, with a high-tech turkey baster. My role was to produce the sperm, and because there's a limited shelf life, I had to actually perform at the clinic. I've masturbated in all kinds of places, so maybe I shouldn't have been squeamish, but the idea of jerking off in a room specially dedicated to that purpose, where hundreds of other guys have left their mark, made me kind of ill.

I suppose part of my reluctance stemmed from the fact that having kids wasn't my idea in the first place. Not that I resisted when Amy said she wanted to start trying. In fact, the added sex was nice, at first, but, as our difficulties mounted and the process became literally clinical, I lost some enthusiasm for the project. It was humiliating enough to learn I was sterile, but the repeated failures, in addition to being expensive, made it feel like somebody was rubbing my face in it.

I was reminded of this experience when I went back to our house. Since my last visit, during the blizzard in December, Amy and I had barely spoken. I phoned her a couple of times, but she must have been screening my calls, because she never answered, even when she should have been home. I would drive by every so often on my way home from school, just to take a look at the old house. Sometimes, if Amy's car wasn't there, I'd pull into the driveway and just sit, while the car idled.

And by February, it was two full months since I'd set foot in the place. I still felt too guilty to take any of the furniture. But I got to thinking I might like to have the hoop on our garage. There was an alley behind my new apartment building, with room for a backboard. It wasn't for me; what with my knee problem, I didn't see myself playing so much anymore. But Morris had a birthday coming up, and I thought it would make a nice gift. I know giving a used hoop sounds kind of lame, but new ones start at 150 dollars, and I thought it might look like I was showing up his mom to spend that much. Anyway, there was nothing wrong with the hoop, and it seemed like a big waste to have it sitting there in our backyard, with no one to use it. The hoop was cool, too, one of those newer models, with the bars that let you raise and lower the rim for easy dunking, and wheels so you can move it. The only trick was going to be disassembling and reassembling it. When I put it together for the first time, it was a real hassle. Even with a neighbor helping, it had taken me several hours. But I figured it would be a good project for Morris and me to work on together. First, though, I had to find the assembly manual. I looked in the drawer in the kitchen, where we used to keep all of our warranties and receipts. There it was, underneath a pile of papers and old pictures.

Before looking at the manual, though, I grabbed a handful of photos and flipped through them. There were pictures from graduate school days, from our wedding and from nearly every Christmas and birthday since then. As I shuffled through the photos, I slumped down onto the kitchen floor. It had only been a few years, but the clothes and hairstyles from grad school were dating already, and since some of the pictures had been exposed to sunlight, they had the washed-out hues of old denim. Looking through the photos bummed me out. We looked really happy in all those pictures, even the recent ones. I stood up and opened the drawer. This wasn't why I'd come back to the house, for a depressing nostalgia trip. I was just here for the hoop.

But as I began putting the pictures back, I caught a glimpse of a colorful sheet of paper, at the bottom of the drawer, which made it impossible for me to keep a lid on the memories. It was a full-color Xerox that Amy had put together for the adoption agency, a "family profile."

I was ready to throw in the towel after three missed tries at the fertility clinic. Amy, though, insisted we keep trying. But after six failures, and most of our life savings, even she saw it wasn't going to work with my sperm, so she began talking about adoption. So we went to a bunch of meetings for prospective adoptive parents. Almost all the people were professionals, in their late thirties and early forties—like us, but with more money—usually coming straight from work, lugging their leather briefcases and smart-phones. What leapt out at me first, when people introduced themselves, was that, for most folks, adoption is not about helping some orphaned kid. Not one person even pretended to have a selfless motivation. In fact, nearly everyone started by saying how long they had been trying to have kids. For some it was like five years or more. And you could just see in their drawn lips and humorless smiles that their whole identity was wrapped up in that fact. That was the moment when I realized just how much trouble Amy and I were in. Don't get me wrong, I can understand why the idea of not having kids is sad. But it's not the end of the world. Life ain't fair. You've got to deal with it and move on. But that night I looked over at Amy and saw the same tortured expression on her face as all the other women, and I just had this bad feeling we weren't likely to get past it.

Anyway, the new thing in adoption is this business they're calling open-adoption. I don't know if you've heard of it or not, but it sounds like an absolute nightmare to me. The idea is that it's bad for the kids to not have any idea who their biological parents are. So the pregnant girls basically audition the adoptive parents they like best, and then from that point on the adoption is open. In other words, you know who the birth mother is, and she knows who you are, name, address etc., and you are supposed to have an actual relationship with her.

The agency trotted out this cute couple, the Pierces, who had gone through it. They showed us a PowerPoint presentation of their adoption experience. Believe it or not, Mrs. Pierce had actually been the labor partner of the birth mother. They went to Lamaze classes together and practiced all that visualization stuff. And one whole side of the Pierce family tree was there at the hospital for the birth. When the baby was ready to go home, he went with the Pierces, though I found out later, by reading the fine print, that the birth mother has the right to change her mind after the birth. Anyway, now the birth mother is like a member of the family. She texts Mrs. Pierce at least twice a week and even spent Thanksgiving with them.

This is all justified by the idea that adopted children sometimes have trouble accepting the fact that their parents gave them up. The social worker who introduced the Pierces explained that now, with open adoption, "Instead of wondering why their parents didn't keep them, they'll be able to call them up and ask them."

That sounded like wishful thinking to me. I mean you've got to wonder how comforting it would be if the real answer was that the kid's mom slept around in high school, and the dad was too high to keep a steady job. But for me the bigger objection was this business about having a relationship with the birth mother. I can imagine all kinds of nightmare scenarios. For example what if your teenager starts saying stuff like, "Dad, you're so lame, my birth mother lets me drink beer at her house." And what are you supposed to do if the birth mother asks you—or worse, gets your kid to ask you—to borrow money? The Pierces' kid was only two, so they didn't have any answers to that, and the social worker blew me off when I asked her.

Amy didn't have any answers either, but she wanted to go ahead with it. So she made this "family profile," which is essentially an advertisement, complete with photos, inspirational quotations and saccharin philosophies on the meaning of life. The profile goes in a big book they give to the pregnant girls who come to the adoption agency. Amy showed me ours before she submitted it. It was like she was entering us in some wholesome family contest. None of the hundreds of photos we already had were good enough, so we had to stand in these silly "I love you" poses, including one where we pretended to be walking and holding hands. And Amy thought it would be a good idea to show the birth mother what the baby's room would look like. So I moved my desk and all of my books out of the study, and Amy painted it in frilly colors.

She was actually going to buy a crib, but I put my foot down, and made her borrow one from a friend instead. Oh, and since there was a shorter wait for minority children, Amy wanted to put in a shot of us with our "black friends." But when I saw the picture she'd dug up, I didn't even remember the names of the people. The woman teaches with Amy, and the husband and I had met at her school's Christmas party, which is where the photo was taken. The husband was a nice guy, and there was some vague talk about us getting together to watch a game sometime, but nothing ever came of it. And Amy gave the photos insipid captions like, *"The more love you give the more love you get."* Or *"The best way to do something for yourself is to do something for someone else."*

Though I wasn't happy about auditioning for a teenager, I agreed to do it. But I didn't do much to hide my reluctance, and I guess that really bummed Amy out. It was right about then that I'd started up with Dara. Not much of an excuse, I know, but the whole children thing had soured our relationship. Amy was depressed all the time, and Dara was so much more fun, so much less complicated. At first, anyway. Fortunately adoption is a slow process, and we were only halfway through the bureaucratic maze when Dara called and told Amy about our affair. It would have been an even worse nightmare if she'd called after we already had a kid.

But now, as I looked at the profile Amy had hidden away, it was a bit hard to put my finger on what exactly was so wrong with it. The perfect family schtick wasn't *so* far-fetched. We had actually been happy for a couple of years there. And then, I wasn't as opposed to having kids as I used to be. Maybe it was because of all the time I'd spent with Morris, but now, I guess I understood a little better why Amy was so desperate to be a parent. Morris was a knucklehead and all, no doubt about it, and he probably always would be, but I'd come to feel he was *my* knucklehead. I hoped that the profile in the drawer wasn't a sign that Amy had given up on being a mother. She'd have been a good one.

CHAPTER 18

"Ahh, God, this is terrible," I said, as Goldstein, Cynthia and I sat down for lunch. "Do you see what Betty gave me?" I had ordered a Sloppy Joe. Disgusting, I know, but I figured there was no way Betty could sabotage it, since the meat all comes from the same tray. I was wrong, though. She must have given me the display sandwich they keep in the window, just below the sneeze-guard, because my meat was cold and the sauce had congealed, the way hamburger fat does, into a greasy paste. Fortunately, as a backup plan I'd gotten Goldstein to order me an extra one. And sure enough it was much fresher than the one Betty had foisted on me, though it still wasn't good.

"Smart move," I said to Goldstein, "getting that salad." He just had a pile of iceberg lettuce and a scoop of tuna, on his plate.

"Well, I'm pretty consistent," Goldstein said. "This is what I get almost every day."

"Yeah, you do. What's up with that?"

"It's kind of an anti-meat thing," he said, looking down at his plate.

"What do you mean? Tuna's meat. Tuna's murder, dude," I said, drawing out the last word into two syllables.

"I know it," Goldstein said.

One of the things I liked about Goldstein was that you could tease him without him getting too riled up. Although, it would have been more fun if he had teased me back. "Well, I guess you could call me a fishatarian, then," he said. "No poultry or red meat."

"What's the point of that?"

"Just for animal rights, I guess," he said softly.

"Well what about the tuna?" I said. "Don't you care about the rights of little Charlie Chicken of the Sea?"

"You're right," Goldstein said. "I would love to be a vegan, but I just don't have the energy for it right now. I'm not such a good cook, and it's really hard to get enough protein. The rule I go by is I'll eat anything as long as the animal is treated relatively humanely."

"What's so humane about killing a fish?" I said.

"Nothing," Goldstein said. "It's not humane, but it's loads better than the factory farms, where we get most of our food."

"Maybe this is a stupid question," Cynthia said, "but why exactly is it called a factory farm?"

"Because of the way they treat living beings, people and animals, like they're inanimate objects."

"How do you mean?"

"Well," Goldstein said, "the cattle are castrated and branded without anesthetic."

I gave a mock cry of horror and reached for my crotch, but they both ignored me.

"Oh, and the veal is the worst," Goldstein said. "They take them from their mothers right after birth and chain them in tiny stalls, like, this wide," he spread his hands shoulder width apart. "And the floors are slatted to keep them from moving, which makes them tender, I guess, but it gives them terrible leg pain. I read somewhere that by the time they are slaughtered, which is at four months, most are too crippled to even walk."

"How horrible," Cynthia moaned, in what I thought was a sexy voice.

"And it's not much better for the workers," Goldstein said. "The cutting women, who are almost all black and Hispanic, get carpal-tunnel syndrome and arthritis from handling all that frozen meat."

"I'll give odds it beats the jobs those folks had in Mexico or Honduras, or wherever they're from," I said.

"I'm not so sure," Goldstein said. "The turnover rate is over 100 percent per year."

"How awful," Cynthia said, staring down at her plate of coq au vin.

"I'm sorry," Goldstein said. "I didn't mean to ruin your lunch."

"Don't worry your pretty little head about that," I said, tearing a huge bite from my clandestine Sloppy Joe. "I'll say this for you, Goldstein, you might be a hopeless bleeding heart, but at least you don't preach much. I've been having lunch with you for months now, and I didn't even notice that you don't eat meat. Lots of these animal rights guys are so full of it. They make such a big stink about the animals, you know that their whole agenda really is about how pure and good they are, and not about the animals."

"Well I'm glad you did say something," Cynthia said, giving him a sweet, big-sisterish smile. "I've never given much thought to what I eat. But it's not something you should hide from. I think it's great you have such strong convictions, Eric."

Goldstein blushed and changed the subject, but lunch was ending then anyway, and we had to get to class. By now Goldstein was doing better with the deltas. Though, at first, they had resisted his group activities and student presentations, they were starting to come around.

He had assigned a major library project, in which each kid researched some aspect of ancient history. But instead of having them write a paper, the students presented their research in a creative fashion. Today was presentation day, and the kids seemed genuinely excited. For one thing, Goldstein had allowed any of the presenters who wished to give their information in the form of a rap. Several of the kids, it turned out, wrote their own rhymes and performed them in the student cafeteria during lunchtime, and they were delighted to be getting credit for it.

Goldstein had given the kids a choice of presenting their projects orally or visually. About half of them had chosen to do the visual project, and to lend the occasion more drama Goldstein decided to make it like the opening night of an art showing. He'd plastered the kids' work around the room and printed little brochures, listing the name of each kid and the title of their project. And to make the showing more festive, Goldstein had purchased some sparkling grape juice, that came in champagne-shaped bottles, cheese cubes and crackers, and several bags of Doritos. The students were supposed to be like art critics, and they had to walk around the room and write down a positive comment about each project.

Federico's turned out to be the best. It was really cool, actually. He'd made a comic book of Ancient Egypt. The history wasn't any good—most of the names of his characters were Greek, not Egyptian—and the story was hard to follow—something about a tomb robber. But the drawings were amazing. He'd used high quality markers, and they gave his pictures a shiny, professional look. The pyramids were shimmering silver prisms, illuminated by torches, under a starry sky. Even better than that were the tombs beneath the pyramids. Filled with snakes and mummies, they were as creepy as anything in *Raiders of the Lost Ark* or *The Mummy*.

Federico stood by his poster, his smile alternating between nervous and shy, anytime one of his classmates gave him a compliment.

"That is *raw*, Joe," Billy Jackson said to Federico, as he clasped his hand. "I didn't know you could do that. You always be so quiet. That's cool, though, you're doing your thing." Billy turned to Anisha, who was following him around the classroom and said, "Yo, if I could draw like that, everybody and his mama would'a heard by now."

Federico squirmed at the touch of Billy's hand. And when Billy finally let go of him, he sighed in relief.

"I think it's fantastic, too," I said to Federico. "Really, I knew you liked to draw, but I had no idea you were so good at it. That stuff you're always showing me, do you do that free hand?"

Federico nodded.

"Wow, you *are* really good. I guess I thought you were tracing it. Are you taking any art classes?"

"No," Federico mumbled.

"Why not? Didn't you tell your guidance counselor you were interested in art?"

"He thinks I'm stupid," Federico said, looking away.

"We've got to get you into something for next term. I'll talk to your counselor." I was already moving away from him, when he mumbled an expressionless, "Thanks."

When the art show was over, it was time for the performances. If anything, the class was even more fired up for the musical performances than the artistic ones. I'd seen the kids on the Internet, whenever we went to the computer lab, looking up rap lyrics, and of course I'd noticed that they all walked the halls clutching an iPod, ear buds blaring, but I guess I hadn't realized how seriously they took their rap. Several of them had multiple pages of "rhymes," as they called it, and a couple of the kids had actually taken the time to lay down a rhythm track for their songs, which they played on my boom-box. Goldstein had Xeroxed the lyrics, and he passed them out so the class could follow along. But even with the lyrics right in front of me, I had no idea what most of them were talking about. One of them went like this:

The Shang Dynasty was raw
Like Kobe Bryant out in Cali

The Chinese had a wall that never saw
Nobody coming over into their alley

Luther wrote a song, not a rap, and though the lyrics made sense, you wished they didn't. Set to the tune of *Amazing Grace*, it went like this:

The Ancient Greeks, Oh how sweet the booty
They molested boys like me
Once was straight, but now are gay
Was straight, but now hits that booty
'Twas Greeks that taught
My butt to fear
And Greeks my fears made true
How precious did that butt-guard seem
The hour I first saved my booty
Past many homos, fags and queers
I have already run
'Twas me that bought a brand new gun
And Greeks will all go home

It was beautiful. Really. Luther has a phenomenal voice, and he sang it straight-faced, as if it were a real spiritual.

Everything went without a hitch, until the end, when Jackie Tompkins gave her presentation on torture throughout history. Aside from Anisha, she was the only other girl in the class. Jackie was a sour kid, and generally a poor student. But her research was actually decent. She'd found some *Time-Life* type books on torture and had made diagrams, showing some of the worst medieval tortures. The class's favorite was the Spanish Donkey, which was a contraption that looked like a sawhorse, except that on top, where the victim sits, there's a sharpened blade. The drawing showed a naked man, with heavy weights tied to his legs, straddling the blade. Jackie's enthusiastic reading of the caption, which concluded with the following phrase, "Hundreds of pounds of pressure often did grave damage to the loins," sent most of the boys into the fits of groaning and crotch-grabbing she'd hoped for.

Jackie's final visual was a picture of a woman, bound and gagged, sitting stoically as flames vaulted all around her. "They call this burned at the stick," she said.

"Stake," Goldstein said, smiling. "Burned at the stake."

"Whatever," Jackie said darkly. "Anyway, they burned up all these witches that were guilty of witchcraft."

"Okay, that was great," Goldstein said, as Jackie took her seat. "Thanks a lot, Jackie. By the way, they say being burned alive is one of the worst ways to die. It's supposed to be incredibly painful."

"How do they know that?" Billy said. "Ain't they all dead?"

"Good question," Goldstein said. "Well, I guess some people have probably almost died from it, and lived to tell about it. And maybe just from watching people being burned at the stake, the people watching get some idea. Did you come across anything in your research about this, Jackie?"

By now Jackie had sat down, and she gave Goldstein an annoyed scowl. "It's not that bad," she said. "I've seen it. It's not like he's saying."

"What do you mean you've seen it?" Goldstein said.

"My cousin burned his dog. Put it out in the alley in a box and burned it. It wasn't that bad."

The chatter and cackling of the class stopped completely.

"Your cousin *burned* your dog," Goldstein said, his face pale.

"That dog was old," Jackie said. "She was dying anyway. The vet was gonna charge my aunt 200 dollars."

Jackie's gaze pivoted about the room, searching for an ally. She found none. And Goldstein no longer tried to conceal his outrage. "That's disgusting," he said. "Disgusting! Some people shouldn't be allowed to have pets."

"You're just as bad as he is," Jackie said, pointing at me before she stormed out of the room.

After class we went down to see Fran Lester, the school's social worker. Fran was an African-American woman of about forty, with a knack for working with the toughest kids. Jackie was just sitting down with her when we got there.

"I heard that foul mouth of yours from all the way down the hall," Fran said, giving Jackie a gentle smile. "So go on and tell me what all this fussing's about." Fran was a skilled code-switcher. She could calibrate her speaking style to put just about anyone at ease, from Ivy League educated parents to West Side gangbangers.

To her credit, Jackie told the whole story pretty accurately. When she was done, she said, "Ms. Lester, you *know* I don't like Mr. Cavaliere, and I thought it was gonna be different with this new man, but he disrespected me in front of the whole class."

"Jackie," Fran said, "how long ago did your cousin burn that dog to death?"

"When I was ten," Jackie said.

"Now, nobody's blaming you for what happened to that poor dog, Jackie. You were just a little kid. But I'm going to be honest with you; it was a *stupid* thing to do. You don't have to go to the vet and pay all that money. Doesn't your aunt know she can take the dog down to the pound and say she found it on the street?" I half expected Jackie to snap at Fran, too, but she held her tongue. I envied Fran her ability to say brutally blunt things in a tone that somehow did not put people on the defensive.

"Listen, sweetie," Fran said, "everybody's got folk in their family that do stupid things. Remind me to tell you about my sister sometime. But, honey, no one made you tell a whole room of people about your dirty laundry. You've got to learn to keep some things to yourself."

"And Jackie," Goldstein said, "I want to just say that I'm sorry I lost my temper at you. I know it wasn't your fault. And even if it was, it's not any of my business. I hope we can still work together."

It was a good idea for Goldstein to apologize. He had really lost his cool over the burning of the dog thing. Not that he was necessarily wrong to do so—I lose my temper pretty often—but since Goldstein was always calm, the effect was magnified, and Jackie must have got a strong feeling that he didn't like her.

Jackie was enough appeased that the crinkles in her forehead relaxed and she looked at Goldstein for the first time in our meeting. But she couldn't quite bring herself to accept his apology, since that would mean ceding the moral high ground—a position she probably wasn't used to. "I'm not going back there," she said, looking away from Goldstein again. "I can't go back to that class with those two white men."

"Save it, honey," Fran said, reclining in her chair, as she laughed out loud. "There are so many horrible white men out there, just waiting for you. Save it! Don't waste it on these two."

Goldstein and I both began laughing, and Jackie looked around suspiciously for a minute to make sure we weren't mocking her. But then the humor of Fran's comment sank in and she smiled—beamed, really. I had never seen her let her guard down like that before; it was great to see.

After school that day, Peter Boyle came by to talk.

"What's up, Peter?" I said.

"Well, uh, there's, uh, there's this person," he said, looking down at his hands as he spoke. "And I, well, I was wondering if you could, well, if you could help me do something for them?"

"Do something for *her*?" I said.

"What?"

"This person is a female, is she not?" I said.

"Uh, yeah."

"And you have the hots for this young lass, do you not?" I said, suppressing a smile.

"Oh," he looked shocked at my use of the word hot. "Well, uh, I really like her."

"Is her name Anne Burch?"

Peter turned bright red, and Goldstein tried, but failed, to stop a chuckle from escaping.

"Very intriguing, Peter," I said, using my most pedantic voice. "This is all very natural. There is nothing to be embarrassed about. You know when a boy reaches a certain age, it's actually quite common for him to have some unfamiliar feelings. Often he will find himself thinking of a certain girl more than he is accustomed to, and hair will start growing in odd places. There's no need to call a doctor. It's actually fairly common."

Peter laughed without smiling. But I wasn't quite done having fun at his expense. "So all of this is unsurprising," I said. "Except for one small piece. I'm having some trouble imagining where I come in."

"Oh, yeah, right," Peter said, unzipping his backpack. "Yeah, well I ripped Anne this disc." He pulled a jewel-box from his backpack. "And I want to leave it somewhere for her to find it, so I was wondering if you could maybe put it on her desk before she comes in tomorrow?"

"Is there some sort of musical recording on this disc?" I said in my mock old fogey voice. "One of these rock and roller bands, that all of the kids are so jazzed up about."

Goldstein laughed, but Peter didn't quite know what to make of my schtick. "I asked her friends what kind of music she liked," he said, "and I burned her some songs from all her favorite bands, and put them on this disc. And I did a little introduction to each song. But I want to leave it on her desk so she finds it, and then she won't know who it's from until she plays the disc."

"Let me summarize your plan," I said. "You have researched the musical tastes of the admirable Anne Burch and made a mix tape—pardon me, I'm dating myself, mix *disc* for her. Now, you are attempting to enlist your history teacher to leave that disc on Anne's desk. When quizzed, yours truly will profess ignorance of the author of the mix disc. But the carefully selected music on the disc contains commentary from you, and at some point in this commentary, the identity of the secret DJ will be revealed. Anne, having solved the mystery of the secret DJ, will be smitten. And then..."

Peter stared blankly at me for a moment, waiting for me to finish my sentence, but when I didn't, he blinked and said, "You don't think it's a good plan, do you?"

"Peter, buddy," I said, dropping my arch tone, "you're over-thinking this. You're plan is too complicated, *way* too complicated. You've got this Rube Goldberg scheme here, with a blueprint of the school, and little action figures representing you and her, and all of her friends, and you're moving them around like pieces on a chessboard. Trust me here, your idea is sweet, but sweet is not what girls want. Not even nice girls like Anne, who think they want it."

"But what *do* they want, then?" Peter said.

He really did not know. "One word, Peter," I said. "Confidence. You have got to be confident."

"Oh," he said. His face darkened and he sank into one of the desk-chairs, as discouraged as if I had told him to grow another eighteen inches. "So how can I, uh, how do I seem more confident?"

"Let's ask Mr. Goldstein," I said. "He's got more of a connection to your generation."

"I'm afraid Mr. Cavaliere is right," Goldstein said, giving Peter a sad smile.

"You don't think I should give her a mix CD?" Peter said.

"Not at the beginning, I guess," Goldstein said. "You know, sometimes, the simplest things are the most effective. How well do you know her?"

"We were in the same middle school homeroom for two years," Peter said.

"Honestly, the best thing is probably just to ask her out to a movie or something like that. You might be surprised how effective it can be just to ask someone on a date. Not too many people do that anymore. But back in Mr. Cavaliere's day," Goldstein winked at me, "that was how you showed someone you were interested. I think most girls would be really flattered by it."

"Yeah, but what if she says no?"

"You know what, Peter," Goldstein said, "either she likes you or she doesn't. And it's almost impossible to convince someone who doesn't like you that they ought to. That usually only happens in movies. The beauty of asking her out on a date is that if she says no, then it will be over and you can move on. If you sidestep around it, you'll let her avoid the issue. She can pretend she has no idea you like her. And with a girl like Anne, as nice as she is, you might just stay in limbo forever. It's probably best to find out, and then you can go on with your life."

Peter's brow furrowed and he thought for a minute, processing everything Goldstein had said. "So I should just text her out of the blue and ask her out?" he said finally.

"Well, maybe not out of the blue," Goldstein said. "What you want is to have some opportunity where you guys are together and it's kind of casual. Not a date, but where you have a good time. Then you follow up, like the next night."

"So how do I arrange this casual thing?" Peter said.

"I'm afraid I can't help you there," Goldstein said chuckling.

CHAPTER 19

As we were waiting for our in-service day to begin, I grabbed a donut from the coffee line and turned to Goldstein, "I hope you're prepared for the stupidity of these institute days." But he didn't hear me. He was talking to Cynthia and her friend, a plain-looking Spanish teacher, whose name was something like Jean or Janet. Goldstein was focused on Cynthia, and it was easy to see why. Since there were no students today, most of the faculty had dressed down, and she was wearing tight jeans that showed off her rock-hard body. I shook my head. It had been too long for me. In fact, now that I was pretty much recovered from my surgery, I decided maybe I could lay a little groundwork with Cynthia, and possibly ask her out. This seemed like a good chance to chat her up, but Goldstein was talking so much I had trouble getting a word in. He was telling her the story of his most disastrous day of teaching, when Billy Jackson had started a debate on whether the Puerto Ricans had ever done anything. Goldstein's a good story-teller, though I'd noticed that in most of his anecdotes he winds up as the butt of the joke. That's not my style, but it seemed to be working for him, because Cynthia laughed in a husky voice. I hoped he wouldn't take it the wrong way, and get false hope. I mean, he was a nice guy and all, but as hot as she was, I didn't see any way she'd give a college kid a chance.

"Is this your first institute day, Cynthia?" I asked when Goldstein finally paused his story to pour coffee.

"Well, we had that one in the fall. Thank you," she said, as Goldstein handed her a steaming Styrofoam cup.

"Oh, right," I said. "Well this one promises to be even worse. This 'Team Quality Management' stuff is a nightmare."

Before I could say anything else, Doug Feeney burst into our little circle. "Hey, Cavaliere," he said in a voice not much lower than a shout. "Did I send you those jokes on email?"

"No," I said, hoping he would go away. Actually I did remember getting a forward from him, but I'd deleted it without reading it.

"I'll tell you now." He tapped Cynthia and her friend on the shoulder. "Yo, listen up. You ladies will appreciate this. Why does a dog lick his balls?"

Feeney gaped at us with his mouth open, I guess hoping somebody would answer. Nobody said anything for an uncomfortably long time, but he was absolutely blind when it came to picking up social cues, and he continued undeterred. "'Cause he can."

Everybody except Feeney was too embarrassed to speak. "Whoosh," he said, waving his palm above his head.

"You know," the Spanish teacher said, scowling, "I heard some idiot comedian make that same joke on cable."

"Hey," Feeney said, holding his hands up as if he was being mugged, "I don't claim to write my own material. I'm just sharing it. Yo, Cavaliere," he clapped me on the shoulder, "got to get to the meeting, but I'll make sure I send you that email."

"Sorry about that," I said to the two women. "He's a jerk. Not my friend."

"He wouldn't be so depressing if he wasn't trying to get laid," the Spanish teacher said. "I mean, if he was just a fat, crude slob, who didn't care what anybody thought, that's one thing. But he actually called me last month and asked me out." She shivered, thinking about it.

"Yeah," Goldstein said, "there's nothing quite so distasteful as the unrequited lust of a middle-aged man."

"That's a really witty line, Eric," Cynthia said, smiling. "You have a way with words. He's going to be a great teacher, don't you think, George?"

"Yeah," I said, "you know, I really think he will."

"Look, Eric, you're blushing," Cynthia said, brushing his forearm with her fingertips.

I wasn't sure if I had embarrassed Eric or if Cynthia had. I'd agreed with her instinctively—what else do you say in that situation—but as we went into the meeting, I decided she was right. Sure, he needed to read more history and to work on his classroom discipline, especially at the delta level, but both of those things would come with time. He was good; really good. Like Cynthia had said, he was verbally quick, a good explainer and very funny. And yet he had an earnestness about him that the students found appealing.

I'd warned Goldstein about the stupidity of these institute days, but even I was surprised by this one. One of the junior administrators, Don Tristan, was in charge of the meeting. "Now, Doris and I spent three weeks last summer at the TQM workshop, and we took away so many great ideas, didn't we Doris?"

Doris nodded.

"Our goal today," Tristan said, "is to try to come up with an action plan, so that we can implement the TQM program this year."

I raised my hand.

"Yes, George, is this important?" Tristan said, "because our time is limited, and I don't want us to get off task here."

"What does TQM stand for?" I said.

Tristan, whom I'd never liked, looked at me hard, as if he maybe thought I was yanking his chain. Which I was. "We copied a lot of the literature for you and put it in your box, George. You were supposed to read it before the meeting."

"Yeah, I didn't do that," I said. "How about a quick summary?"

Tristan looked at Doris, but she just shrugged. "All right, George, I'll give you the *Reader's Digest* version. Team Quality Management," he lingered grandly over each word, as though the name itself were explanation enough for anyone to see the virtues of the system, "or TQM, was developed by one of the leading business theorists in the field, and it's been used by innumerable Fortune 500 companies. In one company, sales and profits went up by twenty-two percent." He looked over at Doris again, "Which company was that?"

Doris shot him a blank stare and fumbled through a pile of papers.

"We'll get that info for you later," Tristan said. "I believe it's in the blue folder. But in any case, all of that should have been covered in the reading you did, and I do want to stay on-task here. We are going to be one of the first schools to bring TQM into the classroom, so we're real pioneers here. And our job for today is to try to graft the organizational template into whole school reform."

Tristan kept prattling on like that, so I pulled out some papers to grade. TQM, at least according to the chatter I couldn't manage to block out, seemed to be a jargony way of saying everybody ought to try to do their job better. One particular exchange was so inane I actually put my pen down and listened. Tristan was giving a PowerPoint slideshow on a screen. He had made these diagrams, with jazzy colors, that showed the various parts of what he called "the circle of success," and several teachers were trying to figure out how exactly to apply it at Edgemont.

"So if the students are the final products, then who is the customer?" a math teacher asked.

"Well," Tristan said, "I guess that would be the community. You know, the businesses that employ our students when they leave here."

"Wait, Don," Doris piped up, "Most of our kids go to college, so wouldn't *they* be our real customers?"

"But colleges don't pay us," a business teacher said. "Shouldn't the customer be the person who pays you?"

"Yes, absolutely," Tristan said, nodding. "The parents should be the customer. After all, they're the ones who pay us with their tax dollars."

"No, I don't think so," Doris said. "The parents are the *supplier*. They send us their children, you know, like raw materials, and we shape them." Several heads bobbed in agreement.

"Wait just a second," Tristan said. "What about the junior highs? Aren't they the real supplier?"

I slipped Goldstein a note, *"Still want to be a teacher?"*

Goldstein must have been thinking the same thing, because he got the giggles and had to bite his lip in order to control himself.

I grabbed the note back from Goldstein and scrawled another question: *"Are you seeing Cynthia, just curious?"*

He wrote back, *"Kind of. We've been on a few dates."*

It had just been a hunch, and, frankly, I was a little surprised. She seemed so far out of his league, but seeing them together today—the way she touched his forearm while she was talking to him. It made me wonder. I thanked God I hadn't asked her out. In fact, something Goldstein had said earlier had kind of got to me. When Feeney left, Eric had called him middle-aged. And neither Cynthia nor her friend seemed to disagree. Well, if Feeney was middle-aged, so was I. We'd started the same year and we were about the same age, not too far south of 40. From where I stand, I'm not sure 38 qualifies for middle age, but I guess from 21 or 22 it looks awfully close. In fact, now that I thought about it, Cynthia was about the same age as Alyssa Taukeuchi.

"Good," I wrote back. *"She's a nice kid. You both are, and I meant what I said about you being a good teacher."*

Eric's eyes widened as he read my note. He didn't look at me, but his cheeks turned pink again.

Mercifully, the TQM nonsense broke for an early lunch after ninety minutes. Since this was an institute day, and all the teachers were eating at once, the line was brutal. But when I got a look at the woman standing behind me, I actually wished it was longer. She had long auburn curls—but not over-permed in that 80's way—and she wore a lime-green blouse that was stretched by a perky bust.

"I'm George Cavaliere," I said. "Are you one of the presenters today?" She was tall, probably five-nine, and a real knockout.

"Oh, no," she said, "I'm a secretary. Today is my first day, actually."

"Welcome aboard," I said, shaking her hand. "I teach history." I'd been trying to avoid Betty, and either having Goldstein buy my lunch for me, or just eating from the salad bar, where she had no control over the food I got. But today, though I had no intention of eating anything Betty served me, I got in line anyway, figuring I didn't have to eat the food, and it would give me the chance to chat up this new secretary a little more. When we reached the counter, Betty glared at me through vicious eyes. "What's the special today, Betty?" I said.

"Stuffed grouper," she said.

"Sounds good," I said.

"Nice to meet you, George," the hottie said. "I'm Lori Belvedere, the new secretary for the guidance office."

"Here you go," Betty said, dishing a surprisingly generous scoop of fish onto a plastic plate.

"Did you say guidance?" I said, turning around to look at Lori.

"I think your fish is ready," Lori said, pointing at Betty.

Betty held my plate over the counter toward me, and as I reached for it, she tilted it at a sharp angle. The grouper skidded down the plate and then the gravy jumped over the lip, drenching the front of my shirt. "Ahh, shit," I shouted as the sauce scalded my chest.

"Are you all right?" Lori said.

"Here's another piece," Betty said with an evil smile.

"No, that's all right," I said. It was all I could do to not curse Betty out, but I stopped myself because it wouldn't help me with Lori.

"What can I get you, honey?" Betty said to Lori.

"Cobb salad," Lori said, turning back to Betty, while I mopped myself up with some napkins. "Yes, I'll be working for Josh Wentworth. Is there something I should know?"

"No, that's great. Josh is great," I said as we moved up the soda fountain. "I just hadn't heard that Dara—that was Josh's old secretary—had changed jobs. Do you know, did she take over the switchboard?"

"No, she left the school. Somebody said she's working for an insurance company."

"Really? She left?"

"You sound happy about it."

"No, not at all. I'm just, uh, just surprised," I said. "Hey, you should join us for lunch. We've got a nice little table. I'll introduce you to everybody, just as soon as I finish getting cleaned up."

"Thanks," Lori said. "I'd love to, but how about next week? Like I said, this is my first day and I want to get back to my desk and try to figure out the computer system."

"That sounds great, Lori," I said. "It's really nice to meet you." Nicer than she knew. Dara leaving the school, a hot new replacement, who was friendly and not crazy, I couldn't have drawn it up on the chalkboard any better than that.

"Hey, Goldstein," I said, as we bused our trays after lunch, "sign my name to the attendance sheet at the next breakout session, will you?"

"Oh, are you not coming?" he said.

"I can't take any more of that crap. I'm gonna go grade papers in my room."

"So just sign the sheet with your name?" Goldstein said, his voice tensing at the thought of forgery. "You don't think they'll check?"

"Not a chance. But your honesty is endearing. You'll go far."

I slipped off to my room, with my stack of papers. In addition to the tedium of TQM, now that I knew Cynthia was out of bounds, there was one less reason to go to the session. At least I had some hopes for this new Lori. In fact, while reading a couple of especially dull papers, I found myself picturing all the things I wished I could do to her smoking body.

But life doesn't work that neatly. Not for me anyway. As I was grading my final paper, a voice came over the loudspeaker and said, "Mr. Cavaliere, please report to the principal's office."

Elaine was sitting behind her desk, clutching a small tape recorder. When she saw me, she didn't come out from behind her desk or even offer me a chair. Instead she glared up at me from behind flaring nostrils and snarled eyebrows. "Why didn't you tell me you were having an affair with Dara Jurevicius?"

I pursed my lips, but didn't say anything.

"Why didn't you tell me, George? Why didn't you tell me you and Amy were separated? It sure would have been nice to know that before I got out on a limb and stood up for you, before I made a fool of myself. Because now Dara's accusing you of sexual harassment."

"Sexual harassment?" I scoffed.

"That's right," Elaine said. "That's what she said in her exit interview, and now the board wants to know why I've been defending you."

"That's such bullshit. Do you know this woman, Elaine?"

"A little bit. As far as I can see, she's very well liked."

"Yeah, she's very popular," I said. "But she also happens to be evil. I mean absolutely out of her skull. Do you know why Wentworth set me up in class? Because of her. She's got him wrapped around her finger. You can't trust her, Elaine. She'll say anything to get me in trouble."

"She didn't make this up," Elaine said, picking up the tape recorder. "And, frankly, it disgusts me."

"What is that?"

"A tape of a voicemail you sent her. Listen for yourself." Elaine pushed a button on the recorder, and I felt my face flush as the machine started humming.

There was a beep and then me talking. Ranting really. My voice was slurred; I sounded drunk and bitter. While it played, Elaine glared at me, eyeball to eyeball. When it got to the part where I called Dara stupid I looked away. And the last bit was pure torture. "I'm sorry I ever slept with you and I never would have done it if I'd known you'd wind up being such a whore. I know about your little scheme to get me. I know you've got all your bitch friends plotting against me at school. It's not bothering me, so you may as well give it up, and, for the last time, leave me the fuck alone."

"Well?" Elaine said, when the tape clicked off.

"It's not as bad as it sounds," I said.

"It sounds terrible."

"We had an affair for about a year," I said, my voice rising. "You know how it ended? She called Amy and told her about us. I guess she was hoping I would shack up with her. So Amy threw me out, and I broke it off with Dara. But I didn't retaliate. I didn't call her husband. I broke it off; that's all I did. And all I wanted was to be left alone. But she just wouldn't let it go. She showed up at my new apartment, called me, emailed me constantly. For weeks I ignored her, but finally one night I lost my temper and left her that one voicemail. Just one. I told her to stop harassing me. Did she mention how she and her secretary friends have been messing with me all year?"

"Messing with you?"

"I can't get a video delivered from AV, the copy woman screws up every article I try to have Xeroxed, they messed up my direct deposit payments, so my checks bounced. Oh, yeah, and if you were wondering, the reason I stink of grouper is because Betty poured my lunch all over me."

"Victim's a new role for you, George," Elaine said, acidly. "I don't think it suits you."

"I'm not trying to be the victim," I said stroking my scalp. "All I'm doing is trying to explain why I got frustrated and used some unfortunate language."

"Unfortunate?" Elaine said, squinting at me out of one eye. "Fuck, bitch, whore." She hurled the words at me like punches.

"I don't know what you want me to say," I said. "Look, it was a relationship that went bad. I wasn't a very good husband, and I'm obviously not the best boyfriend. You must be glad we never got together."

Elaine nodded emphatically at that last bit, and though I couldn't blame her, it really bummed me out. "But I don't see what this has to do with my situation."

"You don't see what this has to do with your situation?"

"No. Not really. I mean, Dara can say whatever she wants, but I didn't sexually harass her. Never. I broke up with her is all, told her to stop harassing me. It wasn't pretty but it doesn't have anything to do with my job; it's not a school matter. She didn't work for me, I didn't pressure her to see me, and I never even interacted with her at school."

"That's not how it's going to look to the board," Elaine said. "Let's be honest, women have more credibility in these situations. Besides, for some reason that escapes me, you chose to verbally abuse her on the school's voicemail."

"I was trying to be nice," I said.

"Nice?"

"Not the best choice of words, I guess," I said. "But I didn't want to call her at home, because of her husband. I didn't see the point of ruining her marriage."

"Well, the fact that you left it on the school voicemail is reason enough for the school to look into it."

"Is Dara demanding something," I said, "or was this just a parting shot?"

"She hasn't filed a formal claim or demanded a financial settlement. But she could."

"What if I could prove she was the one harassing me?"

"Prove it how?"

"She sent me at least ten emails begging me to come back."

"Do you have them?"

"No, I deleted them. But can't one of the techno-geeks from the computer center dig them up on the server. I thought email never really gets lost."

"Probably," Elaine said. "But be careful with that, George. Once you go down that road, everything will come to the surface. If we start looking at some of your emails, then they're all fair game. If you've got any other skeletons in your closet, they're going to come out."

"Maybe you're right," I said, thinking of Alyssa. "I don't want people rooting through my private files and notes. But if I don't tell my side of the story, where does that leave us?"

"There's no us, George," Elaine said. "There's just you. And you're in trouble."

CHAPTER 20

THE NEXT MORNING the phone rang at six a.m., just as I was getting up for school.

"Yeah?" I mumbled.

"George, this is Eric Goldstein." He was hoarse and spoke softly.

"What's going on?" I said.

"I won't be coming in today. Actually probably not for the rest of the week."

"What happened?"

"My father died. Last night," his voice broke. "Pan... uh... pancreatic cancer." He wheezed and tried to keep from crying.

"Jesus," I said. "I'm sorry. Can I do anything?"

"No. Can you just cover the classes until I get back, I guess?"

"Of course. If you need anything else, just call me."

"Thanks, George," he said. "The funeral's tomorrow—Jews bury their dead quickly—but with my mom and all, I probably won't be back until Monday."

"Hey, take as much time as you need, Eric," I said. "And don't worry about school."

"Is Mr. Goldstein sick?" Anne Burch asked, after the bell rang and there was no sign of him.

"No. Not really," I said. "But I'm afraid there's some sad news. Mr. Goldstein's father died last night. He's going to be out for several days."

The class was silent for a few moments, and then Anne said, "What did he die of?"

"Pancreatic cancer," I said. "I guess it's one of the worst kinds. Most people live just a year or two." I'd looked it up on the web, when I got to work.

"Was his father sick for a long time?" Anne said.

"Uh, I don't know." Eric had never said much about his family. "But you know," I said, thinking aloud, "he transferred to Xavier just this fall. I bet his father's illness was the reason. Probably wanted to be closer to home. I can't imagine any other reason to transfer from Harvard to Xavier."

"Mr. Goldstein went to *Harvard*?" several kids said all at once.

"Yeah. Didn't he ever mention it?"

Everyone shook their heads.

"If I went to Harvard, I'd wear a crimson sandwich board and pass out pens to everybody I know," Shelley Krawcyk announced.

"We would've remembered it if he'd told us," Anne said.

"Yeah, I guess you would've," I said.

"It makes sense, though," Anne said, nodding. "He is *so* smart."

"Yeah," I said, "he's a bright guy. You guys do like him, don't you?" I'd never asked them directly before, because Goldstein was always around, but it was useful information. I was going to have to evaluate him and write him a recommendation, and there was a possibility there would be a job at Edgemont for him next year.

Several of the boys said "yeah," or "he's cool," but Anne and a bunch of the girls exchanged looks and giggled.

"What does that mean?" I said.

"It means he's a hottie," Louis said. "The girls all have crushes on him. Couldn't you tell?"

"Is that right?" I said.

Anne blushed. "No, we all just think Mr. Goldstein is, so, uh, so nice. Do you know where the funeral is?"

"No, I don't. I guess it'll be in the obituary. But that won't be in the paper until tomorrow."

"Do you think it would be all right if I went to the funeral?" Anne said.

"Oh, yeah. Boy that's really sweet of you. I'm sure Mr. Goldstein would be very appreciative. You know, I'm gonna go, too," I said, though I hadn't really thought about it before Anne mentioned it. "If anybody needs a ride, I can fit three or four people in my car."

The next morning I checked the obituary in the *Tribune*. It turned out that Goldstein's family was pretty interesting. He was from Hyde Park, where my mom used to work, home to the University of Chicago. It figured; Hyde Park is a weird little world of its own: racially integrated, intellectual and liberal. But it's surrounded by housing projects and black ghettoes. Hyde Park's city councilmen have a long tradition of noisy futility in opposing Mayor Daley's machine (both the younger and older mayor). Though they've never really been able to gum up the workings of boss rule, Hyde Parkers are the type of people who draw some consolation from the knowledge that their virtue is rewarded by the worst snow removal, trash collection and pothole repair the mayor's minions have to offer. And if Stanley Goldstein's obituary was to be believed, Eric's parents were real Hyde Parkers. The mother was a school social worker, and his dad was a professor at the university. You could tell Stanley Goldstein was a real hotshot, because the *Tribune*'s obituary was an actual article, half a page long, not one of those small-print jobs they give most people.

Stanley Goldstein was a professor of journalism who, in addition to writing several award-winning books, had, with the help of some of his graduate students, freed an innocent man from Death Row. He was on the board of several charities and the family had asked for donations to the local soup kitchen in lieu of flowers. A whole family of do-gooders.

Several kids had expressed interest in going down to Hyde Park for the funeral, but since the service was right after school, most of them had conflicts with sports or theatre practice for the big musical. So only Anne and Peter met me after school.

They were both dressed up, of course. Anne looked fantastic, and much older. She had on a black dress, and had blow-dried and combed her hair, which usually was just bunched up in an unruly pile. She was going to be something when she was an adult. And Peter, well, his suit was too short in the legs and his tie was too thin, but he almost looked like a normal kid. Normal, that is, unless you saw him interact with Anne. He turned to stone anytime she spoke to him. And whenever she came within three feet of him, he kept his hands at his side, as if he was afraid that at any moment he might lose control and start pawing her. The easy, laughing confidence that girls find attractive was completely foreign to him. Still, it didn't seem entirely hopeless. I was quiet for most of the ride, while they chatted about all kinds of things like classes, their families and their plans for the summer. Though Anne had way more to say than Peter did, her speech had such an easy rhythm about it that it was hardly noticeable. A lot of teenage girls are like that. They can talk for hours and still manage to say next to nothing; it's really an art form.

I could tell the majority of the people at the funeral were intellectuals of some kind or other, even if I hadn't know Eric's dad was a professor. There was something about them, their conspicuously unfashionable hairdos and the clunky bifocals—I've never understood why more people don't wear contacts—that was distinct to the egghead subset of nerdom. I hate George Wallace with a white-hot passion, but looking around the temple, it was easy to see why his diatribe against the pointy-headed intellectuals resonated so well with the working class. Don't get me wrong, if I'd needed a demographer or a linguist, there's no place I would rather be. But there was a sort of disdainful superiority in the air that made me want to administer a few good wedgies.

The temple was a beautiful building; gray arches, a turquoise mosaic on the inside of the dome and stained glass ringing the balcony. After Anne put her condolence card on a table, where there were already several dozen others, we headed up to the balcony. Pretty soon, each one of the auditorium's thousand or so seats was filled. From all the young faces, it was clear Goldstein's father must have been a popular professor. Eric and his family were seated in the front, near the casket. Cynthia was there, too, holding Eric's hand. As he peered around the congregation, I got a straight-on view of him, but it didn't seem appropriate to wave, so I pretended not to see him.

Just then, Rabbi Perlmutter took the podium. He was a stout man of about fifty, with a wiry black beard and a booming voice. When the murmurs in the crowd stopped, he began chanting in Hebrew, a low hymn so solemn you could tell it was a dirge, even without knowing what the words meant. When he was finished he peered around the audience and said, "As a child of the Jewish aristocracy, there was every reason to expect Stanley Goldstein would leave his mark on the world."

Even from those few words it was obvious the rabbi knew how to handle a microphone. He gripped the podium with both hands, and his voice echoed throughout the hall. I wasn't quite sure what he meant by "Jewish aristocracy," but most of the people around me nodded knowingly.

"Hannah and Norman Goldstein emigrated from Frankfurt, Germany in 1938," Perlmutter continued. "The surging tide of history pushed them from one world to another, out of the orbit of Hitler's Europe, buffeting them through Holland and England, until they found haven on the shores of America. None of that is remarkable. Millions of Jews were scattered across the globe during the war. Yet, there *was* something remarkable, something special, about the Goldsteins of Frankfurt. And it is the same quality that has drawn so many hundreds of relatives and friends here to support the Goldsteins of Hyde Park." The rabbi paused here, looking directly at the family. Eric bowed his head.

"The Goldsteins pushed right back at the tide of history. Quietly, to be sure, never calling attention to themselves, but unmistakably, Stanley Goldstein, like his parents before him, fought for a better world. Stanley was not content to watch as the most basic human rights were denied to fellow American citizens, simply because of their skin color. During the Civil Rights Movement, he traveled to Mississippi to register African American voters.

"Back home in Chicago, he marched for fair housing with Martin Luther King and protested the Vietnam War and the Democratic convention of 1968. And it was there, in Grant Park of all places, amidst flying police batons and swirling clouds of tear gas that he met Sarah. Their first words were exchanged in the back of a police wagon. And from the day of their release, they were seldom apart, until now.

"Despite his tremendous accomplishments, it was hard to get Stanley to talk about himself, for he was a humble man. But there was one subject he would go on and on about, his son Eric. Stanley burst with pride for Eric, not because Eric is tall, not because he is bright or handsome, though he is all of these things. What made Stanley soar with pride for his son was that, ever since he was a young man, Eric has shared his parents' powerful sense of duty to those who do not have the advantages he was born with. All of his short life he has worked to make a better world, by volunteering and teaching.

"And then there was Sarah." Perlmutter smiled at Eric's mother. "Friends would sometimes ask each other 'Are Stanley and Sarah human?' 'Don't they fight, or at least bicker, like everybody else?' For, even after more than three decades of marriage, there was an intimacy about them, expressed in a thousand little gestures. The way Stan held her hand, when they took their dog for a walk, or the tenderness in Sarah's voice when she called him Stanny. Some couples use their intimacy as a refuge, a place to recoup their energy from their frazzled lives. But what was remarkable about Stanley and Sarah was how inclusive their affection was. The confidence of their love admitted all. Watching them sometimes you suspected it was Stanley who was stronger than Sarah, but other times you were sure it was Sarah who was stronger than Stanley. And then, finally, you realized it was the same strength.

"To take the measure of Stanley Goldstein's life, it is not enough to look through the old black and white photos of him, with his wild crown of hair at the protests. Nor is it enough to recite the lengthy list of his awards and publications. To measure Stanley's worth, you must go out into the communities where he taught, mentored and volunteered and see the effect he had. To some, these tasks may have seemed humble in comparison to the turbulent battles of the Sixties, but Stanley Goldstein understood a community is bound together by the unglamorous work of being a good neighbor, teacher, husband and father. The winds of history blow at gale force, and no one person by himself can reverse them. But Stanley Goldstein knew a community of men and women, working together, can build a fortress capable of withstanding the cruel gusts of want, deprivation, hatred and fear. His life was a testament to the idea of what just one man can do."

My feelings about religion are a lot like my views on public transportation: a great idea. For other people. But the rabbi's speech kind of got to me. The thing he said about bucking the tide of history, and how Goldstein's dad had forged his own life—well, my whole career, I'd been teaching kids just the opposite. That our lives are shaped by forces beyond our personal control. But then what the hell did I know. All that reading, all that history—and what good had it done me? I've always been a talker. But for the first time I could remember, I was ready to listen.

There was a reception in the banquet hall of the temple, and I watched the crowd as I went to get a cup of coffee. Goldstein stood on the other side of the room, with Cynthia clutching his hand and watching him with huge, fawning eyes. The two of them were mobbed by a line of mourners. Since I saw him every day, I didn't see the point of waiting in line to talk to him. So I got my coffee and a couple carrot sticks, while I waited for a socially acceptable length of time before leaving. But a few minutes later, Goldstein came into the bathroom, while I was at the sink.

"Hey, George," he said, grasping my hand, before I could tell him I hadn't had a chance to wash yet. "I didn't think you were coming. That's really great of you. You didn't need to do that."

"Oh, uh, yeah, well I wanted to," I said. "I really did. Hey, I never know what to say at these things, but it just sounds like your father was really an amazing guy. A great man."

"Thank you," Goldstein said.

"Hey, did you see who I brought with me? Anne and Peter are out there."

Goldstein took his glasses off and rubbed his eyes. "You're kidding," he said.

"No, really," I said, "I'll show you." We walked out of the john together, and when I pointed them out, he shook his head in disbelief.

"Wow," he said. "That is so amazing, so generous. I can't believe they would come all the way down here for my father."

"They came for you," I said. "You've made an impact."

Goldstein put his glasses back on and made a beeline for the kids, blowing off a couple of people who tried to stop him and talk. He gave each kid a huge hug.

After the kids gave their condolences, we headed to the parking lot and piled into my car. "Hey, guys," I said, as I started the engine, "there's something I'd like to get off my chest. I don't know if you two are aware of this or not, but I'm in a bit of trouble, because of that whole thing that happened with Colleen West earlier in the year."

Neither kid responded, which made me think they already knew all about it.

"You know," I said, "that business about Native Americans."

They both nodded uncomfortably.

"Well, anyway," I said, "I just want to say I know that was not my best moment. I mean, I still think Colleen overrea—" I caught myself. "Sorry, that's not important. Anyway, what I'm trying to say is, I realize I got carried away there. And I don't know if anybody has noticed or not, but since then I've been kind of making an effort to be a little more, uh, more sensitive."

As I put the car in gear and pulled out of the parking lot, I glanced over at Anne, trying to gauge what her reaction was. Her brow was furrowed, and she looked as if she didn't know what to say.

"Anyway, you don't need to say anything about it. It's just something I've been meaning to get off my chest."

"What kind of trouble are you in?" Peter said, his voice flatter than normal. "I mean, they couldn't really do anything to you, could they?"

"Actually there's a hearing in a few days, and they're probably going to cut me loose."

"You mean fire you?" Anne said.

We were on the highway now, and Anne was sitting next to me in the front, so I couldn't get a good look at her, but I stared into the rearview mirror, scanning Peter's face for a reaction.

"But they can't do that," Peter said, his blank expression sliding into a frown.

"Actually, they can," I said.

Both kids were silent for a moment, and then Peter said, "Mr. Cavaliere, you're my favorite teacher."

I tried to say something, but the muscles of my face had all gone soft and my lips felt like they were knit together.

"Not just now," Peter said. "You're my favorite teacher ever."

"Yeah, well," I said, staring at the taillights in front of me, "I could do a hell of a lot worse for students than the two of you."

After we dropped Anne off, I turned to Peter and said, "Hey, you know what we were talking about, the other day. How you should ask Anne out after you hang out causally?"

"Yeah?" Peter said.

"This counts."

"But it's a funeral," Peter said, trembling as he spoke. "I don't want her to think that I came just so I could hang out with her."

"That's true," I said. "A funeral isn't exactly romantic. But don't be too picky. You guys seemed pretty comfortable together. Look, I'm not in a position to guarantee anything, but from what I saw, I wouldn't be surprised if she agreed to go on a date with you. I think the next day or two is your best shot." I hoped I wasn't leading him on too much, but he was so nervous around her, I figured if I didn't give him a little kick in the ass, he might never ask her at all.

"Have you decided where you want to take her?" I said.

"Oh, uh I hadn't really thought about it," he said. "I dunno, maybe for dinner or something."

"Dinner's a tough first date," I said. "I wouldn't encourage it. Not if you're the nervous type. That's a lot of time, with not much to talk about. And you sit face to face, across the table, which might be uncomfortable."

He nodded as if this made sense. "But what else is there?"

"How about the zoo?"

"The zoo?" He squinted at me, trying to decide if I was pulling his leg.

"Really," I said. "The zoo is awesome. Think about it. Every two minutes there's another animal, so there's always something new to talk about. And you're walking constantly, which gives you a chance to burn off some of your nerves. Plus, you won't have to stare at each other. Trust me. The zoo is a great first date."

We were at Peter's house now, but he seemed so preoccupied with the idea of the zoo he hadn't even noticed. He just sat there, nodding to himself for a moment. Finally he said, "Mr. Cavaliere, you're a genius! The zoo it is." Then he slammed the door and went inside without even saying goodbye.

CHAPTER 21

WHEN GOLDSTEIN RETURNED to school a week after the funeral, he walked right over to me and gave me a big hug. I'm not really the touch-feely type, but he seemed so moved I didn't mind all that much. "Thanks for everything you did for me while I was gone," he said.

"Oh, don't thank me," I said. "I really didn't do anything."

"You came to the funeral, and you brought Anne and Peter," Goldstein said, and he looked like he was going to cry, which was the last thing I wanted, so I changed the subject. "Hey, Goldstein," I said, "Elaine is really anxious to see you teach. She wants to come on Thursday. That's all right, isn't it?"

"Sure, what do I care," he said. "Who is Elaine, though?"

"Elaine Jorgenson" I said. "The principal."

"Why would she want to watch me teach?" Goldstein said.

"Scouting you out for a job."

"Really?" Goldstein's eyes deepened. "But I didn't think anybody in History was scheduled for retirement this year."

"Nobody is scheduled for it," I said. "Some choose retirement, and others have it thrust upon them."

"Oh, Jesus," Goldstein said. "You mean yourself, because of that whole disciplinary thing. I'm so sorry. I wasn't thinking. But would she really be scouting me out to replace you, I mean right in front of you? That just seems so... so unseemly."

"It might be unseemly," I said, "but she'd be a fool not to do it. Let's be honest, here, bud, we don't get too many of you Harvard boys in this neck of the woods. Anyway, even if I don't get canned, there might still be an opening."

"Yeah?" Goldstein said. "Why?"

"Well, you never know with enrollments. The rising class of freshmen might be bigger than we expect."

"That would be great," Goldstein said. "I mean it would be such a shame if I wound up working here and you were gone. I mean, I've learned so much from you—"

"All right," I said, "don't get weepy on me yet. I'm still kicking. Anyway, I know it's short notice and all, and if it feels like too much pressure, so soon after this thing with your dad, I could try to postpone it. The only thing is Elaine is interviewing all these candidates, and the sooner you get on her radar the better."

"It's just as well," Goldstein said. "If we push it off, I'll stress out from now until then anyway."

"You'll be fine," I said. "You're good at this."

"Thanks," he said. "Anything else happen that I should know about?"

"Oh, yeah, good news. Peter and Anne went to the zoo over the weekend, for a date."

"A date to the zoo," Goldstein nodded. "I like it."

"Actually the zoo was my idea," I said, with more than a bit of pride. "He emailed me over the weekend to tell me. He was really psyched about it."

"Wow, that's great," Goldstein said. "Good for Peter."

"But we should probably talk through your lesson. What do you want to teach?"

We hashed it out together, and Goldstein decided he was going to piggyback on my press conference idea. To his credit, though, I think he realized he didn't have the stage presence to really pull it off, so he flipped it around so that the students were the ones performing. The lesson was the presidential election of 1912, maybe the most interesting election in our history. There were four serious candidates: Theodore Roosevelt, the former Republican president, who had elected not to seek a second full term in 1908. Then there was William Howard Taft, a Republican and the incumbent president (Taft had been TR's hand-picked successor, but his pro-business, anti-environmental positions had angered Roosevelt so much he had reentered the fray as a Progressive). Naturally, the split in the Republican Party was welcome news for the Democrats and their candidate, Woodrow Wilson, who, in 1912, was the governor of New Jersey. Finally, though he had no chance to win, Eugene V. Debs, the Socialist ex-and-future convict, was perhaps the most intriguing candidate.

Goldstein spent a good part of the week preparing the AP class for the press conference. He arranged it so there were three kids working on each campaign, and they were to have a debate in front of the class. They also produced glossy pamphlets, outlining their candidate's position on the issues of the day.

Goldstein also made a big push to get the students to come to class in period clothing. So on Thursday when Elaine showed up, she was treated to the sight of kids pulling on hoop gowns or pinstriped trousers, held up by suspenders. I've tried before to get kids fired up for costumes, usually without much success. But Goldstein had really knocked himself out. He'd made some kind of arrangement with the drama teacher and gotten the kids access to the wardrobe room, in back of the stage. To clinch the deal, he'd promised extra credit for anyone who did it.

Peter Boyle, of course, was psyched. Unlike most of the other kids, who pulled their rumpled costumes out of their backpacks, Peter had worn his monocle and black tailcoat all day. He was teamed up with his two friends in the class, who were, not coincidentally, both immigrants. I say not coincidentally because it's pretty typical for native-born nerds to make friends with foreign students, since their status as a foreigner makes most American kids reluctant to hang out with them. The sad thing is some of these kids would probably have been decently cool back home. They were fine-looking guys, and the rules of American popularity must have seemed arbitrary to them. Thadeuz, the Polish kid, couldn't get a handle on the American wardrobe. He'd tried to do the designer clothes thing, but he just couldn't get it right. Once he wore a Tommy Hilfiger red and blue rugby style shirt and blue pants that matched the stripes of his shirt. The only problem is that, as almost any American kid, except maybe for Peter, could have told him, wearing two matching pieces from the same designer on the same day was death. He was trying too hard, and it made him look a little like one of those early eighties joggers. The other boy was from China, and he was actually really good looking, but his undoing was his name. His parents called him Desheng, which obviously was a non-starter, so to try to fit in he had chosen an American nickname. Unfortunately he'd tried to be too cool by half and called himself "Harley." Maybe naming yourself for a motorcycle worked in grade school, but Harley wasn't going to have much luck getting the females to take their pants off. The other thing that set both boys off from their American peers was the unselfconscious seriousness they brought to their studies. It must have been confusing as hell to the children of immigrants, from post-communist countries, when they learned that the best way to make friends was to ignore their parents' endless lectures about hard work, and the right to rise, and learn, instead, how to act stupid. So Peter was about the best they could do. Kind of makes you wonder how America ever took over the world.

Anyway, Peter was playing Teddy Roosevelt and Thadeuz and Harley were his lieutenants. Since Peter already had his costume on, all he to do was fasten a gigantic pair of false front teeth and he was ready to go. "Good morning," he said, stepping to the front of the room and reaching for his shirt pocket, where there was a bulging wad of paper. Just as his hand touched the pocket, a shot rang out in the room, and Peter fell to the floor with a thud.

Really.

Well, it was a fake shot. But the class erupted in pandemonium as if it were real. Thadeuz, the Polish kid, stood in the middle of the room brandishing a toy pistol, while Peter writhed on the floor, pretending to be in pain. Shelley Krawcyk gave a shriek, and several desks crashed across the floor.

I sneaked a peek at Elaine; she was making an effort to keep her expression neutral, but I thought I could detect her suppressing a smile. Meanwhile, Harley chicken-winged Thadeuz from behind and yelled in a thick accent, "I have apprehended the would-be assassin."

"I would just like to let everyone know that I have been shot," Peter announced, as fake blood dripped down the front of his coat. "But I shall not let the forces of monopoly and consolidation that have inflicted this trifling injury on me interrupt my crusade for a better America." After that little speech he gave a moan.

By now, even the most clueless of kids had decided it had to be a stunt, but most of them didn't get the connection to history.

"For those of you who don't remember from the reading," Goldstein said, "you should know that Roosevelt was really shot on the way to a speech during the 1912 campaign, and he really did give the speech before going to the hospital. Harley, Thadeuz and Peter have evidently chosen to reenact it. I do appreciate the effort at authenticity, boys," he said dryly, "but in the post-Columbine era, I wonder a little bit about your judgment. Why don't you let me hang onto that gun for a while, and we'll discuss the consequences in more detail after class."

"But it's just a starter pistol," Thadeuz protested.

"Nevertheless," Goldstein said, extending his hand.

Goldstein handled the situation well. He didn't freak at the fake gun thing; he knew the kids well enough to see that it was just a case of overly-testosteroned, but harmless, boys burning off some energy. And by promising to deal with it later, he satisfied Elaine, who gave a slight nod of approval as Goldstein took the gun away.

Peter proceeded to give a solid Bull Moose speech, with pugilistic flourishes against the "commercial interests," that TR would have approved of.

The other candidates were nearly as good. Anne Burch had begged Goldstein to let her play Eugene Debs, who was a special hero of hers. She pulled the text of her speech from her backpack, on which—emulating Woody Guthrie—she had scrawled, "*This bag kills fascists.*"

Anne was the last to go, and her speech was just what you might expect from her, or from Debs: Lots of socialist platitudes about workers' rights, and how the people must own the corporations or the corporations would own the people. After she was done, there was a question and answer session, where the other students acted as reporters.

"Mr. Taft, I would like to know if your obesity has ever caused you any problems as president?" somebody asked. "Just a moment," said Louis Sterling, who was playing Taft. He coughed furiously into his fist. Louis was dressed in an enormous suit, six sizes too large for him, which was stuffed with pillows and sweatshirts. Now, still coughing, he bent over and pivoted away from the class, his stage coughs becoming more exaggerated. As he turned his generous behind, the whole class saw a faucet handle glued to one of the fat rolls on his ass. The joke was that Taft, who weighed 300-plus pounds, once got stuck in the bathtub and had to have the tub cut to get him out. The more knowledgeable students chuckled, and Anne let out a peal of oddly pitched dork-laughter that kept going after everyone else had stopped. For the first time, I could see how somebody like Peter had a shot with her. She was hot, but she sure wasn't cool.

"All right," Goldstein said, "enough goofing around. Let's have some serious questions." There was a good discussion of the tariff, the banking system and woman's suffrage. And as the class was drawing to a close, Goldstein asked the students to summarize the significance of the election.

"I think it's important because Wilson was able to accomplish so many progressive goals," Anne said. "Like outlawing child labor and having the direct election of senators and giving women the right to vote."

"Yeah," Peter said, "but the funny thing is that if Roosevelt hadn't joined the race, Taft probably would have been reelected. After all, there had only been one other Democratic president since the Civil War. It's kind of strange, because Roosevelt hated Wilson, but he's the one who got him elected."

"Why *did* Roosevelt enter the race, Mr. Goldstein?" Louis asked. "I mean he must have known that he and Taft would wind up splitting the Republican vote and that would guarantee Wilson would become president. Why would he do that if he hated Wilson so much?"

"Ego, I suppose," Goldstein said. "You know they used to say Roosevelt was the bride at every wedding and the corpse at every funeral he ever attended. He absolutely could not stand to be out of the spotlight, and I think he regretted retiring from the presidency."

"So one man's ego changed the whole..." Louis stopped for a second, grasping for a phrase, "the whole course of everything."

"I guess you could say that," Goldstein said. "Wilson becoming president changed domestic policy. He had a very different reform agenda than Roosevelt's. And it certainly changed foreign affairs. Wilson was reluctant to get the US involved in WWI, but both TR and Taft would have sided with Britain against Germany from the get-go. Some argue that if we had joined the Allies from the beginning, the war would have ended much earlier, before it became so desperate. And if you buy that argument, it's not such a big leap to say that Germany might not have become so bitter and unstable in the 1920's. Then it's just one more step to saying the conditions would not have been ripe for Hitler's rise."

"Wait a minute," Anne said, knitting her brow, "Mr. Goldstein, aren't you contradicting Mr. Cavaliere's 'Great Man' theory?"

"Yes, I suppose I am," he said.

"Well, Mr. Cavaliere what do you say to that?" Anne said. "Aren't you going to argue with Mr. Goldstein?"

The whole class pivoted towards me like a row of sprinklers, waiting to spit. I thought about how to respond, but every argument I came up with was weak. The kids were right: TR had changed the course of history. And if I'd learned anything over the course of the school year, I guess it was that the best thing you can do when you're wrong is to admit it. "Far be it from me to argue with a Harvard man," I said, giving Goldstein a wink. "Maybe one man can make a difference."

"Well done, Eric," Elaine said, after the kids had left. "A very nice mix of fun and scholarship."

"Thank you very much. I'm glad you enjoyed it," Goldstein said. "Actually, George gave me the idea."

It was cute how Goldstein was trying to help me out with Elaine. There was something really likable about him. I guess it was the easy way he took and gave compliments, like it was no big deal. That was a skill that I'd never mastered, but I thought the least I could do was try to return the favor. So I said, "Yeah, you might not have noticed it, Elaine, unless you know the kids, but what's most impressive about Goldstein's handling of this class is how he turned the peer pressure of the kids to his advantage. He got them fired up about the costumes, and he even gave some extra credit, but there were still a few kids today who couldn't seem to retrieve the poles from their asses. You saw them, the ones wearing their Abercrombie and Fitch uniforms. Those guys are in the popular crew, but the funny thing is there were so few of them without a costume. Evidently they were the ones who felt out of place. Did you see everybody else scowling at them, like they'd farted at the party? And the best thing is the cool group knew it; they were all standing in the corner, looking sheepish and hoping nobody noticed them. The nerds are in control of the culture of this class. That's a real accomplishment, Elaine. Even for an AP class."

"I know it," Elaine said. "I'm very impressed, Eric." She got up and shook his hand, and as she left, she looked at me. "George, you and I need to talk later today. I've got a meeting right now with the board, and one of the things on the agenda is your situation. So come by my office after school."

"Do me a favor," I said, as I walked into Elaine's office at 3:30. "Don't try to dress it up if it's bad news. Just tell me what the deal is."

"All right," she said. "The board voted to initiate dismissal proceedings."

I took a deep breath but didn't say anything, so Elaine kept talking. "The president of the board was rather adamant about it. I got the feeling Colleen's parents had really put a bee in her bonnet."

"What did she say?"

"Just that she couldn't go back to the community and defend a man who had a track record of insensitive comments towards minorities."

"What did you say?"

She stood up and paced behind her desk. "I tried, George. I really did try."

"What did you say?"

"I said you were our most talented, knowledgeable history teacher. I said that I thought you had learned from this episode. That you were liked by almost all of your kids."

I nodded and exhaled. "They didn't care, huh?"

"They said it might be different if you didn't have another fresh complaint lodged against you from Dara."

"That's such bullshit," I said. "How can they take that seriously?"

"I think from their point of view, the way the courts are today, they don't see how they can't take it seriously." Elaine sat back down in her chair. "You will get a formal hearing. They've got to give you one by law, but unless you knock their socks off in that hearing, I think it's a safe guess how they'll vote. If I were you, I would practice being humble. And let's be honest, George, you could use the practice."

"Humility, huh?" I said, as I sat down in one of the leather chairs. "So much shit has happened to me this year, Elaine. I lost my wife, I live in a seedy apartment, and now I'm in the process of losing my job. And I know I brought it on myself. So believe me, I'm a lot humbler than I was a year ago. But I will tell you this; I will *not* grovel for them. If that's what they want from me, they can have the job. As my deltas like to say, I'm not going out like that."

"That's a legitimate choice, George, but don't have any illusions about the outcome."

"So that's it," I said. "They vote to fire me and I'm out of here."

"You could sue them, of course," she said. "The tenure policy protects you, and the burden of proof is on the school to show they have just cause to fire you."

"Give me some odds."

"Not that bad, actually," Elaine said. "Your case isn't a no-brainer. It's not like you hit a kid. But, George, I don't think the question is whether or not you can win."

She paused, waiting for me to ask what the real question was. When I didn't bite, she sighed and said, "The real question is whether you would want to come back here after a court fight. After all, so far this business has been pretty quiet, because it's an administrative matter. But now that the board has acted, it's going to become public. If you take it to court, the whole thing becomes a circus. I don't know," she looked me in the eye now, "don't you suppose you'd be better off starting out somewhere fresh? No matter what happens in court, it's likely to soil your reputation."

"If you want me to leave, Elaine, then show some guts and say so. But don't try to dress this up in that 'it's for your own good' bullshit."

"No, George, it's not that," Elaine said, her voice high and defensive. "It's just that if you do win in court, there are going to be a million headaches. I'm going to have parents demanding to have their kids not placed in your classes. People are going to talk—"

"Look, I don't want this to go to court," I said. "I didn't want any of this, period. But if I leave, what happens to my pension and all that? I mean I put fifteen fucking years of withholding checks into that damn thing. Now it's all gone?"

"Of course not," she said. "It's true if you stop teaching after fifteen years, you'd have to pay a pretty severe penalty to get at the principal. But you can roll it over to your next teaching job."

"Next teaching job?" I said, scowling. "Elaine, are you out of your mind? Which school, exactly, is going to hire me, when they find out I got fired for making racist comments?"

"Why would they have to know?"

"What? Are you kidding me? I teach here for fifteen years, than all of a sudden, I give up my tenure and five years on the salary schedule to move to a new school. For a lot less money, and they aren't going to call some people over here to find out what happened?"

"Well maybe it wouldn't be so easy, but I'm sure you could find something. Anyway, George, fifteen years is a long time to do this job. You know that's partly why I went in to administration. It wasn't the kids; I miss being with them more than anything. But I just couldn't find the energy to grade papers anymore. Most teachers do reach a point where they lose the fire, and maybe it's a blessing in disguise to be pushed into finding other opportunities. You've got the chance to get out before burnout sets in."

"You're amazing," I said without bitterness, "the way you can put a happy face on just about anything. Wouldn't it be great if you could convince people they were actually really lucky to get fired because now they have the freedom to explore other, less interesting careers, at lower rates of pay?"

"This isn't what I wanted either," Elaine said. "And believe me, the board would like to avoid a court fight. They lost a case like this a couple of years ago. I can't say who the teacher was, but he's still in the building. And even if the district wins, their legal fees will cost them a fortune. They wish this would all just go away. What I'm trying to say here, as your friend, but without compromising my role as principal," she slowed down, weighing her words, "is if you pushed for a settlement, they might offer some pretty generous terms."

"You mean I can extort them by promising to shut up and go away."

"Call it whatever you want, George, but it would serve both your interests. You could be sure of getting your pension and enough of a severance package to give you a cushion, while you figure out what you wanted to do. You could even go back to school and get that Ph.D."

"I'll be honest with you, Elaine, I've thought about doing just that, from time to time. But there's a big difference between choosing to do something, and being pushed into it."

"I know, George," she said. "And I'm sorry."

CHAPTER 22

THAT NIGHT, AFTER PRACTICE, I gave Morris a ride home. "Hey, I almost forgot, happy birthday, buddy," I said, as we pulled into a parking spot.

"How'd you know it was my birthday?"

"From your player profile sheet. That thing you filled out on the first day."

"Oh, yeah. Good thing you didn't tell the guys," Morris said, laughing. "I would have got some serious birthday licks."

He probably would have, which was actually a nice thing. Birthday licks are the sort of thing guys do with their friends, and though I wouldn't say Morris was the most popular kid on the team, the other guys had accepted him as sort of a big, dumb mascot.

"No problem," I said. "Actually, I got you a present."

"You're joking."

"I'm not joking."

"Sweet! What is it?" Morris said.

"I think you'll like it. But I could use a hand moving it, actually. It's kind of heavy."

Morris' jaw dropped as he tried to imagine what I would give him that could possibly be so heavy. "Is it a weight set?"

"I don't want to give it away," I said. "But I'd like to move it tomorrow morning. Are you doing anything?" We were back home by now, and I fumbled with the key while I talked.

"I don't think so."

"All right, I'll pick you up at eight-thirty," I said, opening the door. "We have to go over to the U-haul place and get a truck and then go to my old house and pick it up."

"A truck!" Morris shouted. "Come on, coach, you gotta tell me what it is."

"Hey, quiet down a second," I said. "You hear that?"

"What is it?"

"I don't know." We were climbing up to Morris' apartment now, and a harsh rattle, followed by a thud, came spilling over the banister. The sound was too violent to be hammering, or anything like that, so I was suspicious even before I heard a woman's scream. I beat Morris up the stairs to the landing by a few steps. The door to the Spicers' apartment was shut, but the walls in the place were paper thin, and a man's voice came through, clear as a bell. "Fucking cunt!"

"Give me your keys," I said to Morris.

He dug into his pockets and pulled them out, but his hands were shaking so much he couldn't even really let go, and I had to yank them from him. Then I pulled my cell phone from my pocket and hit 911 and send. "Here," I said handing the phone to Morris, "tell the cops to come right now." I heard Morris shouting in the background while I unlocked the door. The locks worked the same as mine, and I had the door open in a second.

The place was a disaster. Phone off the hook, fragments of broken plates littered everywhere, and the sheet that separated Morris' section of the apartment from the rest was furled on the floor. Mrs. Spicer was standing near the sink, next to the cabinet, clutching a blue dinner plate, which matched the fragments on the floor. She made a flinging motion, with the plate, but before she could release it, the man in the kitchen closed the few feet that separated them, raining blows at her head. Now Mrs. Spicer used the plate as a shield, blocking her face with it.

"Get away from her!" I yelled, at the man. It was Andy, Mrs. Spicer's boyfriend, and he was in such a rage he didn't even acknowledge that Morris and I were watching the whole thing. He lowered his elbow on top of Mrs. Spicer's head. She fell to the floor without a sound. Morris let out a gasp behind me.

I went right at Andy, grappling both his arms from behind. As I chicken-winged him, he twisted in my grasp, but I held him tight. I was bigger than he, and crouching to try to use my weight for leverage, I spun us both around and forward out of the kitchen. But my bad knee limited my strength, and he fought me the whole time, kicking with his heels and clawing at my grip with his hands. Finally, I couldn't hold him any longer and he broke clear of me. He whirled to face me, and I got a good look at him for the first time. He was wearing a bedraggled Housing Authority uniform and he had a gun in his holster, but he didn't reach for it. Now I stood between him and Mrs. Spicer, and she rose from the floor.

Morris, bless his heart, had gone to his side of the curtain and got a baseball bat. He held it out in front of him, with both hands, like he was in the color guard, carrying a flag.

Andy ignored Morris and said, "You cunt, Gloria. Are you with this fucking fag, now?" By fag, I guess he meant me and he charged me low, in a wrestler's crouch. We tumbled forward together into the wall, a ball of limbs, amid the sound of falling plaster and Mrs. Spicer's screams. I rolled on top of him, but he squirmed and buggy whipped his legs, throwing me off. Pain shot through my right wrist as I fell hard to floor, landing on it. Now I was no longer blocking the path between him and Mrs. Spicer. She stood by the sink, a kitchen knife in her hands. "Just get the hell out of here, Andy," I said. "The cops are coming."

He stared back at me silently, the smell of tequila drifting from him, across the room.

"Did you hear me?" I said. "The cops are coming."

"Fucking cunt," he spat.

"Don't talk to my mom like that," Morris said. He was clutching the bat so hard his hands had gone white.

"Fucking retard," Andy snarled. "That bat make you feel big? Come this way and let's see just how big you are."

"No!" Mrs. Spicer screamed. "Leave my Morris out of it." For the first time, I was able to get a good look at Mrs. Spicer. Blood was seeping from her scalp, through her matted brown hair, and the flesh around her eye was puffy. In the morning, it would be black.

Andy took a step toward Mrs. Spicer, and I was just about to jump him from behind again when the doorbell buzzed. I was standing right under the console, and I jabbed the button. "That's the cops, Andy," I said.

Andy whirled toward the door, and then back toward me, confused. Feet pounded on the steps, and then a policeman burst into the apartment. For some reason, nobody said anything to him. The cop looked around the room, at Andy in his uniform, at Morris with his bat, at Mrs. Spicer with her bruises, and then finally at me.

"Hey!" a woman's voice rang out from the hallway. I twisted to try to see who was shouting, but as I did, my gaze stopped on Andy. His hand was on the holster of his belt. There was a hissing noise, and then I was on the floor, eyes burning and gasping for breath. Mace. Now somebody wrestled me over onto my face, and I felt a boot stomp me in the back.

"You're under arrest," the female cop said. The handcuffs felt like ice on my wrists, but I was coughing too much to care. She must have got me full in the face with the pepper spray, because when she flipped me over and I finally opened my eyes, I saw that neither Morris nor Andy was having anything like the reaction I was. Mrs. Spicer was hugging Morris and Andy was standing silently, cuffs on too.

"Should we cuff this one?" the female cop said to her partner, pointing at Morris.

"Everybody but the lady."

"He's just a kid," the woman said.

"The kid had a weapon," the male cop said, pointing to the bat. He snapped a pair of cuffs onto him.

"No, no," Mrs. Spicer said. "They didn't do nothing. He's my son. And his coach there, neither one of them. They was just helping me, because that one was drunk and I didn't call him back. And he won't leave me alone." She talked so fast and with so little coherence I could hardly follow her, even though I had seen most of the incident.

The cops were completely bewildered. "Listen, ma'am," the female cop said, "you've been through a lot. But you're safe now. We're going to take you to the ER and get you some stitches. And then we'll go down to the station, and you can catch your breath and explain it to me down there."

"No," Mrs. Spicer said, "don't arrest my Morris. He didn't do nothing."

But Morris was beaming now, and he said, "Look, Ma, how raw is this?" He contorted his body so she could see his hands. "Ma, go and get the camera. I'm gonna show the guys on the team."

"Morris!" she said, "I'm not gonna take any pictures of you like that."

"Come on, Ma!" "Morris said. "I might never get arrested again."

Finally she laughed and said, "The camera's dead and I don't have any batteries, Morris, but maybe they'll give you a copy of the mug shot."

Much to his disappointment, neither Morris nor I got to pose for a mug shot. Once we got down to the station, they were able to straighten it all out pretty easily. Andy tried to blame the whole thing on me, but he was still drunk and he turned out to be just as bad a liar as he was a boyfriend. Because Mrs. Spicer had to stop at the ER to get her head stitched up, it was nearly midnight by the time she got down to the police station, and they didn't finish processing us there for a couple more hours. They held Andy overnight and said they would charge him in the morning. The Spicers and I got in a cab at about two-thirty in the morning, but only after the female cop gave Mrs. Spicer a lecture.

"You've got to get a restraining order against him," she said. "I've been on too many of these domestics, and I can't hardly stand it anymore. It's always the same story. Tomorrow, he's going to call you up, all weepy, and tell you he's sorry. He's gonna say he's changed, he's learned his lesson. *Don't you listen to that nonsense.* They don't change. Never. People just don't. The bad ones are built like that. If you saw what I've seen, you'd get rid of him faster than a hiccup. I've been called back to the same apartments six and seven times. Always the same story, except the beating gets worse every time. He blacked your eye and gave you some stitches tonight. Next time he'll wait for you in the parking lot, and you might get a broken arm. And the time after that, this boy of yours could wind up an orphan."

I like speeches, and this was a good one, but the cop was wasting her breath. Mrs. Spicer had the same glazed look in her eyes that Morris got when I gave one of my halftime pep-talks.

"I mean it about this restraining order," the cop said as she walked us to the door. "We're going to send a social worker over to your house in the morning. She'll explain how to do it."

"Thank you, ma'am," Mrs. Spicer said dully.

The cops had taken our statements separately, so when we left I still didn't know exactly what had happened between Andy and Morris's mom. As we rode back in the cab, I asked her what had set Andy off like that.

"After last time," she said, "when he hit Morris, I told him I didn't want him coming around no more. He kept away for awhile, but he was always calling me. So tonight, when he rang the doorbell, I didn't let him in. But I gave him a key a few months ago, and he came barging in, smelling like a wino." She shook her head in disgust at herself. "I never should have gave him that key, or at least I should've set the chain, after he rang the bell. Anyway, when he came in the apartment, he didn't get violent at first. He just wanted," she peeked over at Morris. He was asleep. "He, well, I guess he wanted to be with me, if you know what I mean. But I promised myself I was through with that, after last time when he hit Morris. So that's when he started getting rough. And, thank the lord, that's when you and Morris came along."

"I'm glad we were able to help," I said.

"Mr. Cavaliere, I really don't know just how to thank you," Mrs. Spicer said, her voice thick with feeling. "With what you already done for Morris and now this, it almost seems like you're too good to be true."

"Thank you for saying so." I glanced at Morris to see if he was still asleep. He was snoring and his head was slumped against the door. "But I feel like you and Morris have done lots for me, too. I haven't said much about it to Morris, but you know I've been having a tough time lately myself. My wife and I just separated, and you might have noticed I haven't had all that many friends coming over, even after my surgery. I've barely had any dates since Amy threw me out. So I guess I don't have all that much going on in my life right now. Really just school and basketball, and Morris is a big part of that."

"Well you're kind to say so, Mr. Cavaliere. Very kind."

"Call me George," I said.

"My name is Gloria," she said, smiling.

We got home so late that, the next morning, I slept through my alarm. By the time Morris and I left the apartment for my old house, it was almost one in the afternoon. It was a bitch of a day, temperature in the low thirties, leaden sky and a fierce wind pouring in off the lake. I'd forgotten gloves, so I tried rubbing my hands together, but my right wrist was sore and swollen, where I'd fallen on it.

Except for the sound of the wind thrashing the trees, we drove in silence. I didn't really know what to say about last night, and Morris seemed kind of down in general, though he did perk up when we got to the truck rental lot. The last time I went to the house, I had disassembled the hoop, only to find out the pole didn't fit in my car.

"It must really be big," Morris said, as we piled into the cab.

"It's big," I said.

As we pulled onto my old street, I saw the lights were on in the bedroom of our house, and Amy's car was in the driveway. "Shit," I said. "She must be home."

"Who must be home?" Morris said.

"Amy."

"Is that your wife?"

"Yeah."

"Oh," Morris said. "But I thought you said this was her house."

"Yeah, good point," I said. "The thing about it is when you're separated, sometimes it's a good idea to keep your distance from each other. That way you won't fight so much."

"Do you and Mrs. Cavaliere fight a lot?" he said, staring down at his feet.

"No, no, no," I said. "Not like that. I would never hurt a woman."

He didn't seem convinced, though, and he kept studying the floor mat. I guess I couldn't really blame him, since the first time he'd seen me was during my blowout fight with Dara on the stairs. "I wouldn't fight a man, either," I said. "Not unless he was a wuss."

"You fought Andy," Morris said, brightening, "and he's not a wuss."

"Yeah," I said, "and look how I messed up my hand. You know, that was the first fight I've been in since sixth grade, and I lost that one."

"Really?"

"Really."

"You did pretty good, then."

"Thanks," I said. "Anyway, Amy is pretty pissed at me about the whole separation thing. She likes me to call first, so she can clear out of there if I come over."

"Is she mad because you broke up with her?"

"Not exactly. Actually, it was her choice."

"So why is she mad at you, if she broke up with you?"

"It's a long story," I said. "I did some things I shouldn't have, so she broke up with me, but she's still really mad about the thing I did. You know, when you're married, it can get pretty complicated."

"Oh," Morris said, in his 'I have no idea what you're talking about' voice.

"You know, the thing of it is I actually did call, but I said we'd be coming over at eleven, and it's almost two now. That asshole screwed up our whole schedule."

"I'm sorry I made you late," Morris said.

"Jesus, Morris. Would you shut up with the apologies already? When are you gonna get it in your head that it's not your fault your mom dates an asshole?"

"Oh. Yeah," Morris said.

"I tell you what," I said, "there might be some arguing, and you've probably had your fill for the week, so why don't you wait in the truck for a bit, while I smooth things out with Amy."

She must have seen the truck in the driveway, because she met me at the door, before I had a chance to ring the bell. "Goddamn you, George," she said, sticking her head through a crack in the door. "When you say you're going to be somewhere, then be there."

"I'm sorry," I said, gripping the molding on the outside of the door, "it's a long story. Really. I had to help out a friend. I'm here now, though—"

"Well it's not a good time," she said. The lines of her knuckles had gone taut from gripping the doorframe.

"I'm sorry," I said. "It couldn't be avoided."

"It can be rescheduled, though," she snapped. "Come next week."

"Hey, wait," I said, slipping my fingers between the door and the frame, before she could pull it to. "Look, I'm sorry about showing up late, but could you just trust me that I had a good reason for it."

"Can I just trust you?" she sneered, flinging the door open and arching her back like a cat. She was trying to look ferocious, I guess, but her rounded shoulders made her breasts point directly up at me, and I had to force myself not to look at them.

"Could I just *trust* you?"

"Sorry," I said, "poor choice of words. But I brought this kid with me," I pointed to the truck. "Anyway, I dragged him all this way, and I'd feel bad making him come back. He's had a rough day already."

Amy took a long look toward the truck, and her chest sagged back towards the ground as she exhaled. "You asked a student to help you? Couldn't you find anybody else?"

"He's not my student," I said, letting go of the door. "He's, well, it's kind of a long story, but he's my neighbor, and anyway the hoop's for him, and it's his birthday. But if you could just let us around back."

For the first time since we'd been talking—the first time I could remember, actually—she looked at me without frowning.

"It really isn't a good time, George," she said. "Honestly it's not. I have company."

"We won't bother you," I said. "I don't even need to get inside the house. The thing is already disassembled. All we're gonna do is load it into the truck. If you'd just open the gate, we'll be out of here in ten minutes."

"It's a man, George. A guy I'm seeing. Craig. His name is Craig."

She was trying to hurt me, and I suppose she had every right. My lips went soft and my stomach clenched. But if she was determined to hurt me, I was determined not to let her know how easy it was. So I said, "Yeah, that's fine. Like I said, we aren't gonna come inside."

"I don't know, George," she said. "It's just too weird. I mean I don't know that I want my boyfriend to meet my ex-husband."

That word ex-husband hit me like a body blow. The divorce hadn't gone through yet. Amy knew it. "Hey," I said, "you're certainly entitled to see other people, and he doesn't have to meet me. I just want to get in the yard. We'll be gone in ten minutes."

"Are you still seeing what's her name?"

"Her name is Dara," I said. "I'm not seeing her anymore. I'm not seeing anybody."

"That doesn't bother you? That I'm with somebody?"

"Do you really want to do this, Amy?" I said. "I mean we can sit here and pound each other all day long. But believe it or not, I've got better things to do. And it sounds like you've got something decent going on in there, with uh—with this, uh, Craig. So will you please just let me pick up the hoop, and then I promise I'll leave you alone."

"Fuck you," she said.

I sighed. "Amy, I fucked everything up. I know it and I'm sick as all hell about it. And I know it's just as bad or probably worse for you. The only thing I want to say is I hope that we can—"

"Fuck you! Don't even say it. We're *never* going to be friends again—"

"Listen, Amy. Please—" I held up my hands.

"Never! You weren't my friend for the last year of our marriage, when you were fucking that, that secretary. And you weren't my friend when you turned your back on me, after we found out we couldn't have kids." She was crying now.

"Amy—"

"So don't try to make me feel like I'm the one who's—"

"Jesus Amy, would you just listen. That's not what I was going to say. I know we're not going to be friends. I was just going to say that I hope, someday, when we think about each other, it won't be this painful."

She was still crying, but at least she had stopped shouting.

"That's all I was going to say. Oh yeah, and one more thing. For the record, the thought of you with another guy is absolutely killing me. If I didn't have the kid with me, I'd probably cry."

"Take the hoop and get out of here," she said, slamming the door in my face.

We'd probably had a hundred fights over the last three years, but that was the first one in which I could remember feeling I'd been a bigger person than Amy had. The shitty thing about it was that it was no consolation at all.

* * *

I'd followed Altgeld's progress throughout the year, and what they'd done to us in that first game was no fluke. They hadn't lost a single game; in fact, they'd won by more than ten points every time. So I wasn't under any illusions about our prospects for the season finale, but we still prepared as best we could, mostly working on their 1-3-1 trap. Since we couldn't simulate Altgeld's size and speed in practice, I had six and sometimes seven defenders running their zone. But other than that, I kept it pretty loose because I didn't want the whipping we were bound to receive to leave a bad taste in the mouths of my guys and ruin a successful season. So for our final practice I had all the guys bring in their Nerf hoops, and we played a wild game of knee ball in the field house.

I spotted Goldstein and Cynthia, sitting in the last row of bleachers, just a few minutes before tip-off. I had tried to persuade them to choose a game where they might actually get to see us win. But this was the only one that worked with their schedules, and I was touched they'd come back at all.

Altgeld started the game in their trademark 1-3-1 trap, and even with all of our preparation, it was a shock for my guys. We turned the ball over on the first two plays, and, with only thirty seconds elapsed, it was already 4-0. Fearing we were headed for another disaster, I called a time out.

"Easy guys," I said. "Remember what we talked about. Colin keep wide and use the whole court. You've got tons of room out there. When they try to squeeze you between the forwards, back away from them and really stretch them out. And Morris, you've got to come strongly to the ball. Use your voice and your arms, and make yourself a big target. Colin can barely see over those guys. And when you get the ball, don't wait for the defenders to attack you. Split the double team and hit Mitch on that fly route to the hoop."

The next time Colin did it right, and by spreading the defense across the whole width of the court, he was able to slip a bounce pass to Morris. Then Morris found Mitch, who took it straight to the goal. Altgeld's big guy came over to help, but he was late and had to foul. Mitch sank his free throws, so we were on the board, 4-2. From that point forward our guys gained more and more confidence against their zone. We still turned it over occasionally, but the zone just wasn't as effective on our bigger court, and we actually got the big guy in foul trouble. When he went to the bench, with three fouls, the second string center came in, and he was good, but not nearly as dominant.

On defense, we had no hope of really stopping them from scoring, but we did much better than in the first game. The reason was because we were playing zone instead of man. Actually, Fasso had convinced me to try it. "Mr. Cavaliere," he'd said, pulling me aside before the game, "you know, I didn't really follow what you were doing with that man-to-man at the beginning of the season. I figure we probably could have won a couple more games with zone. But now I get what you were talking about. You did what you said you were going to do. They really have learned how to play man-to-man."

"Thanks for saying that," I said. "We should both feel good about it."

"So since they learned it already," Fasso went on, "don't you think we could play zone just this one game. It would give us the best chance to win."

I was so used to ignoring anything Fasso said, that it took me a minute to process his point. That last phrase he used, "best chance to win," kind of got to me. He was right. It did seem only fair to give our kids the best chance to win; after all, this was our last game. And there was no doubting that, with our size disadvantage, zone was our best chance. Not that we could win anyway. The 2-3 zone is a passive defense, which relies on the other team to miss their shots. And it would take a miracle for Altgeld's players to miss enough shots for us to win. Still, the zone slowed them down, forcing them to reverse the ball, side to side, and burn some clock. At halftime we were only down eight points.

We marched into the locker room with our heads held high. "What's our best game of the season so far, boys?" I said. They were used to my rhetorical questions, so they waited patiently for me to give the answer.

"Really," I said. "I mean it. Which game was our best?"

"Harrison," Mitch said. "We won by twenty."

"How about Grant?" Colin said. "You can't beat winning on a last second shot."

"Could be," I said. "But you know what, I think it's this game. Right now, what you've just done in that first half. If we can duplicate that effort in the second half, this will be our best game by far."

"If we duplicate that half, coach, we lose by 16," Wex said.

"If we play like that and lose by sixteen," I said, "I will be thrilled. Absolutely thrilled. I believe that's the best half of basketball we've played all year. We ran our stuff on offense as well as we've ever done it. The picks are crisp, Mitch is making all of the right reads, and our spacing and timing are as good as I could ask for. How many offensive rebounds does Altgeld have, Coach Fasso?"

"Three," Fasso said, looking down at his clipboard.

"Boys, that's the best we've boxed out this year. You know what, Wex, Altgeld *is* winning, and I'm going to level with you now. They will win this game." Some of the kids frowned, but I kept on going. "But it doesn't bother me one bit. You know why? Because we can't control the opponent. It is simply out of our control that those guys are on average six inches taller than we are. It is out of our control that they have some of the best basketball players I've ever seen at this age. But what we've done so far is to ignore all that and worry about the things we can control. And we've done it. Now, listen good, you too, Morris—" Morris shook himself and came back from wherever he'd gone. "This is the last speech you're going to hear me make as your coach. If we play another half like that, we still won't win this game, but I promise you there is no way in the world that Altgeld's coach will be any prouder of his team, than I'll be of mine."

As soon as the speech was done, I began second-guessing myself. While I felt an obligation to them to be honest about our chances, I didn't want to discourage them, by telling them we couldn't win. But our effort never flagged, and my guys didn't back down. We didn't win the game, but it was closer than I'd dreamed it would be. The final was 44-29, and the other coach didn't feel comfortable taking out his starters until there were just two minutes left in the game. After the first game with Altgeld, my guys had raced through the handshake line, before fleeing the court with their heads down. But this time they stood tall, nodding and chatting with the Altgeld players. And their big guy said something to Morris that made them both laugh. Then the two of them exchanged shoulder bumps and a snap handshake.

Coach Macintosh and I were the last ones in the handshake line, and he swallowed my right hand with both of his. "You guys have come a long way," he said. "That's a fine piece of coaching."

"Same to you," I said. "That's a special team you've got there."

"I know it," he said.

Goldstein and Cynthia waved to me as they made their way down the bleachers. "Hang on a second, Goldstein," I called.

I threw my arm around Morris' shoulder. "Come with me for a second, Morris. There's somebody I want you to meet."

"Who's that?"

"A friend of mine."

When we reached the other side of the gym, I said, "Eric, this is the fellow I've been telling you about. This is Morris Spicer. And Morris, this is Mr. Goldstein and Ms. Juniper. They're teachers at the high school."

"It's nice to finally meet you, Morris," Goldstein said. "Mr. Cavaliere has told me all about you."

"Really?" Morris said, turning a shy smile toward me.

"Really," I said.

"Hey, you played a great game today," Goldstein said.

"Thanks," Morris said. He still wasn't much of a conversationalist.

"So Morris," I said, "let me explain why I wanted you to meet Mr. Goldstein. I haven't told you this yet, but I'm probably not going to be at the high school next year."

"You're not?"

"Don't worry," I said, "I'm not moving or anything, so you'll still see plenty of me. Just probably not at the high school."

"Okay," Morris said.

One of the things I liked about Morris was his total lack of curiosity. Even if they didn't have the guts to ask, most people would be dying to know why I was being fired. But Morris just accepted everything the way it was. It made him easy to be around. "Anyway," I said, "I want you to go check in with Mr. Goldstein every once in a while. Just tell him how you're doing. If you need help with anything, he's a great man to know. And be sure to tell the guidance counselor you want to take his class, World History Delta."

"Okay, coach," Morris said. His blue eyes were clear and sharp.

CHAPTER 23

You could tell the board had made up their minds in advance, just from the arrangement of the room. There was a huge blond table at the center, and the surface of it glistened white from the light, streaming out of cans suspended overhead, making the room feel as bright as a television studio. And all five of the board members and their lawyer sat on one side of the table, tribunal style, with just me, alone, on the other. There was a row of chairs to the side of the table, for visitors to sit in during public meetings. But since this was a personnel matter, the public wasn't invited, and Elaine was the only person in the audience. As I took my seat, she shot me a little nod of encouragement. I winked back at her and planted my Old Hickory tankard on the table next to me.

Sally Katz, the board president, opened the hearing by thanking me for coming, but she said it coldly, and she didn't waste any time on small talk. "The first item I want to address is the issue of the complaint filed by Ms. Dara Jurevicius. Mr. Cavaliere, you should know that everyone on the board has heard the voicemail you left for Ms. Jurevicius. But I think it's worthwhile reading a transcript of the phone call."

There was some shuffling of paper, while the board members dug in their folders for the document. The room went silent as they read it. When everybody had finished, the whole board looked at me, a wall of stony faces. "Is there anything you want to tell us about this, Mr. Cavaliere?" Katz said.

Katz seemed to be making an effort to avoid eye contact, but I locked gazes with her. "Let me just say," I said, speaking slowly at first, "I'm not proud of any of that, and I apologize to you for having you see it and hear it. And I'm not going to defend it. I'm deeply ashamed of what I did and said."

"Oh," Katz said. She had kind, hazel eyes, and they widened as she processed what I'd said. She seemed surprised by my contrition, and it flustered her. "Oh. Well, we will take those comments into consideration," she said. "But I must confess, the language you used here, well I don't know quite else how to say this," she peered down the table at the other board members, "but it makes me question whether you are the sort of person we want to entrust our children with."

Katz squinted through her glasses at me, as though trying to read my face, but she gave up and said, "Now, I'd like to spend some time detailing exactly what you are alleged to have said to your AP class. Matthew, will you step in here?" Matthew, the attorney, was a tall guy, real well dressed, but he had a grating voice that would have been death in the classroom. He recited the whole long story from the beginning, repeating the taco stand comment and the thing I said about black men and all the stuff I said when I was playing Andrew Jackson.

At the mention of Jackson's name, I pulled the tankard closer to me and studied the scene painted on the front, while Matthew spoke. The caption embossed above the painting said, "*Dickinson Out Dueled By Old Hickory!*" Charles Dickinson, reputedly the best shot in Tennessee, had made the foolish mistake of impugning Jackson's wife, Rachel. In the picture, the two men were shown facing off on a dueling field. A bullet was poised to strike Jackson in the side of his coat, while Old Hickory aimed his own pistol at Dickinson. As the story goes, Jackson, who was slim, selected a billowing great coat from his wardrobe that day. Fooled, Dickinson misjudged Jackson's girth and, though his round went through Jackson's coat and into his chest, it inflicted only a minor wound. Jackson had strength enough left to aim and discharge his pistol with precision. A few moments later, Dickinson was dead. Jackson healed soon, but he carried the bullet to his grave.

"Well, Mr. Cavaliere," Matthew said, his eyes pivoting from the page to me, "do you wish to take issue with my account of these events?"

"No," I said. "That's pretty much how it happened."

From the corner of my eye, I could see Elaine fidgeting over in her chair. I glanced in her direction, and she scowled at me, almost pleadingly. "Say something!" she mouthed at me. I shot her another wink.

Katz took off her glasses and massaged the bridge of her nose. "There's nothing you feel you want to say in your own defense?"

I spun the tankard around to the side inscribed with one of Jackson's quotations. "*I have lived in vain,*" he said, "*if it be necessary to enter into a formal vindication of my character.*"

"No," I said. "Not really. Not in my defense."

"Oh, well," she stared back at me, confused. "In that case—"

"But," I said, cutting her off, "if it's all right, there is something I want to get off my chest." Katz leaned back in her chair and gripped the armrests, as though bracing herself for a verbal assault.

"I know what's happening here," I said. "I know you've made up your minds and this hearing is just a formality. I know you've got to go through the motions to protect yourself. And I know you're going to fire me."

"Let me assure you, Mr. Cavaliere," Katz said, "that we have not come to any final decision."

"Look," I said, "I'm lots of things, but I'm not dumb. It's over."

She frowned and opened her mouth as if to protest, but I said, "It's all right. I'm not bitter. I deserve it. I know I brought this all on myself. So let me just say one last thing." I breathed deeply and stared up into the ceiling lights. When I looked back at Katz, my pupils shrunken, her face bobbed in front of me like a patchwork of dark and light circles. "You know all these years, I've taught my kids that people are powerless against social forces. That they can't change their own destiny. But I've been rethinking that this year; I've been rethinking lots of things this year." As my sight unclouded, I saw that the whole board was watching me now. Matthew, the lawyer, stopped taking notes, and his brow furrowed. All those eyes, staring across the table at me, made me dizzy, and the temperature in the room seemed like it had gone up twenty degrees. I wished I'd brought some papers to shuffle or a notebook to doodle in, while I talked, to give me something else to look at. And then I remembered I had an envelope in my back pocket. I pulled it out, twirling it around in my fingertips, as I spoke. I'd scrawled Sally Katz's name on the front of it, and my eyes lit on the K in her name, mesmerized as it turned in my hands like a pinwheel. "Anyway, I've spent my entire adult life working with kids. A lot of them probably can barely remember my name. But there *are* a bunch of them I've made an impact on. These kids are better off because of me. And there's a few that might even say I've changed their world." I looked up from the envelope, unsure of what kind of reaction my speech was getting.

Katz gave me a quizzical look, and over on the side, Elaine winked. Encouraged, I pressed on, "Anyway, I feel like I've had a great run. And I know this, I've enjoyed the hell out of it."

Katz tilted her head to the side a bit, wondering if I was going to continue. But when she saw that I wasn't, she nodded and said, "Is there anything else you'd like to say, Mr. Cavaliere?"

"No," I said. "I've said my piece." I stood up. But as I turned to go, I said, "Oh yeah, one last thing. Let's make this simple." I held the envelope out toward Katz. She looked baffled, and she extended her hand slowly as though reluctant to touch it.

"Go on, take it," I said. "It's my resignation."

"Are you sure you don't want to consult with an attorney, Mr. Cavaliere?" she said. "Because I would just urge you to not do anything rash."

"I don't need one," I said.

"Are you sure?"

"Pretty damn sure," I said. "Unless you're planning on suing me. Because I'm not going to sue you."

The room stayed hushed. "Take care," I said. I took one last sip from my tankard, put it back down on the table and walked out of the boardroom.

In the hallway, I weaved through the red and blue maze of lockers. Near the exit by the gym, where I park my car, I slowed my pace, soaking in the peace of the empty hallway. During school hours the halls are congested with young bodies, and there's a din from clanging lockers and obscene exclamations. But it was 8:00 now. All the lights were out, except for one emergency bulb at the end of the corridor, which bathed the trophy cases in a hazy glow.

I moved toward the exit, and pushed down on the arm of the door. The door was all glass, and it was so gusty outside that when the wind raged, the breeze came right through the pane. I propped the door open and stood there, letting the wind chafe my hand, until my palms began to chap. Soon, the glass on the door had fogged up, but I wasn't ready to leave yet. Where would I go? Not home. There was nothing to do there. No, I wasn't ready to leave. I turned around and walked back through the hall, past the line of trophy cases and over to the gym.

I opened the double doors and shuffled to the center of the court. The gym was hot and dark, except for one yellow light, nestled up in the rafters by the championship banners. Old gyms have a music of their own that modern facilities, like the one at Garrison, with its computerized thermostat, can't match, and for a while I sat at center court listening greedily to the spitting of the radiator and the light buzzing over my head.

The phys-ed staff keeps the basketballs over in the rear of the gym, in a metal cabinet, just past the bleachers. My key didn't work, didn't even fit into the tiny padlock that secured the handle. So, without remorse, I reared back my good leg and stomped on the lock. It gave a weak metallic yelp as the bolt broke, and I opened the cabinet. The ball I plucked from the shelf felt glassy and light in my hands.

Since my surgery, I hadn't taken a single shot, but now I bent deep on my knee. It felt good. I went to the free throw stripe and lined up, square to the backboard. My first shot came up way short, missing the rim completely and bouncing under the basket support. The gym was so dark I could barely see the hoop, and I could tell the ball missed, more by the sound than the sight. As I retrieved it from over by the bleachers, I stripped down to my undershirt.

With no collar or necktie pulling at my shoulders, the next shot was smoother, but it still was short and bounded off the front rim. On the third shot, everything clicked, and I knew the ball was going in from the moment it left my hand. If there's a cleaner, more pure, sound than the thwack of leather rippling nylon, I haven't heard it.

Though I could bend my knee enough to shoot, I wasn't in any kind of shape to move about the court. So I stayed camped at the free throw line, going through my routine before each shot: three dribbles, spin the laces parallel to my body, take a breath and release on the exhalation. After a few minutes I got a good rhythm going, and a light sweat beaded my forehead. I shot a hundred times, making eighty-two. Pretty good for a one legged man, but

I still wasn't ready to go home, so I took a silent vow that I would stay in the gym until I hit ten in a row. The first six went in and I started to wonder if I'd set the bar too low, but I missed the seventh, and I didn't get close again for a while. Then after twenty more minutes of futility, I hit eight and then nine straight. On the tenth, I did my routine and let the ball go, closing my eyes as I exhaled. The sound of rippling twine and echoing ball filled the gym. I stayed frozen for a minute, eyes shut, listening. When I looked up, I saw that the net had flopped up and over the front of the rim. A perfect shot.

I walked under the hoop, staring up at the net. The folds were crisscrossed all over each other and tangled over the edge of the rim. To me, it looked like a pair of webs, spun by dueling spiders. Before I got hurt, I would have been able to jump up and fix the net, but with my bad knee there was no way I could reach it, so I grabbed a folding chair from the corner. Wobbling on the seat of the chair, I stretched my hand toward the net and braided my fingers through the web of nylon. A flick would have righted it. But instead I pulled back my hand and stared up at the little nest of mesh I'd made.

* * *

Even though my teaching career is over, I've found a way to keep my hands in the history business. Elaine hooked me up, actually. She knows a guy at one of the big textbook companies, and she recommended me for a job writing the curriculum materials that go with the books. They've got me doing some free-lancing right now. The money's not as good as I was making while teaching, and there's no Cadillac pension, but it's enough to live on. So right now I'm working on a World War II mapping project. It's a cool gig just going to the library, creating lessons, and, best of all, no grading.

Oh yeah, another piece of good news: as far as I can tell the people at Garrison haven't heard about my problems at Edgemont yet, and they've promised me the job coaching there next season. And if the rumors I've heard turn out to be true, it should be a pretty sweet year. Morris talked to the big guy from Altgeld over the summer, and he said that the two best players on the Altgeld seventh grade team, twin brothers, have moved into the Garrison district. Gotta love twins. And Morris, well, he's still a bit of a knucklehead, but he did graduate from Garrison, and Goldstein's looking out for him at Edgemont. Whether he makes it through high school is anybody's guess. But much as I love the kid, I'm not losing any sleep over it. Some things in life you can control, and some you can't.